The Bastard's Battle:
the toughest fight is with yourself

The Shadow Sword Trilogy - Book Two

Vanessa Victoria Kilmer

an EVERLASTING LEGACY PRODUCTIONS book

Erika Kilmer Freidly - Editor

Cover Design by Erika Kilmer Freidly

Published by

Everlasting Legacy Productions

Florida, USA 2023

Inquires can be sent to

EverlastingLegacyProductions@gmail.com

First Edition

ISBN: **979-8-9850134-1-2**

To all those who told me I can.
I know who you are.
My heart is full.

Other Books by
Vanessa Victoria Kilmer

Revena's Revenge: not a pretty love story
The Shadow Sword Trilogy - Book One

CHAPTER ONE

Tender Hearts

Eryk pounded on the storeroom door with the pommel of Shade, his sword. It nicked the ancient oak planks, but the door did not budge. He used his shoulder and rammed the door several times.

The girls, three foundlings adopted by Revena and Kellan last summer, pulled at his sleeves and tunic hem.

"Hurry," said Ema, twin sister to Ava. She cried giant doe-eyed tears, her pink cheeks wet.

"Save them," said Ava, a former scullery maid, along with her sister, Ema. She cried as hard as her sister, sucking in gulps of air.

"Please," said Gisela, the child sent to Revena by Daisy, the swamp witch. Her cry pierced his ears like the wail of a banshee.

Eryk stopped slamming into the door, breathed deep and calmed down.

"Girls," he said, untangling their fingers from his clothing. "I can't break the door down if I'm worried about hurting you. Go stand over there." He pointed his sword at the opposite wall. The three girls moved away from him to the spot he showed them.

Noise from the storeroom grew in intensity. The girls hugged and wept as if life had ended.

Eryk took a deep breath, shook his shoulders, and assaulted the door. It popped off its top leather hinge, falling into the other chamber at an angle.

The screeching sounded like winds barreling down from the alps.

The girls got quiet and held their breaths.

Eryk wedged his sword under the bottom leather hinge. His father rolled over in his grave. Not meant to be used as a simple tool, Shade was a gift from Allan, Count Thorne, to his youngest son. Bastards rarely received blades from their fathers. Swords were too valuable, making a statement of legitimacy.

Eryk's father was different in so many ways. He broke the rules when he thought the rules were wrong. He married Eryk's mother, Maryn, born a serf, despite not having the King's blessing. They held the ceremony in their local chapel in the woods, with the priest and all their people in attendance as witnesses.

And here, Eryk was abusing the sword his father gave him. He hoped his father would understand that it was for a good cause, soothing the tender hearts of young maidens.

He hacked at the cured hide: the material tore as it was old and needed replacing. The heavy slab of wood fell into the room. The slam and bang startled the troublemakers. Silence emanated from the room.

Ema, Ava, and Gisela ran past Eryk.

"Girls, slow down and be careful. You might get hurt."

The girls ducked under shelves, behind barrels, and over sacks, their quarry challenging to capture. Little girl giggles filled the space along with the howls of the kittens, lost and afraid.

Ava got hold of the black and white one. She held it wrapped in her skinny arms and it quieted when escape became impossible. Ava took her captive out into the yard. She went to the barn to reunite the puffball with its mother.

Ema worked hard for the tabby kitten. It ran away from the giggling girl until she cornered it behind the bags of flour. She held up her prize for Eryk.

"Take the little minx to the barn and calm down." Eryk sat on a sack of grain.

Gisela collapsed on the floor beside his feet, her prize wrapped in her apron. The all-black kitten with blue eyes so light they appeared white matched the maiden. The child gazed at him with admiration.

"Go join Ava and Ema."

The girl left, nuzzling her malkin under her chin.

All this over some kittens. If his brother Kellan, the true heir of Thornewood, saw how Eryk took the stewardship of his holdings, he'd take the land back.

Eryk expected news from his brother, half-brother to be exact, and the legitimate son of their father. The world played a joke, and he'd be home soon to take over the care of the estate. He knew it wasn't likely to happen. Kellan was a man of his word, and Kellan had gotten the King's approval, in writing, to transfer the holdings. The Holy See legitimized Eryk's parents' marriage, making Eryk a legal heir.

Eryk knew Kellan's wife, Revena, had a hand in it. She helped to get the legal documents in front of the King and approved with his official seal. She even legitimized her brother, Adam, the son of her father, and the swamp witch. Adam was now Baron Beust and in charge of the estates Revena inherited from her first husband, Surat Beust, Kellan, and Eryk's cousin. Revena inherited that property when she executed him by running him through with her sword, Shadow.

No one missed Surat, the evil piece of shit, and Revena was well within her rights to kill him for what he did to her. No one knew she had done it except everyone on all the estates under her purview, but they were more than willing to keep it quiet.

"Hello, mother," Eryk said to Maryn as she entered the stockroom. He wiped his sweaty brow on his sleeve.

"Haven't I taught you better manners?" She swatted his shoulder, but the strike carried no force.

He stood. His mother looked and acted like a lady. He treated her like one, even though she was born into the lowest caste of society. Everyone that knew Maryn loved her, and while no existing law prevented a count from marrying a lowly serf, society discouraged it.

"I see the girls have you wrapped around their fingers. Thank you for getting the door open."

"The warped door needs replacing. The kittens got in that way. Cats must stay out of the pantry."

"Since when?" She brushed a speck of oats from his shirt. "It is their job to patrol the place and keep out the mice."

He blushed and averted his head. Maryn reached up and raised his face back to her.

"Do not fear your tender feelings. I am glad to have three sweet little girls to spoil after raising you boys. They remind me of Nicolette." Maryn rearranged a box on a shelf, her back to Eryk. He sighed. She turned to him and hugged him.

"You did a good deed by removing them from Hilltop while that pig in silk, Henri, is visiting."

Eryk growled. He worked a load of phlegm up in his mouth, pursed his lips, saw his mother's face, and swallowed it.

CHAPTER TWO

Imposter

The blackthorn hedge bloomed in rampant white flowers, heralding spring. The shrubs gave Thornewood its name, served as a formidable natural barrier around the household, and provided dark blue fruit for sloe jam, one of their unique exports.

Thornewood's house crest was a blackthorn branch with dark wood, thorny protrusions, and white flowers. Kellan gave Eryk their father's blackthorn broach made of black gold, deep purple crystals, and white opals, the badge of office meant for display by the current Count. Eryk had never worn it.

Eryk stood in the April sun, eyes closed, and inhaled, filling his body with the sweet scent of the bushes. He stretched, rolling his shoulders. He needed to remind the girls to keep away from the blossoms with the warmer weather. The delicate lacy petals with their pink centers would tempt after the darkness of winter and the drab brown colors.

Eryk was Count Thorne and bored. He shook his head, still not believing it. He felt like a fraud and knew most people considered him one. It didn't matter that he had parchment with the King's seal that said otherwise.

"Born a bastard, always a bastard," the blacksmith said when he didn't know Eryk approached the forge. He didn't get mad at the man because he agreed with him deep in his soul.

He played a role, like the actors who visited the area for fairs. They stayed for a night or two, performing small farces for food and lodging. While they served a purpose, no one considered them upstanding members of society.

In some ways, life was worse for him now that he wasn't just Kellan's bastard brother. He was free of responsibilities then, with plenty of friends. The men he used to work with gave him sidelong looks.. They didn't trust him.

When Kellen joined the men in the field during haying or by the paddocks to repair fencing, they joked and did not mention his status as their overlord.

They isolated Eryk, though.

"Let me lift that." One man took a pole from his hands.

"Perhaps you'd be best reading a book." Another man sneered.

He'd sat with them while they drank, yet now they avoided eye contact. They punished him for his good fortune.

He put up with it for his mother's sake. She deserved all the best that his new elevated status brought her. The subtle abuse he absorbed kept it from her.

He accepted it because of his brother. Kellan presented Eryk with the papers from the King and beamed. He always thought the best of Eryk and considered the royal legitimacy of his birth Eryk's due.

For his mother and his brother, Eryk pretended to steward Thornewood to protect his mother and return it to Kellan because Eryk vowed never to marry or have children. They would subject no one he loved to the whispers.

Eryk reached inside the neck of his tunic and rubbed the stone hanging from a leather thong. Touching the smooth, dark-brown amber relaxed him. He kissed it, then hid it under his shirt. It was his secret.

"Enough of this self-pity. To hell with what anyone thinks."

Jon and Stefan had brought down a wild boar this morning. They were skinning the animals behind the slaughterhouse with several other men. He would be sure of their warm welcome, especially if he brought dinner and a full wineskin. His stomach rumbled at the thought.

He glanced up. The sun floated overhead. Early for the meal, but what the hell? They rose before the sun to start the hunt..

Eryk tamped down the anger in his chest when he considered they had not invited him to join them. Instead of joining his friends in ordinary manly pursuits, he had been ridding the pantry of kittens for some little girls.

He stomped his foot in disgust over these uncharacteristic thoughts. No wonder no one else wanted his company. He couldn't stand himself as he marched to the kitchens for bread, cheese, and drink.

His friends stood around in a group as he approached them, as if ready for a fight.

Stefan looked up from slicing the skin from the pig, blood smeared on his face, neck, and bare chest.

"Oh, ho, tis the mighty Count Thorne, here to see the spoils of our labors."

Eryk turned red. He dropped the victuals and turned on his heel.

Jon blocked his retreat. His mouth quirked up on the left, dimpling his cheeks. His enormous hands reached out, grasped Eryk's upper arms, and turned him back to the group.

Eryk tried to shake him off, but even angry and taller than Jon, he wasn't strong enough to dislodge himself from the big man.

Jon tugged at Eryk's shirt, pulling it up. It enclosed him for a moment, causing him to panic, until it came off over his head with a yank, freeing him. Jon shoved him at the small of his back, knocking him to the ground.

"Come here and get dirty. You've spent too much time indoors. You're as pasty as a bit of unbaked dough." Stefan's laugh shook the leaves on the surrounding trees. He tossed Eryk a knife.

Eryk approached the swine and Stefan, watching the man. Stefan had an impish look.

Stefan grabbed his wrist and pulled Eryk close. He plunged his hand into the pig's stomach, pulled a bloody gob out, and smeared it over Eryk's face and body.

"Now you look like a man; all women will love you." He released Eryk and pointed to the fences, where young women stood watching.

Stefan waggled his fingers at the women, who giggled and waved back. He nudged Eryk with his elbow.

Eryk grinned, his teeth flashing through the animal muck on his face. He dropped the knife and pushed Stefan on his ass.

Gray eyes narrowed, and teeth bared, the blond man surged up and punched Eryk on the chin, knocking him into the dirt and on his back.

Silence settled around them.

"Shit."

He didn't know who said it.

Stefan's eyes widened, and his mouth hung open.

Eryk rubbed his jaw and wiggled it. He guffawed and grimaced.

"About time someone treated me like normal." The clouds flitted across the blue sky and held up his hand.

Stefan clasped it and pulled him up. Eryk punched Stefan, who staggered a bit but kept to his feet.

"That was a sucker's punch," said Stefan.

"Serves you right for not bringing me on the hunt," said Eryk. "Since when do you hunt razorbacks without me?"

"Is this the reason for your recent standoffishness?"

The men stared at each other.

Sitting on a stump, Jon smacked his lips and burped as he lifted the wineskin in salute to them. He ripped a chunk from a loaf of dark brown bread and chewed, his eyes closed in ecstasy.

Eryk clapped Stefan on the shoulder. "Do we understand one another again?"

Stefan nodded.

"Let's go get the food from Jon before he eats it all, the greedy giant."

Eryk flung his arm around Stefan's neck and hugged him.

CHAPTER THREE

Can't Have Everything

Eryk felt better after spending the afternoon with Jon and Stefan. Inside jokes, playful punches, and hard work characterized their friendship. He went to his rooms, shivering from cleansing in the stream that washed away the last of his dark mood.

He fell into bed, exhausted, and finally allowed himself to think about Nicolette. He knew he couldn't keep her from his mind once his mother mentioned her. Nicolette's dark amber eyes followed him to sleep, where he relived the last time he saw Nicolette three years ago.

In his dream, Eryk plucked a stave of wild wheat from the ground next to him. He closed his eyes and lay back, putting the stem between his teeth. He brushed his thick, rusty brown hair from his forehead. The small pond at the back of his father's lands soothed him. He loved his family, but sometimes he needed to escape them.

This morning, Kellan brought up the future with him again. His older brother didn't understand. As the eldest and only legitimate child, he only experienced good and saw the best in life.

Eryk admitted he had it better than most bastards, but his only future was his half-brother's benevolence.

Kellan would beat the shit out of him if he knew he used words like half-brother, bastard, and illegitimate. His brother insisted these words had no meaning between them. Kellan only ever called him a brother, even when Eryk wasn't around to hear.

Reeds rustled by the pond. Eryk sat up, hiding in the tall weeds around him.

"Shit, what the fuck is she doing here?"

He crawled closer to the water, crouching low like a stalking animal. He came here today specifically to avoid thoughts of Nicolette. He knew he could not have her. And if he couldn't have her, he didn't want anyone.

She hiked her skirts to the middle of her thighs and tucked the hem into her belt. Her dark brown hair, thick and curly, fell below her waist. She had it uncovered and unbound, and it danced around her in the cool spring breeze. Eryk got painfully hard as the water licked her naturally tan legs. The sunlight sparked in her eyes, the amber color like gold. He knew from memory they were as deep as a pool.

Nicolette raised her hands above her head, twirled, and laughed. She fell backward into the water, submerging her whole body. After several breaths, she broke the surface like the goddess she was to Eryk.

Her gown clung to her curves, highlighting every lush part of her. Eryk had never seen a lady act with such abandon. One reason he wanted her was because she didn't act like other high-born women. She laughed often and from deep in her belly. Her laughs included her mouth, cheeks, and eyes.

The first time he saw her when they were nine, she had fallen while trying to mount a battle horse. Her oh-so-proper sister, Isuet, had tried to get the younger girl in trouble.

He couldn't stand Isuet, who was so different from Nicolette. Different mothers made them opposites in physical appearance and in temperament. Isuet looked washed out and anemic, with pale blond hair, a thin frame, and a constipated expression; she yipped at people like a deranged lap dog.

Nicolette got astride the destrier, and the warhorse bucked and threw her to the ground.

Eryk ran over and offered her his hand. His giant paw dwarfed her tiny fingers. He pulled, not knowing his strength, and she collided with his chest. He looked into her bottomless eyes, lost until Isuet shrieked.

"Get your filthy bastard hands off of my sister," Isuet screamed, hitting him with a broom she grabbed from a passing scullery. They were enemies from that moment. She never missed an opportunity to embarrass him whenever they were together.

Nicolette's family visited every summer after that. Count Tomas, her father, hoped Kellan would marry her. Kellan was always polite, but distant. Allan, their father, never entertained the idea because of Kellan's restraint.

Eryk spent summers in agony and ecstasy: seeing Nicolette was pleasure and pain; seeing Isuet was simply a pain.

Kellan had not seen his humiliation that day he fell in love. That's why Kellan didn't know that Eryk had no future.

Eryk collapsed onto his belly, burrowing his face in his arms. If he could cry, he would. His heart, body, and soul cried out for the young woman cavorting in the water just feet from where he lay in the grass. She had no business coming here, disturbing his solitude, his escape attempt.

Kellan should have mentioned that they would visit them early this year. Why would Kellan mention Nicolette when he didn't know Eryk yearned for her?

Eryk cursed his father, Allan, dead now for two years. He loved his father but couldn't thank him for leaving him when Eryk was sixteen and becoming a man. Being viewed as a mistake and an abomination by the world, despite his father's love, was difficult to accept. He had everything at his fingertips, but nothing to hold in his hands as his own.

Passion, as well as reason, lived in Allan. He loved his first wife, Lillian, and his heart broke when she died six months after Kellan was born. He grieved by running away from his son and his other responsibilities. Maryn, Lillian's maid, took over nurturing Kellan and running the household. She was heartbroken, too, having grown up with Lillian. The women had been lifelong companions. Maryn saw a need and filled it.

When Allan returned home from his year-long mourning pilgrimage, he found everything as it ought to be. His gratitude to Maryn soon became love, as Allan was a loving and dedicated man. He petitioned the King, his friend from childhood, to allow Allan to marry Maryn. The King denied his blessing. The best he got was the King's agreement not to make Allan marry someone else. And so, Allan and Maryn married in the chapel in the woods, which granted Maryn certain privileges but prevented Eryk, born three years after Kellan, from any inheritance rights.

He was healthy, well-educated, loved by his father, mother, and brother, and trained better than most firstborn, legitimate sons, but he couldn't have the woman he wanted.

Eryk woke with moonlight shining across his face. He brushed his fingers across his brow and rubbed his eyes, wiping away his tears before falling asleep until sunrise.

CHAPTER FOUR

Charmed, I'm Sure

Nicolette, eyes closed, breathed in the scents of baking bread, mint, and honey. Her stomach rumbled. They had not broken their fast yet this morning as they rose at first light to finish the end of their journey as soon as possible.

Maryn's kitchen felt like home to her. Scrunching her eyes tight, Nicolette held back her tears. She clasped the pendant she always wore, a two-sided silver disk with the esoteric symbols of her mother's people, Berber and Basque from Iberia. Her mother wore the necklace until she died, bequeathing it to her daughter. Touching her mother's gift steadied Nicolette's nerves.

Maryn held Betsey on her lap, as the six-month-old slept for the first time in weeks..

Nicolette rolled her neck and stretched her shoulders.

"Tell me your secret."

Clarissa, her oldest friend, squeezed Nicolette's fingers with one hand while pushing a bowl of chamomile tea toward her.

Maryn nodded at the tea.

"Drink, relax. Children can sense our moods." She combed her fingers through the white streak in Betsey's hair. "When did you last rest?"

"Not for several weeks." Clarissa sipped her tea.

"We did not take a direct route here."

Nicolette wrapped her fingers around her warm cup. "There is danger for the child and her mother. We needed to take great care while on our travels."

Betsey whimpered in her sleep. Maryn rocked her tall, thin body from side to side, and the baby settled.

"You will stay here for a bit. We have Revena and Kellan's daughters here for the summer. They would love playing with this little doll while you recover, and your visit will help keep them out from under Eryk's feet."

"Eryk is in residence?" The blood drained from Nicolette's face. "I heard he traveled to Rome."

"How do these rumors start? I will never know." Maryn shook her head.

"I have been out of touch with the lives of others for many months," said Nicolette.

"She has been comforting me in my bereavement," said Clarissa. "Losing my parents and new husband came as a shock to me."

"Of course, but Eryk has been here all along. He plans to learn every bit of the running of Thornewood. He feels his father's eyes upon him and feels himself lacking."

"That can not be so," said Nicolette. "I've known no one as capable as he." Her cheeks turned warm, and she looked down. "From what I remember, he excelled at all his lessons. But it has been three years."

Maryn smiled. "He is the only one who believes him deficient."

Nicolette saw Eryk in her. Taller than most, thin but well-formed, with rusty brown hair and the softest brown eyes.

Nicolette wondered how he might have changed since they last saw each other several years ago. She ached to see her dearest friend but feared his reaction to her showing up after all this time just to drop a child off to be fostered and then to leave again.

Clarissa cleared her throat. "We would like to pause our journey for a few days," she said, "a brief holiday, perhaps."

"Clarissa and I can not stay," said Nicolette. "You were always so kind to me, and I will repay you by asking for a boon." She wrung her hands. "Betsey's mother can not care for her. She refuses to mention the father's name but admits he is dangerous for mother and child if he knew of the girl's birth." She sucked in air. "I vowed to find Betsey safe fosterage and beg you to take on this task."

The baby stretched, yawned, and yowled.

Nicolette jumped up and reached for her.

"Sit," said Maryn. "The babe needs a nappy change and some food."

A short, round woman entered the kitchen, her plump cheeks hiding her eyes as she laughed.

"Give the child over," she said, taking Betsey from Maryn. "I'll set her to rights." Two girls joined her. They laid cloth on a side table along with a large bowl of warm water and clean clothes.

"It's been so long since we had children in the house," said Maryn. "We are overjoyed, are we not, Jen?"

"Aye, we are," said Jen as she cleaned and redressed Betsey. "I have milk warming on the stove, and the bread is out of the oven, so the wee one can fill her belly."

"Jen and her daughters are the best cooks in the kingdom," said Maryn. "Their skills are a blessing."

"Tis a blessing for us to be here," said Jen, "and no lie. When my husband died, I despaired for my daughters. Count Eryk saved them. He saved us all."

"Count?" Nicolette's voice squeaked at the title—so many changes.

"A long story," said Maryn. "The three of you will remain here, take your ease, and recover. You all need respite and care. The fullness of time will tell all stories."

Maryn rose from her bench.

"Come, refresh yourselves with cool water. Wash the road from your face and hands. Loosen those gowns and remove a few layers of clothing. You know we don't stand upon such ceremonies here. We are a family home."

Jen's daughters helped Nicolette and Clarissa remove their overtunics. They stripped down to chemises, and a single overdress.

Clarissa giggled. "I feel wicked. I believe I will adopt this mode of dress at home."

The women took the travel garments out back to beat the dust from them and draped them over bushes to freshen in the sun.

The cook placed bread, butter, and a pot of honey on the table. Stewed apples flavored with nutmeg, a plum tart, slices of smoked sausage, and mugs of warm brown ale rounded out the meal. Betsey sat on the stone floor, gumming a piece of bread slathered with butter and honey.

Nicolette laughed. "She will need cleaning again."

"You leave her care to us for the rest of the day," said Jen. "Wait until the little misses clap eyes upon her. Make no mistake upon it."

"Do I smell food?" A clattering of boots on the wooden floors of the hall accompanied the jovial question.

Nicolette froze at the sink, her back to the doorway. She spun around when she heard a male grunt.

Eryk crouched in the doorway, his body too tall to get through while erect. Betsey crawled to Eryk and clasped his trousers. She wiped her sticky face on his leg.

"Oh, ho, little one." He entered the room laughing and scooped the little girl up to his face. She laced all of her syrupy fingers into his bushy beard and pulled.

As Betsey bussed him on a hairy cheek, he howled like a good-natured beast.

"Who be you, my sweeting?" He wiped jam from the child's pudgy cheek.

He scanned the room full of laughing women and girls for an answer, his eyes traveling to each one until they rested upon Nicolette.

He clenched his jaw, narrowed his eyes, and stilled.

Nicolette walked to him and brushed her fingers on his hand as she glanced up at his face.

He jerked, eyes blinking.

They stood there, alone in the churning sea of eternity.

"Let go of the child, Eryk," said Maryn from across the room, breaking the spell.

CHAPTER FIVE

Old Friends

After taking Betsey from Eryk, Nicolette turned her back to him. Her chest felt tight, her arms and legs shaking. She sat at the table and buried her face in the child's neck. She didn't think she would see him on this trip. She wanted to be away and back to hiding on Clarissa's estate, Black Bear Lodge, on the edge of the great Bohemian Forrest.

It took her a moment to notice the silence.. Then her ears popped, and the sound came rushing in on her.

"Eryk Allan Thorne," said Maryn. "Where do you think you are going?"

Nicolette had never heard that tone from the older woman before.

"Away," he said, his voice muffled.

Nicolette glanced over her shoulder.

Eryk filled the doorway as he bent to leave.

"No, sir, you are not," said Maryn.

He stopped, his fingers gripping the wood frame, his knuckles white.

"Mother." His voice was quiet.

Maryn crossed the room and caressed his shoulder.

"Son, please join us."

He sighed, shook his head, and let his hands drop. He backed into the room, stood to his full height, and turned.

"Ladies, I apologize for my behavior." He gritted his teeth and bowed. "It's good to see you all." He took a stool from near the wall and placed it at the furthest end of the table from Nicolette.

"Clarissa. Nicolette. A pleasure to see you again." He looked at Clarissa and smiled. His eyes scanned the ceiling above Nicolette's head.

"To what do we owe the honor of your visit?" He sipped the cider Jen placed before him. "After all of this time." He mumbled into his cup.

Nicolette looked up at him. His cheeks flushed red on pale skin and his features were still as granite. His upturned lips did not crinkle the corners of his eyes. Eryk never acted this rude or this out of sorts. He always laughed and smiled when people were around, especially women, appearing carefree and even-tempered.

Her throat constricted. She couldn't swallow.

Maryn frowned. "Eryk, I ask that you be civil."

He banged his cup on the table and glared at her. She gazed back, and they played a few moments of the staring game. He lost.

He stood up, pushed the stool back with his legs, and knocked it over.

"Pardon me a moment."

He stepped outside through the backdoor.

"He must have gotten out of the wrong side of the bed this morning," said Maryn.

"I think we should leave," said Clarissa.

"Certainly not," said the three of them at once: Maryn from her chair, Nicolette over Betsey's head, and Eryk dripping water on the stoop as he returned to the kitchen.

Eryk brushed his russet hair and beard with his fingers.

"My apologies for my inexcusable reception." Eryk crossed the room in two strides, his long legs eating up the distance. "I am, of course, and always glad to see you both."

He flashed one of his beautiful and genuine smiles, even connecting with Nicolette's eyes. Her heart fluttered, and she couldn't speak, dazzled by a look that would never be hers alone.

"While you are most welcome any time and for as long as you wish, tell me why you have come."

Clarissa cleared her throat, coughed, and turned to Maryn.

"The ladies came to ask us to foster this child. There is a certain need for secrecy."

Eryk leaned forward. "Why? Who does the child belong to?"

"The mother's name must remain unknown to all but Clarissa and me," said Nicolette. "We promised."

Jen plucked Betsey from Nicolette's arms. "Come wee one. Let's take you to the nursery." Her daughters, Fronika and Libbe, followed with buckets of warm water to bathe the little girl.

"Our errand must remain hidden," said Clarissa, "so that the little girl's trail grows cold." She pulled at the cuff of her cornflower blue dress that matched her eyes and complimented her blond hair.

"Mother and child may not remain together," said Nicolette. "It is too dangerous for them."

Eryk's brows came together. "The father?"

"He does not know and must never know. He would kill them both if he ever found out."

"I know you are now Count, and the decision is yours, but I have already told them they may linger here, and we will take the child and protect her."

"I," said Nicolette, "we understand if you do not wish a scandal. Being a count brings about different responsibilities." She wrung her hands.

"First," said Eryk, addressing his mother, "you may always make invitations and decisions as you see fit. Thornewood is your home and always will be. We will not even consider the laughable idea that anyone but you ran this place for nigh on twenty years, even when my father and brother were called Count."

"Or my son."

Eryk picked a splinter from the table and brushed off some crumbs.

"Yes, well, anyway, your invitation is more than enough, mother. But even so." He stretched his hands out to Clarissa and Nicolette. "Just so we are clear. I invite you both; we will happily care for the child. Not much good being a Count if I can't help my friends and their friends."

Little girls' squeals and laughter reached them.

"What did you say the girl's name is?" He chuckled.

"Betsey," said Nicolette.

Giggles drifted down from the upper floor.

"She will fit right in. I am completely outnumbered and surrounded by women. Just the way I like it." He bit a slice of sausage and grinned.

"Come, ladies, I will show you to your rooms," said Maryn.

Clarissa followed her out of the kitchen.

Nicolette stopped by Eryk. Seated, he barely needed to tilt his head to look her in the eyes.

"Thank you," she said.

"Hey, what are old friends for?"

CHAPTER SIX

Rest for the Weary

Cool morning air drifted over Nicolette's cheeks. She snuggled under the feather-filled comforter, luxuriating in the joy of staying abed. The window shutters remained open, and bright sunlight coaxed her from slumber.

The day they arrived at Thornewood, Maryn took charge of Betsey and sent Clarissa and her to their rooms to bathe in private.

"We can wash in the laundry shed," said Nicolette. "Tubs in our rooms are too much work. We have disturbed your household enough by coming here."

"Nonsense," Maryn said as she directed men to place saddlebags and other baggage from their voyage. They had brought little with them in their haste to travel in secret.

She had one extra shift in the saddlebags, which were wrinkled and smelled like the bag's leather.

"We'll just air this out," said Maryn, "while you soak in the tub."

More men came with a large barrel of oak planks sealed with tar to prevent water from leaking. They placed it in a spot of sunshine near the window. The afternoon turned warm on occasion late in April, and they took advantage of the spring weather.

Nicolette gazed out her bedroom window as seven young girls filled the tub with hot water in three trips each. She felt guilty idling by as they worked, but the view soothed her.

Thornewood Castle overlooked the Inn River. Fishermen plied their trade from the shoreline, and boats bobbed on the slow-moving, wide waterway. Barges pulled by mules carried salt to northern cities. It looked like a market town.

Nicolette wondered if the change was because of Eryk's management. He always had more energy than Kellen and liked to keep moving.

Someone behind her cleared his throat.

She brushed dandelion seeds from her sleeve, made a wish, and followed them as they floated on the breeze.

"Yes?" She turned back to the room.

"Your bath is ready, and all your belongings have arrived from the stables, lady." A man dressed in brown wool clothing twisted a red hat in both hands. "The girls will help you unpack." He backed out of the room.

Two girls, about three years younger than her eighteen, waited for instructions.

"I'd prefer to take care of myself," she said. She smiled, hoping to take some of the sting from her words.

"Beg pardon, lady," said the girl with pale skin and black hair. "Maryn instructed Grite and me to take your clothing for airing, washing, and mending."

Grite, brown-eyed and with two brown braids that reached her hips, gave a little curtsy.

"We," Grite nodded to the other girl, "me and Kathe are learning household skills. We'd be ever so grateful if we could help you."

"I would appreciate a hand putting all to rights," said Nicolette.

They spent the next hour unpacking a hemp chemise, several tunics with tight sleeves and braided bands at neck and sleeve, and one overtunic from a packsack. They discovered this coat, with its wider and shorter sleeves, had tears in the seams and no decorative bands.

"May we fix this coat?" Kathe held the peach-colored tunic to Nicolette, showing her the loose stitching.

"And add bands to neck, wrists, and hem?" Grite stroked the woolen fabric. "You will need something prettier for the festival."

"What festival?" Nicolette examined the soles of her extra pair of shoes. "These need new soles," she said, distracted.

"Walpurgis Night is in nine days," said Kathe, her eyes sparkling.

"Beltane," said Grite in a whisper. The girls giggled.

"We get to go this year," they said in unison and hugged each other, laughing.

"I will not be here in nine days," said Nicolette.

"Maryn told the household that you and Lady Clarissa will stay for at least a fortnight," said Grite.

"And we must be sure you have all you need while you are with us these two weeks," said Kathe.

The girls held hands and watched her with wide eyes.

She would talk to Maryn. She would let these two earnest young women care for her for now.

"If you could assist me in the tub, I will have my bath now."

They undressed her, and each held one of her hands as she stepped into the now-warm water. It smelled of lavender and rosemary. She breathed deep, dunked her head under the surface, paused for the count of ten, and came up for air.

"Should we stay?" Kathe had her arms full of Nicolette's clothing.

"No, I'd like to be alone."

"We will return in a bit to dry you off and dress you in a clean chemise," said Grite.

"When you bring the garment, I'd like some bread, cheese, and ale. I'd like to go to bed soon."

Tomorrow would be the time to go over their plans with Maryn.

The girls left with all her things and returned with a clean undergarment and a food tray.

She lazed in the water until she shivered as the water cooled, and the breeze from the open window made it feel colder.

Wrapping a large linen towel around herself when she stepped from the bath, she nibbled on dark rye slices topped with soft smoked cheese and washed it down with a thick brown ale. She stretched and yawned after only a few minutes of eating.

She slipped into the borrowed chemise, crawled into bed, and didn't wake until mid-afternoon the next day.

Kathe and Grite brought her warm water to wash the sleep from her eyes. They had arrived as soon as she woke, and she wondered if they had been listening at the door.

They called for the troop of girls and men to empty the bath and remove the tub while she sat in bed eating thin wheat cakes wrapped around sloe jam and cream. She felt lethargic and was more than happy to lounge.

Once the room was clean, she attempted to rise.

"Have you brought back any of my clothes?"

"No, lady," said Kathe. "We will need another day to set them to rights."

Grite brought in a zither and laid it on a bench.

"That's mine," said Nicolette. She picked it up and strummed the three strings. It was out of tune. "Eryk made it for me many years ago."

"Maryn thought it would occupy you for the balance of this day," said Grite.

"She wants you to recover from your recent hardships," said Kathe. "Tomorrow is soon enough to venture about."

"I must see to Betsey," she said, running her hands along the rectangular sound box of her instrument.

"Fronika and Libbe have taken over her care, along with the three lasses." Grite held the door for Kathe, who carried out the bowl of wash water. "The nursery is full and happy. They don't need the rest of us."

And so it was that she spent the rest of the afternoon playing the old gift from Eryk and serenading herself into one more good night's sleep.

CHAPTER SEVEN

For a Song

Music floated down from the upper floor of the castle and settled in the enclosed garden where apple trees grew, and the honeybees built their hives sheltered from the cool winds off of the river Inn.

Eryk's chest tightened, and he held his breath. He recognized the sound of the zither he had made for Nicolette years ago. He worked on the long narrow boxed instrument for months, using the black walnut he cured for over a year.

It took him two summers before he found the right silk thread from a merchant who traveled here from the Far East for the three strings. He waylaid every troubadour that came through the town to get the instrument tuned right.

When he finished, he waited another ten months before giving it to her the following summer on her next visit. They were both twelve.

She left it behind after her last visit three years ago. Eryk hid it, unable to look at it without sadness.

How had she gotten it? It must be her playing. "Under the Lime Tree," learned from a passing minstrel, was her favorite song. From her mother's birthplace in Berber Hispania, it was about a maiden that meets her lover under the gaze of Tándaradéi, a nightingale who never tells the secret.

He learned to play one tune on the instrument before hiding it away. The song "Must I, Then" was about a man forced to leave the love of his life, but he vows to remain faithful to her until he returns to marry her.

His mother took the women away yesterday. They didn't come to the hall for the evening meal or this morning to break their fasts. He couldn't decide how he felt about not seeing Nicolette when she was so close. He lay on the grass in the garden, letting the music from their past torture him.

He closed his eyes. The bright spring sun did not warm him enough to chase away the anger he felt at what he would never have. Nicolette was more beautiful than before. She no longer looked like a sister as he tried, with little success, to think of her. She was a woman. A woman old enough to marry.

Her father must be working on making a match for her. Was her sister, Isuet, contracted to marry Prince Henri? He knew there were negotiations, but he didn't track the situation. As soon as they made that match, Nicolette would be married off to someone.

He couldn't bear the thought of Nicolette with another man, forever out of his reach. Of course, she was out of his reach because he was a bastard, new title or not. Her father would never allow his favorite daughter to marry someone like him.

Pounding the ground with his fists and feet, he growled at the world's unfairness. He was having a tantrum like a toddler. He sat up and looked around to be sure no one saw him. He even glanced up to be sure no one peered out of the windows above him.

He realized silence settled around him. He hadn't noticed when the music stopped. He missed it. He realized there had been no music in the castle since Nicolette had left. His one melody didn't count, since it was more like a lament, an act of mourning.

His maudlin mood disgusted him. He paced along the walls of the garden enclosure, trailing his fingers along the stones. He spent too much time brooding at it of late, and it would not do.

Action always helped any situation. At the very least, it would take Eryk's mind off things he couldn't control. He ran through the list of tasks he knew needed doing, looking for something that would take him from home for a few days until Nicolette and Clarissa left.

A messenger lingered at the garden gate. How fortunate.

Dressed in red and gold, the boy stood at attention, as should a representative of the Margravate of Bavaria. Kellan and Revena sent a page. Eryk picked up speed, fear gripping him.

The boy, about twelve years old, watched with wide eyes as Eryk approached him. He tugged at his brown hair and left it sticking up. Eryk almost laughed, but didn't want to insult the boy's dignity.

"Be calm," he said to the boy, whose forehead barely reached his chest. "Relax and tell me your words."

"Margravine Revena," he said, looking up at Eryk, "is with child." He blushed and cleared his throat. "Begging your pardon, Count Thorne. She bade me speak plainly."

"Of course she did," said Eryk. "There is more?"

"Yes." He nodded. "Margrave Kellan bids you come at once. They have matters they wish to discuss with you."

"Is all well?" Eryk gripped the boy's shoulder where an embroidered bumble bee appeared.

"Yes, yes. I wasn't to worry you, and now I have." He looked at the ground. His shoulders sagged.

"No, no," said Eryk. "You have done well. Is there anything else in the message?"

"I am to ride back with you. And my Lady and Lord said you were to say naught to anyone as it is early days yet, and the Margravine is well aware of her mother's history of mishaps with child-bearing. You are especially not to tell your mother. That's what Lady Revena said, sir."

Eryk laughed. If he told his mother, she'd pack up and move in with Revena and Kellan. Not that she forced herself upon her children, but Revena expecting a child was an exceptional circumstance. Despite his worry now, he calmed down to not give anyone he might meet a clue that something was up.

"Go back to the stables," he told the boy. "Did you come alone?"

"No, Count Thorne. They sent me with a soldier."

"Good. Go back and encounter no one. I wish to leave in stealth."

With lips down-turned, the boy nodded.

"Do not look so crestfallen," said Eryk. "Rest and tell your companion to do so. I will gather a few things and bring food and drink."

The boy nodded again, and his eyes brightened. His neck must hurt, thought Eryk.

"While the accommodations in the stable might not be the best, the repast is. Just be sure to stay hidden."

Looking around the corner of the wall, the boy slipped away, nodding.

Eryk would leave a message with one of the stable hands to tell his mother of his visit to Kellan. To be delivered after he escaped, of course. He'd be at Hilltop Fortress before dark, stay a few days, and then return to a Nicolette-free home.

CHAPTER EIGHT

Coward

"He ran away?" Nicolette covered her mouth. She hadn't meant to blurt it out loud.

The table full of women and girls looked at her.

"We must be too much for a man used to living alone." She waved her hands at the faces with raised eyebrows, grins, and smirks.

Maryn patted her hand.

"You didn't let me finish," Maryn said. She sipped her rosehip tea, added more honey, tasted it again, and smiled. "Kellan asked him to visit. Why, I do not know, but he should return in a few days."

"Clarissa and I will be gone by then," said Nicolette. She looked at her friend for support.

"I heard there will be a festival," said Clarissa. "I have not been to a fair in years. Could we not stay for it?" She yawned and rubbed her eyes. "Truth be told, I am weary."

Maryn, Clarissa, Jen, and her two daughters sat at the kitchen table in their night shifts with blankets wrapped around them as shawls. Fronika held Betsey while Libbe supervised Ava, Ema, and Gisela. Without a man in residence, and eased into the day.

"I insist you stay until after May Day," said Maryn. "You both look exhausted and too thin. Let me mother you a bit before sending you back out into the world and back to the duties of young women of nobility."

"But I did not wish to make our presence here known," said Nicolette. "I wished to break our connection to Betsey."

"And so you shall," said Maryn. "This castle is secure, and those who come and go are faithful to this house. We expect no visitors within these walls."

"Visitors will crowd the town for the festivities and the market." Nicolette pulled her blanket close around her. She shivered. "We can not attend."

Clarissa pouted and stuck her tongue out at Nicolette. Nicolette laughed. Her friend knew how to cheer her up and always get want she wanted.

"We still practice the old ways," said Jen, adding a board of small apple tarts to the table.

The three girls jumped up and reached for them at once.

Maryn cleared her throat.

They looked at her, eyes big in their round faces. They sat, hands on laps.

"May we have a tart?" asked the twins.

Maryn raised her left eyebrow.

"Please," they said in unison.

"They look very delicious, Mistress Jen," said Gisela, her white-blue eyes glowing under her black curls.

Ava and Ema, with their brown hair, brown eyes, and naturally tan skin, did not look like their adopted sister, Gisela, whose skin was so pale you could see the blood vessels in her cheeks. Still, they acted so much alike that one forgot their physical appearance and thought them related by blood.

"You may help yourselves, ladies," said Maryn, "But slowly. I do not wish to treat aching bellies later today."

Gisela lifted the serving board and held it out to Libbe and Fronika.

"Please choose first," she said, all delicate manners.

"The girls will not be going into town," said Maryn, turning back to Nicolette and Clarissa. "They are much too young yet. We will have a puppet theater and musicians in the castle for the children."

"We're making masks," said Ava.

"And costumes," said Ema.

"And practicing a song," said Gisela.

"And dancing," said all three together, collapsing into laughter and hiding their faces behind their hands.

"We celebrate Beltane," said Maryn, "and as long as we pay our respects to Saint Walpurgis, the church elders are satisfied."

"Eat, Lady Nicolette," said Jen. "Look, your friend does not insult my cooking by avoiding it."

"Oof," said Clarissa, around a mouthful of tart, the cream dribbling down her chin. "If my cook at home was as good as you, I'd be fat and happy. The men would be falling at my feet to have me, despite being the daughter of a lowly merchant."

"Ha," said Nicolette. "Don't let her fool you. Since becoming a widow last year, she's had no less than ten marriage offers. And it's not just her father's abundant wealth they are after."

"Yes, they overlook the filthy trades when the gold can pay off their debts, just like Lord Black did when he made me a Lady by marrying me and allowing my father to clear the mortgage on Black Bear Lodge and its lands," said Clarissa with a smile.

"You must still have a care," said Nicolette, "while the widow of a Lord would not usually come to the King's attention, word of your overflowing coffers might."

"Nonsense," said Clarissa with a dismissive wave of her hand. "I am not like you, the daughter of a Count and thus beholden to father and sovereign." She caressed Nicolette's hand. The women exchanged a look.

"I live quietly out in the woods with no one to force me into another match. I did my duty, and now I shall do as I please." She wiped her face. "And it would please me to stay for the fair." Clarissa stuck out her bottom lip. "Please."

"Oh, stop with the face," said Nicolette, laughing.

Clarissa leaned into her, her cheek on Nicolette's shoulder, and batted her eyelashes.

"We will busy ourselves by making costumes and masks," said Maryn. "There will be dancing around bonfires and wreaths of roses woven to bring a loved one into our lives."

Clarissa shook her head.

"Only for those who wish for such things," said Maryn.

Jen's daughters giggled.

"Go on with you both," said their mother. "No need to be rushing yourselves, either."

"No one will see you," said Maryn, "and no one will know you are here. We will keep to ourselves these coming days. You will allow us to coddle you."

"Fine," said Nicolette. "I give up. I know when I have lost the battle."

The women and girls pounded the table.

"Hurrah," they shouted together.

Betsey, asleep in Fronika's arms, woke and started crying. Fronika rocked her and hummed. Then she sang:

"Sleep, my child, sleep. Your father tends the sheep, your mother shakes the apple tree, as falls down a dream for thee. Sleep, my child, sleep."

Betsey stilled.

"She will be well here," said Nicolette, watching the baby.

"Yes," said Maryn, her voice low. "We will take good care of her, I promise. And you may come to see her whenever you are able."

"May we go dress?" asked Gisela.

"And work on our masks?" asked Ava.

"And practice our dance steps?" asked Ema.

"Oh, yes," said Gisela. "I so wish we had music for dancing."

"Nicolette was tuning her zither yesterday," said Maryn. "Perhaps you can talk her into playing for you."

The girls swarmed Nicolette, full of little girl energy.

"If Eryk ran away from this exuberance, who could blame him?" Nicolette laughed.

CHAPTER NINE

A Warning

Hilltop Fortress was a quaint name for the Margravate's castle. The entire stronghold encompassed the crown of a flat-topped mountain, and travelers from foreign lands called it the longest fortress in the known world. While the King lost his warlord, Revena's father, last year, he gained more competent management of the local resources, focusing on the white gold that came upriver from the alpine salt mines.

Eryk stopped Smoke, his horse, and sat admiring the rust-red tile roofs of the town's buildings nestled between the Salzach River and the hill on which the garrison sat. Under Revena and Kellan's administration, the town grew into a small city and a market destination, bringing increased income to the area.

Kicking his mount forward, Eryk, the young messenger, and his bodyguard proceeded down to Mautner Castle, where the salt was offloaded from barges and boats and transported inland. He'd take a ferry across the river to the road leading to Kellan's new home.

Townsfolk worked in the evening while the sun still shown in the west. Dusk on the eastern side made the path up the hill murky and gray. They posted soldiers at intervals with torches lit in their braziers.

The boy slumped over his horse's neck, and the bodyguard's stomach rumbled. Their day was a long one.

"We will be in the courtyard soon," said Eryk. "Once through the gates, you may be off to your victuals and bed. I know my way."

He sidled up next to the child.

"Boy," he said, realizing he had never asked either of their names. "Wake before you fall. We are almost there."

The child slid sideways away from Eryk. He reached out to grab his tunic sleeve and missed. The soldier caught him and pulled him across his lap.

"Thank you," said Eryk, clutching the bridle of the empty horse. "Your name, sir?"

"William, Sir," said the big man. He lowered his chin to his chest, "and this is my boy, Williamson."

"Well met," said Eryk.

"And you, sir." William shifted his sword to give his sleeping son more room. "The trip was a welcome one for me as I am used to being far from home with the army and not hanging about an enclosed fortress."

"I understand that well." Eryk shifted in the saddle on his gray Senner horse. He wasn't used to riding after several months at home. Although he had never been to war, he felt the itch this man spoke of. "You miss being out on the marches?"

"Some," said William, "but remaining home has benefits." He wrapped his arm tighter around his son.

Eryk felt a pinch in his chest. He missed his father. Would that pain ever go away?

"A son is a special blessing," he said, smiling, although he didn't think William could see it in the waning light.

"Aye," said the soldier. "I have a new wife, as well. So home is a good place to be. And I am needed here. Not all dangers happen in strange lands."

"What say you?" Eryk sat up straighter. "Are there dangers here at Hilltop? To the Margravate?"

"Aye."

That simple, clipped word felt like an ax to the neck.

They reached the gate to the outer rampart. William spoke to the guards, and they entered the castle's grounds. They passed through the curtain wall, under the barbican, past the gatehouse, and into the bailey.

"I will leave you here," said William, holding his hand out for his son's horse.

"If I wish to speak with you further," said Eryk. "where may I find you?"

"Aye," said William. "Ask at the keep. Cate, my wife, be about most days and knows my whereabouts, as most wives seem to do." He chuckled. He leaned towards Eryk.

"Mind your back and your brother's with his special guest," said William. "The Margrave has his mind on his wife and quickening child and may not see all there is to see with those professing friendship."

William woke his son, lowered him to the ground, and dismounted. He led his child and the two horses off to the right, along the curtain wall, where houses butted up against it.

Eryk rode off to the left, his heels encouraging a trot from Smoke. He wanted to kick into a canter, but too many people were in the yard. William's words twisted his stomach in knots. He thought this a simple visit to his brother, and now some sort of danger stalked the couple, and Kellan didn't appear to be aware of it.

He reached the keep's doors, slid off his horse, grabbed his saddlebags, and tossed the reins to a groom who appeared without being called.

Howard, the steward of Hilltop Castle, opened the door as Eryk lifted his fist to knock. His hand never touched the wood of the great oak door, carved in relief with scenes from hunts: a Royal stag with its twelve-pointed antlers reaching skyward on the left panel and a great wild boar with its upper tusks curling around to its forehead on the right.

"Where is my brother?" Eryk pushed past the steward.

"A moment, Count Thornewood," said Howard. The man followed the two more steps Eryk took before stopping.

Eryk faced him.

"I need to see my brother immediately." He handed the steward his bags and looked around.

"Begging your pardon, Sir, but it is late for her Ladyship, in her condition," he said, his voice ending in a whisper, "and his lordship retires with his Lady Wife."

"Ugh," Eryk grunted in his frustration.

"If I could show Your Excellency to his rooms," said Howard, with a slight bow, "I can see if His Lordship is available this evening."

"Yes, of course." He forgot where and who he was in the grand scheme of things.

"I will send up some warm water for you, and a tray and have the fire lit as it gets cold still up here." Howard moved as he spoke, walking up the stairs to the private chambers, waving at various serfs who seemed to know what his gestures meant.

Once in his usual room, with wash water and warm roast boar, roasted turnips, and apple strudel, he calmed a bit. He washed and changed into clothes he kept in a trunk for his visits, thus making travel between them more manageable. He settled before the fire and waited, his left knee bobbing up and down without his notice.

Just as he felt himself nodding off, a knock sounded, and Kellan burst into the room, grabbed Eryk as he rose, and hugged him.

"Brother, I have missed you."

"And I, you. Now, talk of this danger that besets your house."

CHAPTER TEN

Danger in the House

"I won't keep you, but one day," said Kellan as he paced the length of Eryk's permanent guestroom. The shadows caused by the firelight and his pinched eyebrows made him look uncharacteristically stern.

"I will stay as long as you need me," said Eryk. "I have nothing that requires immediate attention other than what agitates you." Anything to keep me away from home while Nicolette visited, he thought.

Kellan strode to his brother and grabbed his shoulders.

"I've never been so scared," said Kellan. "This constant waiting and worrying." He shook his head. "I don't know how people do this."

Eryk wrapped his arms around his older brother and hugged him tight. Kellan stiffened momentarily, sank into his brother, and closed his eyes.

A rap on the door broke the men apart.

The steward brought in a Bohemian glass bottle filled with local wine, a jug of cider, and a ceramic pitcher of cold water. He placed them on the table between the two chairs in front of the fireplace.

"Will you be needing anything else, Your Grace?"

"No, Howard," said Kellan. "Send everyone to their beds. And yourself, too. Do not stay up just in case I might need you."

"Yes, Your Grace." Howard's lips twitched up, but he caught himself before he smiled. He backed from the room.

"Sit," said Eryk as he poured a glass of wine and put it in Kellan's hand. He poured himself a glass of water and took his chair.

His brother sighed.

"Tell me what worries you so." Eryk sipped the chilled liquid.

Kellan twirled his cup between his thumb and index finger, staring into the amber liquid. He expelled another lungful of air and rolled his neck.

"You know Aenor's history with pregnancy," said Kellan.

"Some of it," said Eryk, "but no more than most."

"Revena's mother was with child seventeen times. Revena was the only child that she birthed." Kellan twisted the stem of his glass, and it snapped off, cutting his thumb.

"Give me that," said Eryk. He exchanged the broken glass for a cloth.

Kellan wiped the blood from his hand and wrapped it around the wound.

"You see what all of this is doing to me?"

"What is 'all of this'? I know you are worried about Revena and your baby."

"We have the best of midwives," said Kellan, "and Revena has forbidden the physicians at her bedside. She doesn't trust them, and I support her choice."

"As you should," said Eryk with a grin.

"Yes, and she looks and feels well. Her women say she is in good health, and I think she looks beautiful." Kellan blushed as he said this last.

Eryk smiled at his brother's clear love for his wife. He shouted down the jealous voice in the back of his mind.

"And all of us agree Aenor lost all of her babies because of the beatings from Muirdach. For a man that claimed he wanted children so much, especially a son, Revena's father sure did his best to beat all life out of Aenor."

"The death of the former Margrave of Bavaria was a blessing to us all," said Eryk. "I don't think even King Hugh misses his Iron Fist much."

"The Eastern Marches are quiet right now," said Kellan. "The King needs peacetime leaders to run cities and towns and organize the people and their work. Muirdach only knew war, death, and theft."

Eryk nodded.

"A Warlord here in the heart of the King's territories was more threat to his crown than he wanted to admit." Kellan chuckled.

"When Revena and I traveled to his Seat in East Francia last harvest, the King put on a good show with his grief over the death of his warlord." Kellan picked at the cloth covering his hand.

"The pleasure he expressed over the increase in Bavaria's coffers since that death seemed more genuine. As his signature legitimizing you and Adam in the Seat's annals, approving the transfer of titles to you both, and the wedding gift of the hunting estate of Wolfram attests."

Kellan rose and took up his pacing.

"Revena says I am anxious because I am to be a father and nothing more." He stopped and looked at Eryk. "Nothing more, she says. Isn't that enough? Me, a father. I can't fathom it." He took up his movement, stomping like a toddler.

"Truth to tell," he continued, "I do fear for Revena more than the child. I don't know how I lived before I met her. I know her mother survived all the times she expected, but you know how often women die giving birth. My mother died not six months after I was born from an infection after childbirth."

He came back to the chairs.

"Where is my wine?"

"You broke your glass." Eryk got up and retrieved a wooden mug next to his wash bowl. He rinsed it out, filled it with wine, and wrapped his brother's hands around it.

"Try to hold on to this," he said, tilting the cup to his brother's lips.

Kellan emptied its contents and reached for more, grumbling as he drained the bottle. He glanced at Eryk before raising the cup to his mouth.

"Revena is strong. You will not lose her."

Eryk would go to hell for making such a promise, but he felt it in his soul, and the statement seemed to be what Kellan needed to hear.

"You will have a fine babe and be the best of fathers." Unlike you, you will never be a father. That damn jealous voice spoke up again in his head. He gulped some water and rubbed his temple with his free hand.

"I do not know my child yet," said Kellan, "so it doesn't seem real." He wiped the palms of his hands down his thighs. "There are moments when I envision a daughter or a son cradled in my arms."

A sudden downpour filled the night sky, strong winds blowing water into the open window. Thunder rolled down from the mountains and along the Salzach River.

Kellan pulled the shutters closed to keep out the rain and lightning. He laughed.

"What has amused you?" Eryk handed his brother a bathing cloth to dry his hair.

"I rarely believe in portents and omens," said Kellan, "despite my wife's witchy ways." He tossed the towel over a drying rack. "I remained calm these last few months. It wasn't until Prince Henri's visit I seemed infected with thoughts of pending doom and death."

CHAPTER ELEVEN

Gift Horse

"His Highness has certainly overstayed his welcome," said Eryk, "even for a Prince of the realm." He took a bite from the apple strudel from the food board. "Doesn't he have his castle he must attend?"

"He claims to leave soon. It's been almost two moons since he arrived to survey the efficiency of our salt distribution and the functioning of the castle," said Kellan. "I'm told he spends most of his time sampling our wines and wenches."

"That seems more like him." Eryk laughed. "So, besides his usual debauchery, what has you vexed?"

Kellan placed a couple of logs on the fire. He picked up the iron poker beside the fireplace and stirred the embers to light the unburnt logs.

"He makes comments while we dine. 'If I held this Duchy, I would charge higher tolls for using the river crossing. If the Duchy were under my control, I'd raise the price of the dues on the guilds.' He points out we seem to be doing a passable job managing the territory." He tossed down the rod. It clanged on the stone hearth. "Nothing overt. He laughs and says he's just making helpful suggestions, but my gut tells me he's threatening us."

"I never discount your stomach, brother," said Eryk, "whether 'tis for food or lurking danger."

"How a son could be so different from the father is beyond me," said Kellan, as he ran his fingers through his dark blond hair, tucking it behind his ears to keep it out of his amber eyes. Kellan looked so

41

much like Allan that his confusion over Prince Henri and King Hugh was understandable.

Eryk favored Allan's father, a reformed raider from northern Germania, with his towering height and wild rusty brown hair. "But your soft, kind brown eyes come from your mother," he heard his father's voice as he shook his head to dispel the ghost.

Perhaps Henri looked more like his mother, whom Eryk had never seen.

"Does he take more after his mother, Queen Adelaide? Did you not see her when you and Revena went to court last fall?"

"I did, and he does not." Kellan collapsed into his chair with a sigh. "While the king and queen have dark brown hair, they also have dark brown eyes. Henri has those bright violet eyes. And he's so much taller than his parents or his siblings. I think that's why he gets so nasty when he sees you. You still tower over him."

Eryk hunched his shoulders.

"I can make myself less threatening."

Kellan punched his shoulder.

"In your dreams."

The brothers laughed.

"Now that we've established how much the prince loves me," said Eryk, "what am I doing here? How can I help?" He pulled his dagger from its sheath at his waist and tossed it, catching it by its handle while watching Kellan.

"Do you ever miss?" Kellan pointed his chin at the twisting blade.

"Not anymore." He chuckled. "Quit stalling. Tell me."

Kellan grunted.

"The bastard wants your horse," he said and sneered.

"He wants Smoke?" Eryk asked. "When did he ever see my gray? Or does he just randomly want what's mine?"

Kellan shook his head.

Eryk tossed his knife at the woodpile where it stuck and shivered. He furrowed his brow and smoothed his mustache and beard.

"Are you ever going to shave that hairy face of yours and join the rest of us civilized men?" Kellan stroked his bare cheeks.

"Never. The women love this wild man. I can not deny them the pleasure of running their delicate fingers through my heathenish locks."

Kellan burst out laughing, doubling over and holding his belly.

"I've never seen a woman do that," said Kellan. "Do you ever tire of pretending?"

"How do you mean?" Eryk turned his face away from Kellan.

"While I can't deny any woman who meets you falls instantly in love with you," he poked Eryk's arm, "I don't think the same can be said for you."

Eryk cleared his throat.

"Nonsense. I love women," he said. "The horse, what horse does his princeliness covet?"

Kellan frowned at his brother, but Eryk looked back at him, daring to continue the subject of women. For all his jokes and apparent openness, Eryk had a stubborn streak several acres wide, especially regarding women. He just wasn't the type to kiss and tell, despite being surrounded by the fairer sex. Oh, well. Everyone deserved some secrets of their own.

"It's the big, black destrier he wants." Kellan rose to pace the room. "He began hinting at it the first week he was here. He went to the stables for something and spent the entire afternoon and well past the evening meal discussing it and asking questions."

Eryk shook his head and shrugged his shoulders.

"I have a horse in your stables?"

"Oh, for the love of...." Kellan picked up a short whip and cracked it in the air. "Sometimes I despair of you. The monster you got in your bet with that minor Baron who came through here about six months back."

"Oh, the Baron from Frisia." Eryk laughed. "One of the many Ratbods. He couldn't wait to rid himself of that horse. As I recall, the animal bites anything that comes near it."

"That's the one," said Kellan. "The man couldn't shoot for shit. You split his arrows thrice."

Eryk laughed.

"Poor guy. Someone lied to him. Although his eyes should have told him the truth of his abilities."

"He did provide us with an afternoon of entertainment."

Kellan held up the jug to Eryk.

"Apple cider? It's unfermented," said Kellan.

Eryk nodded and held up his cup. He took a sip and smacked his lips.

"I should plant some of Revena's apple trees at Thornewood," he said.

"You'll need another enclosed garden and several years before you get any decent fruit," said Kellan. "Lucky for you, dear brother, I like you. I had our brewer put up a couple of skins for you to take home in the meantime."

"And some cuttings?"

"Of course. Revena insisted."

"Your dear wife is a gem." Eryk put down his cup, rose, and clasped his brother's hand. "She will be fine, as will the babe."

"She's asked for our mother to come," said Kellan.

While Maryn was Eryk's mother and not Kellan's, she raised him from a baby. Kellan simply called her mother.

"You know she will be happy to come," said Eryk.

"Once Henri leaves, I will send for her," said Kellan. He took a deep breath and rolled his shoulders.

"I will bring her." Eryk smiled and squeezed his brother's hand. "If it takes Dirk to get rid of him, I will give the Friesian up. I have no attachment to the animal."

"It's called Dirk?"

"A perfectly awful name, but it came with it. Baron Ratbod claimed the horse came from one of William Longsword's beasts."

"So I heard. As did the stable hands, who told the prince. I think that's why he wants Dirk." Kellan groaned.

Eryk laughed.

"Let him have the animal, although I don't think he can handle him. Has he tried to mount him?"

The men snickered.

"We're such children," said Kellan. "We point out he was battle bred and that we tried to retrain him for more civilized riding."

"Good idea," said Eryk. "I think I left some papers with you on the animal's lineage. Those men from Frisia take their horse breeding very seriously."

"That will make Henri want it even more."

"Oh, no doubt," said Eryk. "Especially when he reads the part about the battles it's been in and the number of its kills."

"That's in writing?"

"Yes, seven pages worth," said Eryk. "You know how bloodthirsty the Normans are. He'll be unable to wait to get Dirk home and show off its pedigree."

"Any idea where the papers might be?" Kellan opened the shutters on the window a crack. "I'm sorry," he said. "The sun is brightening behind the mountains, and I have yet to let you sleep."

Eryk waved him off.

"Who needs sleep?" He yawned and tried to hide it.

Kellan didn't notice as he continued to look out the window.

"They aren't in with the Hilltop documents." His voice escaped on the morning breeze.

Eryk snapped his fingers. He jumped up, went to the chest in the corner, lifted the lid, and tossed some shirts, a leather belt, and a sheepskin rug. He rummaged around and came up with a whoop, waving a sheaf of parchment.

Kellan turned back to the room, leaving the shutters ajar to allow the fresh air to enter.

"Will Henri be able to read them?" Eryk asked as he handed the records to Kellan.

"Yes," said Kellan. "King Hugh educated all of his children. More of our father's influence."

"Makes it more difficult to be cheated." The men quoted their father at the same time.

Kellan leafed through the documents and whistled.

"Are you sure you don't want to keep the animal? It could fetch you a tidy sum of gold."

"It cost me nothing," said Eryk. "You've been feeding it for the six months I forgot about it. Take it and do as you wish. Use the opportunity to get rid of two troublesome animals." Eryk rose and stretched.

"Just make him think he's stealing something I hold dear," he said. "He'll covet it all the more and leave all the sooner."

CHAPTER TWELVE

If Things Were Different

Eryk woke after a few hours. He had left the shutters open on his window to allow the fresh air to help him sleep. Sunshine slanted in and fell across his face just before midday.

He washed and put on a fresh tunic and breeches. He intended to slip out of Hilltop without encountering Henri until he went into the great hall to break his fast and found the prince fondling a maid by the food board.

The girl squeaked when she saw Eryk.

Henri raised his head over her bare shoulder, his brows coming together, his eyes narrowed. He released the girl, who ran off to the kitchens.

Eryk walked over to where Henri took up a wooden board and looked over the sliced smoke sausages, small bread loaves, cheeses, and fruit compotes. Eryk edged just up to Henri's side.

Henri was unusually tall and typically the tallest man in the room, but Eryk rose above him by a head. Normally, he would do things to reduce his size, like not getting too close or keeping seated in a group, but Henri's treatment of the girl made Eryk want to make the Prince feel small, so he moved in as close as possible without touching.

Henri tilted his head back at an uncomfortable angle to meet Eryk's eyes.

"Ah, if it isn't the newly minted ... Count," said Henri.

Henri's eyes traveled from Eryk's face, lingering at his beard, and dropped to his simple T-shaped shirt, worn wool leggings, and scuffed boots. Henri stroked his clean-shaven chin and grinned. His beringed free hand rubbed the gold-brocade trim on his forest green tunic.

"You look quite at home," said Henri. "I had not heard you intended to visit."

Eryk reached across Henri, picked up a black walnut plate, and filled it with a couple of fried white sausages, a crusty roll sprinkled with salt, and some stewed pears flavored with honey and cloves. He took his seat at the table.

Henri finished making his choices and sat at the head of the table in Kellan's chair. He reached for the wine bottle near his place and filled an Italian glass cup. He sipped, closed his eyes, and smiled.

"They have amazing wines here," said Henri.

"They tell me it's the hills at the base of the mountains," said Eryk, reaching for a jug near his hand. He filled a wooden cup with milk.

Henri raised a dark eyebrow. It disappeared into the white streak in his hair.

"No wine for you?" Henri twirled his glass, watching the light dance through the colors decorating the bowl and stem.

"A little early for me," said Eryk. "And I'm still a growing boy." Eryk grinned.

Henri laughed.

"It's too bad," said Henri. He tore a roll in two, covered one half in butter, and topped it with current jelly.

"What's too bad?" Eryk rested his elbows on the table, picked up a sausage, dipped it in a grainy brown mustard, and bit off one end.

"It's too bad you are you, and I am I." He spoke around the food in his mouth. "I could like you if it weren't for the fact that I don't."

Eryk chuckled.

"There is that," he said. "You wouldn't be too bad if you weren't an ass."

Henri stared at Eryk with violet eyes, his mouth turned down at the corners, quiet for a moment.

returned Henri's gaze as he continued to eat, and the Prince continued to drink.

"I will be king one day," said Henri as he refilled his goblet.

"Someday," said Eryk. He nodded. "It's just the two of us here right now. Perhaps we could speak plainly."

Henri shook his head. He leaned back in his chair. He had eaten little but had drunk two full glasses of wine.

"You do like to pull on Satan's whiskers," said Henri.

Eryk sat up straight.

"Why are you here and still here?" Eryk drank his milk. "When are you leaving? Surely, even you have something better to do than linger here."

"I impose myself upon your brother and his wife, but even after two months, they are unfailingly polite and accommodating." Henri shrugged. "I'll be leaving soon. I've become bored." He crossed one leg over the other. "The women here are not as accommodating as in other places, and they seem good at hiding from me." He tapped his fingers on his left knee. "Once Kellan agrees to give me the black Friesian he has in his stables, I'll be on my way."

"That's my horse," said Eryk. He frowned. "It has papers that document its sire and dame. You know how the horse breeders are from Frisia. It's quite valuable. I'm rather fond of it."

The fingers tapping, Henri's knee sped up. He clenched his jaw.

Eryk met and held his gaze. They sat in silence for several minutes, looking at one another. Henri looked away first. His face turned red, and he slammed his glass on the table. It toppled over, and red wine stained the white pine.

Henri stood up, placed his fists on the table, and leaned towards Eryk.

"I will need to extend my visit," he said. "I suspect there are some irregularities in the tax amounts given to the King." He jerked his arm and swept his wine glass onto the floor. It shattered.

Eryk lowered his gaze. He may have pushed Henri too far.

"And I think I must bring my future bride here," said Henri. "I do so miss the Lady Isuet."

Kellan walked into the room, stretched, and paused when he saw the two men poised with tensed muscles. He saw the broken glass in the hay rushes on the floor, the spilled wine, and uneaten food.

"Good Sirs," he said as he got food for himself and sat at the opposite end of the table from Henri. He put some sliced smoked ham and a soft cheese between two slices of dark rye bread, bit into his food, and chewed as he watched Eryk and Henri. He drank a watered-down brown ale.

Henri picked up a goblet from another place, filled it with wine, and returned to his chair.

"How is your wife this day?" Henri spoke to Kellan while watching Eryk.

"She is doing well," said Kellan.

"I hope nothing disturbs her in her delicate state," said Henri.

Kellan startled.

"I know the signs," said Henri. "I have a few bastards running around the countryside. But not to worry. Your secret is safe with me. I won't deny a man the joy of announcing his posterity if it comes to fruition."

Henri glanced at Kellan.

"It's a good thing you waited a while before becoming fruitful, as the priests say," said Henri. "There will be no question as to whether the babe is yours or Revena's previous husband."

Kellan gripped the arms of his chair.

Eryk threw him a look.

"Henri was just telling me he's heading home on the marrow," said Eryk. "He expressed his interest in Dirk and offered to purchase my horse, but I decided, in the interest of friendship and goodwill, to gift the Friesian to Henri."

Eryk smiled and stood.

"It is, after all, an animal fit for a prince and future king." Eryk gave Henri a little bow.

"It is good to have an understanding between men," said Henri.

"I'll go get the papers with the animal's history," said Eryk. "You'll be pleased with them. The scribes took their time and illuminated the vellum in a fine northern style. It may even be an Irish hand that decorated the documents."

"It's a shame your brother is who he is," said Henri to Kellan as Eryk left the room, "and I am who I am. I could quite like him if things were different."

CHAPTER THIRTEEN

Happy Widow

Nicolette sat in a chair lined with down-filled cushions. The April sunshine fell upon her face and shoulders, making her drowsy despite the cool breeze coming in through the open windows.

A thick-woven hemp shawl, dyed with the woad plant to a dark blue, covered her neck and back, the fabric soft from beatings with rocks.

She took a deep breath and blinked, focusing on the cloth in her lap.

Clarissa cursed and sucked on her finger.

"I don't think I'll ever get good at this," she said, her words garbled around her digit. She squeezed the tip and watched a bubble of blood appear. She held it out to Nicolette.

"Look," she said, a whine similar to the ones she produced as a ten-year-old.

"You forget who you're talking to," said Nicolette. "We've been sewing together for years, and you're better at it than I am." Nicolette reached over and wiped off the blood with a scrap of cloth. "You just prefer to be outside."

"The girls will appreciate your efforts," said Maryn, her head bowed over a ribbon she wove, the red poppies, blue gentians, and yellow anemone flowers coming to life as it got longer.

"Libbe and Fronika are the only girls coming of marriageable age in the castle. These Beltane gifts will please them well."

"I know," said Clarissa, "and I'm happy to do this small thing for them. I know the joy of a special shift for your wedding night." She sighed as she continued the tiny stitches on the fine linen in her hands. She created a lacework around the neckline, more skilled than any coming out of Italy.

While Nicolette sewed the nightdresses with care, Clarissa had the talent to make clothing beautiful.

"I'm just so tired of sitting," said Clarissa. "The past year and a half has been too much isolation, too much inactivity for the both of us."

Nicolette coughed, doubled over, and pounded her chest. Clarissa and Maryn glanced at her with concern.

"Sorry." She cleared her throat. "Swallowed wrong." She narrowed her eyes at Clarissa.

"Yes," said Clarissa. "Mourning is confining." She reached over and patted Nicolette's hand. "If it weren't for Nicolette's company, I would have gone mad."

"You are not under any constraints of social norms here," said Maryn. "Feel free to come and go as you please. You are a grown woman, a widow, and certainly of sound mind. I think you are perfectly capable of taking care of yourselves."

Clarissa glanced at Nicolette, and their eyes met. Maryn watched their silent understanding.

"We would never dream of worrying you by venturing alone into the markets," said Nicolette. "We would, of course, bring an escort if we went beyond the walls of Thornewood."

"And we would need someone to carry our parcels," said Clarissa, giggling.

"There is no need to take such care within our grounds," said Maryn. "You may feel perfectly safe here." She held up the ribbon, checking it for missed stitches.

"That's so beautiful," said Nicolette. "I've never seen such bright colors."

"We have an excellent dyer who produces the vibrant threads. Jen's daughters can use these to decorate fine dresses."

"You are so generous to your serfs," said Clarissa.

"We are quite prosperous here at Thornewood, and the family has a long history of sharing the wealth with those who help produce it." Maryn rolled up the band and placed it in a basket at her feet. "We'd like you both to consider yourselves part of our family."

"You are sweet and kind," said Clarissa. "As I no longer have any family, I will gladly consider you so." Clarissa stretched her back. "I'm not calling you mother, though." She shook her head.

Maryn laughed.

"I give you permission to use my name," said Maryn. "Kellan and Eryk calling me mother is more than enough, especially when they do it with that exasperated tone."

"Surely they mean you no disrespect," said Nicolette. She widened her eyes, her cheeks pink.

"Oh, no," said Maryn. "My boys are the best of men. None could treat me better. But I occasionally forget that they are both grown and no longer need my apron strings." She smoothed the skirt of her tunic. "I am glad to have a house full of children, though. And girls. Eryk is so generous that he indulges my desire to give them all gifts and spoil them beyond all reason."

Clarissa and Nicolette smiled at the apparent joy Maryn showed for taking care of the girls.

"Betsey will be in the best hands," said Clarissa, smiling at Nicolette. "Thornewood was a good choice of a haven for the child."

Nicolette nodded as she looked away. She sniffed.

"How are you faring in your grieving, Clarissa?" Maryn faced the young blond woman. Her eyes were the same color as the cornflowers dotting the fields around the estate.

"To be honest with you, I am relieved." Clarissa held up the shift to the light. She smoothed the fabric and folded it. "That's one done." She handed it to Maryn, who added it to her basket.

"You have a fine hand," said Maryn.

"Thank you," said Clarissa.

"How long were you married?" "Maryn rose, poured unfermented apple cider into a wooden cup, and handed it to Clarissa.

"A month," said Clarissa. She sipped her drink. "Long enough to enjoy a honeymoon and too long to realize it was over." She frowned. "I did my duty to my parents, husband, and church. As my parents' only child, I fulfilled their hopes of rising in society. I garnered a title and allowed them to lord it over their fellow merchants. My husband got a cleared mortgage, and his debts paid, not to mention a young, pleasant bride." Clarissa blushed. "I beg your pardon. I've been too long alone with Nicolette. We often speak plainly with one another."

"You may do so with me," said Maryn. "I'm too old to take any offense with plain talk. Plus, there's less misunderstanding when we are honest."

Nicolette looked from one woman to the other. She rolled her shoulders.

"I understand the pressures placed upon women of title and wealth," said Maryn.

"Well, now I am my own woman," said Clarissa. "I sold my parent's customs business, donated to the church, and retired to Black Bear Lodge. We are quiet there, and I place little burden upon the people, so we are all happy."

"When we leave here," said Nicolette, "we will part ways, and our idle will end."

Clarissa pouted.

"I can't convince Nicolette to come home with me."

"Unfortunately, hiding in the Bohemian Forrest is not an option for me." Nicolette sighed. She put away her needle and thread and folded the shift she finished assembling. "Isuet's wedding is soon. My father has sent letters I must come home to take part, and then I must decide on who I will marry. He has several men chosen for me to decide on."

"It's not fair," said Clarissa, banging her fist on the arm of her chair.

"At least I'll have some sort of choice in the matter," said Nicolette, some anger tinging her voice. "Your father gave you no choice at all."

Maryn handed Nicolette a cup of cider.

Clarissa jumped up.

"Let's go for a walk in the orchard. Play under the blossoms instead of thinking of the gloom of the future."

"Yes," said Maryn, "go be young and carefree. We'll leave tomorrow for the future."

CHAPTER FOURTEEN

If Wishing Made It So

Nicolette and Clarissa strolled arm-in-arm through the apple orchards of Thornewood. The sun stood directly overhead, and the sky covered them in a brilliant sheet of blue unblemished by clouds.

They leaned on one another, hugging and supporting, warm and quiet in their comfort and companionship grown through eighteen years of friendship.

Nicolette held her face to the light, and Clarissa guided her over roots and tufts of new spring grass.

Clarissa closed her eyes, breathing deeply, as Nicolette steered her around tree trunks and gopher holes.

The women sighed at the same time and giggled.

"It's wonderful here," said Clarissa.

"I've always loved it," said Nicolette. "I'm glad we could share it one last time." She bent and picked a buttercup. She held the bright yellow flower under Clarissa's chin. "You love butter."

"I won't deny it," said Clarissa. "But surely, your outstanding predictive abilities do not extend to our futures. Why would we not visit here again?" She plucked the flower from Nicolette's fingers, twirled it, and tossed it into the air.

"You know, once I marry, I will not be able to visit Black Bear Lodge or Thornewood," said Nicolette. "Travel for pleasure is not in my future."

"Surely, your future husband, whoever he may be, will not deny you your friends?"

"You, of all people, know better than that," said Nicolette.

"But your father loves you. You're his favorite, not an only child or the oldest." Clarissa kicked at a clump of grass, dampening the toe of her cloth shoe. "And Isuet, by her standards and those of the rest of the world, has made an excellent match. Surely, your father will let you choose your heart's desire."

"The best he will do is allow me my choice from among several men he has picked for me." Nicolette untangled herself from Clarissa, reached up to pull down an apple branch, and smelled the white and pink blossom. She didn't want to think about what lay ahead of her. She wanted a few more days to choose how she spent her time.

Clarissa had told her what it had been like to be married. At first, all seemed well, and she thought herself lucky. His Lordship, the baron of Bernstein, was young, only twenty-two, well-formed, fit, with dark black hair and blue eyes. He looked a dream and made her a lady.

His manners before their marriage were courtly. He treated Clarissa and her parents with respect and deference. His smile dazzled her, their betrothal a whirlwind of girlish dreams.

Once the bands were completed, the mortgages and debts paid, and Clarissa secured in Black Bear Lodge, Lord Bernstein's true nature showed itself.

Clarissa did not spare Nicolette any of the details. The Lord considered her beneath him and resented needing her father's dirty money.

He gave her a tender night for her first time but, come morning, paraded witnesses through their wedding chamber so there would be no question of consummation.

Then he began drinking. Once drunk, he beat her in punishment for having saved his estates.

"Has your father spoken of his choices?" Clarissa plucked a flower from the tree and tucked it into Nicolette's hair.

"No," said Nicolette.

"Then perhaps he has not settled on anyone. You could ask him to allow you to marry Eryk."

Nicolette faced Clarissa.

"You know I will never do that."

"But…"

"No," said Nicolette. "I will not do that."

Clarissa stroked Nicolette's cheek.

"You've known each other for years."

Nicolette pursed her lips and shook her head.

"He's yet unmarried. You are friends. You have affection for each other."

"It can never be. We've discussed this."

Clarissa huffed in exasperation.

"Then ask your father to allow you to come with me," said Clarissa. "I can care for you as well as any man. I have plenty of gold for us to live on for the rest of our lives. We can travel." She danced around Nicolette. "I'm sure we could talk him into it."

Nicolette grasped Clarissa's hands and pulled her to a stop.

"I broached the idea with him a couple of months ago," said Nicolette. "He said he would not allow it and would explain his reasons when we are together again."

Clarissa tugged on Nicolette, pulling her in a circle. They spun faster and faster and collapsed on the ground, arms spread out, laughing at the heavens.

Clarissa rolled onto her side, facing Nicolette, who rolled towards Clarissa, her fist propping up her head.

"There has to be a solution," said Clarissa. "I can't bear the thought of never seeing you again. Or my wonderful sister-of-my-heart trapped in a loveless marriage for the rest of her life."

Nicolette brushed a blond lock from Clarissa's forehead.

"The best I can do," she said, "is a delay for perhaps two years. Time to meet the men on my father's list and make my choice. Time for the negotiations over property settlements. Time to announce the bands and time to plan the wedding."

She fell over on her back and spoke into the air, hoping her whispered words would be an incantation. "You know my deepest, dearest wish." A breeze blew away her words.

"I have a secret," said Clarissa.

"No," said Nicolette, shrieking in pretend outrage. "You swore you never would."

Clarissa laughed and swatted her on the shoulder.

"Well, it was only for a day." She sat up. "I took some of your hair from your brush when we cleaned them yesterday."

Nicolette glanced at her with raised brows.

"Well, I have to do something, and I think I'm more desperate than you. You seem determined to accept whatever fate has in store."

"Not fate," said Nicolette, "just my father. And perhaps Isuet."

"Do you think she has a hand in play over your father's decisions?"

"He hinted as much."

"Oh, that evil c...."

"Clarissa!"

"Cow, I was going to say, cow."

They groaned in unison and spit over their left shoulders, as they always did when speaking of Nicolette's older half-sister.

"Well, then, I'm glad I did what I did."

"What did you do exactly?"

Clarissa tucked her feet under her and covered her knees with her cornflower blue tunic.

"I took your hair and rolled it into a sheet of beeswax with a wick in the middle." She looked off into the distance. "I lit it in my room last night and made a wish for you, just as you did for me."

She leaned close to Nicolette's ear, so their secret did not escape into the wind.

"You freed me," she said. "I intend to free you, with or without your help."

"You can't possibly believe that silly spell I did was responsible for the deaths of your husband and parents."

"Maybe." Clarissa pounded her fist on her knee. "I will do anything. I will do whatever I have to do. You've suffered enough. I will not turn you over to those who did not protect you."

The women rose to their knees at the same time and hugged.

CHAPTER FIFTEEN

Sweet as Honey

Ava, Ema, and Gisela ran into the orchard, laughing and twirling, their bare feet flying across the shorn grass. The hems of their tunics only reached their knees.

All three girls dressed in varying shades of blue, their hair tied back with ribbons of red that vied with the rosy red of their cheeks.

They barreled into Nicolette and Clarissa, knocking the women over.

"Oh, no," said Ava. She slapped her hands over her mouth.

Ema buried her face in her lap and cried.

Gisela stared wide-eyed at the women.

Nicolette grabbed Ema and hugged her.

"Shush," she said. "Tis alright. No harm done." She stroked the girl's soft brown hair.

Clarissa grabbed Ava and Gisela, tickling them under their chins.

"Such a lovely surprise," she said. "Our afternoon was too solemn for such beautiful weather."

They sat the girls around them, calming them and assuring them all was well.

"What game were you playing?" Nicolette squeezed Ema, who hiccuped.

"Chase," said Gisela.

"We each wanted to be first to tell you about the surprise picnic," said Ava, who pointed in the direction they had come.

They all followed Ava's finger.

Fronika carried a basket covered in a red cloth. Two boys about the age of ten walked to her right. One had an arm-full of blankets, and the other laden with cushions almost blocking his eyes.

Libbe carried Betsey.

"Come," said Clarissa, "let us help."

They jumped up. The girls ran over to the newcomers and pulled on the items, causing them to fall. They scrambled to pick up the things like prizes won at a fair. Laughing and giggling, the five children spread the blankets on the grass and piled on cushions.

Fronika placed her basket down, took Betsey from her sister until Libbe sat, then handed the baby back to her.

The boys stood by, shifting from foot to foot.

"Join us," said Nicolette. "I'm sure there's plenty of food for all of us."

"Oh, yes," said Fronika. "Mother packed enough for a week."

"She's afraid we might starve if not overfed," said Libbe. She reached for a small shortbread cake, broke it in half, and gave a piece to Betsey.

The boys sat in the grass next to the blankets, eyeing the food in front of them.

"You may help yourselves," said Clarissa. "This is an outdoor party."

"We really should get back to our chores," said the black-haired boy. He sat on his hands.

"The Ladies have permitted you to stay, Jerad," said Fronika. "You may take your ease and spend the afternoon without care."

"Brint promised to show us the caves," said Gisela, pointing at the brown-haired boy.

"Shush," he said, his cheeks turning pale. "I told you they is a secret."

"They won't tell," said Ava. She glanced at Nicolette and Clarissa. "I bet they want to see them, too," she said, nodding.

"Secret caves?" Nicolette raised her eyebrows. "Eryk never mentioned them to me."

"They is meant to be secret, my lady," said Jerad, "begging your pardon. They is for hiding in emergencies."

"Now I am very curious," said Nicolette. She handed a chunk of ham to the boys. They hesitated. "Please," she said, "we do not stand on ceremony, this band of adventurers. We'd be very pleased if you showed us."

Fronika unpacked the basket and placed all the food on the blanket: sliced apples, ham, shortbread cakes, honeycombs, and hard, sharp cheese. Three goatskin pouches holding apple cider rounded out the victuals.

Clarissa held one of the drink bags up, tilted her head back, and squirted the liquid in her mouth.

The group laughed and clapped.

"I want to try," said Ema. Her quiet voice eased through the loud noises of the others, the first she had spoken in many minutes.

"Of course," said Clarissa, handing her a pouch.

The girl copied the older woman as best she could, but when she squeezed, the juice splashed on her cheeks and ran down her neck, staining her tunic. She paused, stunned.

"Try again," said Ava, who poked her in encouragement.

She did and got some in her mouth. More clapping, and she drank again.

"Let me try," said Gisela.

Brint picked one of the drink pouches, pointing the spout up. He squeezed, ducked, and caught the liquid in his mouth.

Oh's and ah's, and applause from the girls and women. Jerad bumped his shoulder into Brint's.

"Nice," he said.

"Will you show us the caves?" Nicolette nibbled on an apple slice. "We will keep them a secret."

The boys nodded, unable to talk because of their full mouths.

"If you are venturing," said Fronika, "I will fetch you a waterskin for each of you. While not very far, the land is uneven and tiring."

"Best fetch the girls their hose and shoes, too," said Libbe. Betsey lay asleep in her arms.

"Will you not join us?" Clarissa leaned forward and tucked Libbe's shawl over her shoulder.

"We know where they are," said Libbe. "Anyone born to the estate knows where they are in case they attack us."

"They must be large," said Clarissa. She glanced at Nicolette.

"Oh, aye," said Jerad. "We mean them for the women, children, and old folks."

"Kept stocked, too," said Brint.

Nicolette looked up at the sky.

"Perhaps we should go now so that we may be back well before the sun begins to set," she said, "as soon as Fronika returns."

"Oh, but the honeycombs," said Ava.

"You may take them with you," said Nicolette, "and enjoy them as we walk."

The girls clapped. The boys grinned.

Nicolette helped Libbe stand. Jen's daughter took the baby back to the family's quarters to be cleaned up and placed for a nap.

Fronika returned with water pouches for each of them and a spare for cleaning the sticky faces and hands of the girls. She handed the fabric to the boys, who cleaned themselves up.

The girls slipped on their hose and shoes. The boys averted their gazes and packed the leftover food into the basket.

Shoes on, they all stood, brushed off their tunics, strung water bags on their shoulders, and accepted a honeycomb from Fronika.

They strode off towards the hills at the back of Thornewood, Jared, and Brint in the lead, Nicolette and Clarissa bringing up the rear.

CHAPTER SIXTEEN

Letters from Home

Nicolette woke up the next day with sore legs. She rubbed her tired muscles as she stretched and yawned. The previous day was fun and informative: glorious weather, happy children, and a secret expedition into the woods.

The boys pointed out the clues and markings that would make a return trip to the caves easy. Once you knew what to look for, the markers read like a map.

When they returned, they all joined in pinky swears and then used the tip of Nicolette's knife to poke fingertips and seal their secret with blood oaths.

Jerad and Brint performed the ceremonies with solemn faces, and Ava, Ema, and Gisela joined them with solemn vows. They parted as conspirators, feeling older and responsible beyond their childhood years.

The boys received bread and smoked meat in oiled cloths to take home with them, as they will have missed their suppers.

Washed and in clean shifts, the girls ate porridge and berry compotes in their shared bedroom, then gladly climbed into their cots to dream of more adventures.

"An escape route," said Clarissa to Nicolette, her voice a whisper, as they parted for the night.

Nicolette wrapped a soft yellow woolen blanket around her shoulders and padded to the window on her bare feet. She pushed open the right side shutter. The wind grabbed it, and it banged on the wall, rain spraying her face.

She pulled the shutter closed and shivered. It was midmorning, and the sky was dark with storm clouds.

She brushed her dark brown hair, trying to smooth out the curls. She would only tame them once she braided them, the yellow ribbon looping through the strands and tied at the ends.

She splashed her face with cold water from the bowl on the washstand. She covered her shift with a yellow tunic, designed in a simple T shape with no adornments.

Libbe came in with a ceramic mug of chamomile tea and honey.

"Tis almost like winter outside today," she said as she handed Nicolette the cup. "Sit, and I will help you with your hose and shoes. The floors are beastly cold."

Nicolette wanted to tell Libbe she would clothe herself, but after the first day, she no longer bothered.

Maryn taught all the girls working in the hall how to care for ladies and their clothing. She planned to bring all those who didn't want to work the fields out of serfdom.

"The other ladies are in the kitchen where the fire has chased away the chill," said Libbe as she tied on Nicolette's soft leather slippers.

When she reached the kitchen, Nicolette found one chair from the solar waiting for her next to the enormous fireplace used for roasting large haunches of venison or pork.

Jen handed her a wooden board with two small pies. Nicolette sat, picked up a pasty, and bit into a juicy, fruit-filled delight. Apples and berries seasoned with cloves and honey made her stomach grumble in pleasure. She finished both pies, sat back, and rubbed her belly.

"That was so good," she said, looking over her shoulder for Jen.

The cook smiled.

"I'll have you plump and robust in no time," said Jen.

Nicolette sighed in contentment.

Clarissa handed her a goblet of red wine.

"Drink up," she said.

"It's morning," said Nicolette. "I'll be asleep before midday if I have wine now." She tried to hand the glass back.

"There are letters here for you," said Clarissa, "from your father and Isuet. I think you may need something to fortify your nerves."

"Have you read them?"

"No," said Clarissa. "Would you like me to?"

"I am not so much a coward as that," said Nicolette. She gulped her wine and held the glass out for more. "Where are they?"

Clarissa pulled on the drawstring of her plain tan purse, opened the bag, and pulled out two pieces of folded parchment. She handed them to Nicolette.

They both seemed worn: one folded in four and tied with a string that was thin in spots and looked close to pulling apart, the other folded in sixths with her sister's sigil, a fox, pressed into a beeswax seal, cracked and peeling from the parchment on one end.

"They look well-traveled," said Nicolette. She took another sip of wine, not looking forward to reading either letter.

"The rider has been following us from place to place," said Clarissa, "and only just now caught up to us." She placed her hand on her friend's knee and squeezed. "He is one of my men and took his time, knowing we wished time on our own and our route obscured."

"He deserves a reward for his loyalty," said Nicolette. She patted Clarissa's hand.

"I've already taken care of him. He will head back home in a very roundabout way."

Nicolette took a deep breath.

"Would you like to take them to your chambers to read privately?" Maryn rose.

"No," said Nicolette, "Please stay by the fire. The letters will not contain any big secrets I can not share with my friends."

She read Isuet's letter first. It was bound to be the more unpleasant of the two. She broke her sister's seal, unfolded the paper, and squinted at her sister's small scrip.

"Isuet's letter was dated three months ago," said Nicolette. "My dear sister does not waste time with platitudes." She snickered. "They set her wedding date for the day of the full moon in May."

"That is but a month from now," said Maryn.

Nicolette nodded as she continued to read. She tilted the paper towards the flames for better light.

"I am bid to return, as I must participate in the royal ceremonies. She commissioned a dress for me. I need to do nothing else except be there as she does not wish my interference, so I should not be there until seven days beforehand."

"Sweet, sweet, Isuet," said Clarissa. "Her love for you shines through in her words."

"Well, she has done me a favor by keeping me away until the last possible moment, but we will not tell her so."

"You have a fortnight before you must leave me," said Clarissa. "I am thankful for that."

"I, too," she said. She dropped her sister's missive in her lap and took up the other. She broke the twine and unfolded the one from her father.

He never learned to read and write. He was ever so proud that both of his daughters did, though.

His scribe wrote in precise, bold strokes, never really believing Nicolette and Isuet, being women, could read what he wrote.

Her father's voice came through in the words he dictated:

"I miss you, daughter. I do not begrudge you this adventure, but it is time to come home and take up your responsibilities, as Isuet reminds me daily. Once she becomes a princess, it will be your turn to make a wonderful match. I have chosen several men I think are fine and will provide well for you. Isuet has added a few in the nobility that she knows and believes will be perfect for you. Come home before the wedding so we may spend time together. We will then travel in each other's company. Your loving father, Tomas, Count Welf."

Clarissa laughed. "As if you don't know who your father is."

"Well, that's clear enough," said Nicolette.

"Isuet picked out grooms for you?" Clarissa shivered. "Can you imagine what they must be like?"

Nicolette groaned.

Maryn slapped her knees and stood.

"We have fourteen days until you must leave us," she said. "We will do all we can to make them special."

"Yes," said Nicolette under her breath, "fourteen days until my life is over."

CHAPTER SEVENTEEN

The King's Call

The stables at Hilltop held twenty horses, not all owned by Revena and Kellan. Half of the animals belonged to Prince Henri, and now with Dirk, Eryk's black Friesian, Henri had eleven.

Eight horses grazed in a lower pasture, waiting for the Prince to depart and move back to their stalls.

Eryk leaned back onto a wall to reduce his height and avoid Henri's men, who fawned over the prince and his prize. They congratulated him on his cleverness at getting one over on Kellan and Eryk.

Eryk felt naked without his sword, Shade, but no one, except the prince's men, carried a weapon around the future king.

He felt eyes upon him, the prince's violet eyes holding Eryk's gaze. He suspected Henri knew he and Kellan had given up the horse too quickly.

The light from outside moved across the floor and caught Eryk's attention. He looked above the heads of the twenty or so men crowded in the barn.

A young man dressed in King's Livery halted in the doorway, blinking to adjust to the dimmer interior.

Kellan noticed the direction of Eryk's gaze, turned, and saw the squire. Kellan spoke to Henri, standing next to him.

Henri nodded and said something Eryk did not hear, but the men parted and created a passage from the messenger to the Prince. Henri gestured with his fingers, and the young man marched up to him and bowed his head with a shallow nod.

Henri's face turned red. He waved his hands at the people around him, gesturing for them to leave. He didn't want them to hear his father's message. Curious.

The young man began speaking before the room was empty.

"His Highness, King Hugh," he said in a voice practiced to travel over all other noises, "bid me tell you he wants you at the capital immediately."

The squire stood straight in his red and gold finery, chin raised, eyes level with Prince Henri's.

Henri clenched his fists.

"I am to inform you to make all haste," said the young man, a small smile turning up the left side of his mouth.

Eryk slumped back against the wall, half hidden in shadow and unmoving.

Kellan stepped back against a stall. He could not leave the prince alone.

The other men walked to the door in slow and measured steps. The King's message would not be a secret from anyone.

"You are insolent, Kevan," said Henri, his voice like a hiss.

"Prince Kevan," said the squire. He reached into a pocket, withdrew his hand, and passed something to Henri.

A ring rested in the palm of Henri's hand.

Henri pursed his lips, frowned, and cleared his throat. He smiled at the squire. It did not reach his eyes.

"I do as my King and Father bid me," said Henri. "All is well. I intended to be on my way home today. It is of no matter to divert my party to the capital."

Eryk watched as Henri relaxed his whole body. He passed the King's ring back to Prince Kevan.

Eryk wondered who this prince might be. He didn't think he was one of Henri's brothers, who all had dark brown hair like the King and Queen, and he didn't look like Henri, either. He had black hair and dark eyes framed with black brows.

"Shall we go into the hall where you can refresh yourself?" Henri gestured towards the door to usher Prince Kevan out of the stables. "My men can pack and prepare for our trip while you take your ease."

Prince Kevan shook his head.

"I have a message for the Margrave," he said, staying in place.

Kellan blinked and came forward a step.

"By all means," said Henri, turning towards Kellan.

"It is a private message from his highness." The squire stood straight, and although he must be half Henri's thirty-two years, he seemed more calm and substantial than the older man.

Something odd was going on. Eryk was curious why this squire dominated the King's heir.

Henri waved Eryk to join him as he moved to the exit.

"Count Thorne may remain," said Prince Kevan, "if the Margrave so wishes."

"Yes," said Kellan, "I'd like Count Thorne to stay."

Henri paused.

"Please prepare for your departure, Prince Henri," said Kevan. "We will be but a few moments and will join you shortly. Have your men move away from the building. I will let them know when we finish."

Henri turned to Kevan and smiled.

"Of course, dear cousin," said Henri. He showed his teeth, meant to be a smile, but looked like a predatory warning.

Henri walked out into the sunlight like he didn't have a care in the world. He closed the barn door as he left.

Prince Kevan turned to Kellan once they were alone.

"Margrave of Bavaria," he said, bowing more fully than he had done with his cousin.

"Well met, Prince Kevan," said Kellan. "You seem to have grown into your title."

So, Kellan knew the young man.

"Yes, well, for the time being," said Kevan. "There may come a time when I must leave these provinces for a place beyond Prince Henri's reach. Serving my dear uncle, the King, is not endearing me to his son."

"Sometimes loyalties do conflict," said Kellan.

"I have no conflicts," said Kevan. "My mind is clear. King Hugh holds my heart and mind and sword."

Kevan glanced at Eryk.

Eryk joined Kellan and Kevan in the middle of the stable.

"They said you were a giant of a man," said Kevan.

Kellan introduced them

"Prince Kevan, eldest son to the King's favorite brother, this is my favorite brother, Eryk, Count Thornewood."

Prince Kevan held out his hand to Eryk.

Eryk quirked an eyebrow and smiled.

The men grasped forearms and shook.

"Well met," said Prince Kevan. "The King speaks well of you both." He relaxed.

"Margrave," said Kevan.

"Kellan, please."

"Of course," said Kevan. "Kellan, King Hugh bids you and your brother join him in the capital as his guests. He needs you regarding events occurring across the continent that have a bearing on the stewardship of his lands."

Kevan shuffled on his feet. He looked younger suddenly.

"Prince Henri's wedding is being moved to the capital where the King's troops hold a greater force. He wants you to attend the ceremony as his guest. This will be his excuse for having you near and discussing matters of great portent."

Kellan glanced at Eryk.

"The both of us?" He frowned.

"Yes," said Kevan. "He wishes you to arrive a few days before the ceremony. Bring a small party. Bring the Lady Revena if she wishes to attend."

"My wife is with child," said Kellan. "Unless the King insists, we would prefer she not travel now."

"As you wish," said Kevan. "And congratulations. We hope all goes well."

"Thank you," said Kellan.

"The King particularly wants Count Thorne and Adam, the baron of Beustel, to attend as the three of you form a protective triangle in these parts, and a threat may come from the south."

"We will do as the King commands," said Eryk. "Do you know any more about these dangers the King expects? Should we begin fortifying?"

Kevan let out a breath.

"The King will give you all the necessary information and instructions. I know no more."

"We will quietly make arrangements to buttress and secure our lands," said Kellan.

"I will ride over to Beustel and let Adam know he will need to brush up on his courtly manners," said Eryk.

"As if he needs any improvement," said Kevan. "He already has a reputation at court as a friend to everyone."

"He does have a special talent to make everyone feel special," said Eryk.

"I look forward to seeing you all in Verdun," said Prince Kevan. "Now, I must beg you for some victuals for the road. I came with pack mules and an assortment of the King's men. We ride without resting during daylight and sleep on the road. Henri will not be happy."

CHAPTER EIGHTEEN

Sweet Nothings

The rain stopped, but the chill remained. The women and girls stayed in the kitchen for the rest of the day.

Maryn placed quilts on the stone floor, and Ava, Ema, and Gisela lounged on them with linen dolls. They had an assortment of wool threads, beads, and scraps of material they used to decorate their poppets.

Fronika, Libbe, and Clarissa sat with them, stringing wooden and glass beads on bright woolen threads for necklaces and bracelets.

Jen sat by the fire, dozing. Dinner would be a simple stew. There was no fresh bread as the cook was taking a rest day.

Maryn sat across from Jen, mending sitting in her lap, untouched. Her attention was on the people in the room. Her gaze roamed from one to another, and she smiled, looking satisfied with what was before her.

Nicolette felt Maryn's gaze rest on her as she sat in the third chair by the fireplace.

Nicolette held Betsy in her lap, cradling the baby while she slept, stroking the child's hair.

"She is a sweet child," said Maryn to Nicolette.

"Yes, she is," said Nicolette. "She has the sweetest disposition. She rarely cried as we traveled here."

"I imagine her mother will miss her sorely."

"Yes, she will," said Nicolette. She shifted the baby's weight in her arms. "But she loves Betsey beyond all reason, so she knows she must part with Betsey to keep her safe. I know she can not be in better hands."

"Your faith in us warms my heart," said Maryn. "We will not disappoint you. Betsey's mother may rest easy, knowing her child protected and raised with the best we have."

"Thank you," she said. "I know I ask a great deal, especially of Eryk. He is kind to do this for an old friend."

"Ha," said Maryn. "Old friend indeed. More like family. I wish we could make that a fact."

Nicolette startled. Betsey stirred, blinked, and fell back asleep.

"Shush, little one," she said, stroking her fingertips on Betsey's cheek.

She shook her head.

"Do not even entertain the thought," said Nicolette. "Tis not possible. There are better choices for Eryk."

Maryn frowned but said no more on the matter.

"We will make the most of these two weeks," said Maryn. "Forget your cares. Eat. Stroll the grounds. Decorate the hall. Play with the children. Sleep. Do as you wish. We want the next fourteen days to be a holiday for you."

"I am grateful for this respite and the care with which you treat us," said Nicolette. Nicolette looked over at her friend. Their eyes met, and they smiled at one another.

Maryn sighed.

"Your friendship reminds me of my one with Lillian, Kellan's mother." Maryn looked into the fire, her gaze and thoughts going to another time.

"Despite being born into very different social levels, we were friends from childhood and did everything together. Just like the two of you."

"We are true sisters of the heart," said Nicolette. "We know all of each other. She has not had an easy time over the last year."

"Nonsense," said Clarissa from her spot on the floor. "This has been a grand adventure, and having you with me this past year has been a distraction, a support, and more fun than I would have thought possible."

"Well, we will make these final days of your togetherness special and relaxing," said Maryn. "I plan to send you off in your different directions in fine health and proper good moods to fortify any trials and tribulations the future may hold."

Libbe returned from the pantry with shortbread cookies flavored with almonds that she had passed out.

Fronika got milk from the larder and handed out cups of the liquid.

They nibbled and drank in quiet for a while.

Jen snored and woke herself up. She grumped and grumbled through her smile as she accepted some of her cookies.

They all giggled.

"What have you all been on about?" Jen brushed some crumbs from her apron.

"Just talking about these two." Maryn pointed her chin at Nicolette and Clarissa. "I want them to take their ease while here. No thoughts of the world beyond our borders."

"Too true," said Jen. "A fine respite you must have. Do only those things you want to do."

"Will you show me how to make these cookies?" Clarissa rubbed her belly. "They are so good. Are they not girls?"

"Oh, yes," said Ava.

"Mmmmmmmmmmmm." Ema had a mouthful.

"Delicious," said Gisela. "Divine."

"Oh, ho, look at you with your special words," said Jen. "But these are from a secret recipe. I don't think I can give it up."

"She hasn't even shared it with us," said Libbe.

"She said we can have the recipe when she's dead," said Fronika, "but it's not written down."

"I plan to come back as a ghost and whisper it in your ears while you sleep."

The three young girls shrieked in mock fright.

Clarissa stuck out her bottom lip in her famous pout.

"But I am so far away in the Bohemian Forrest. Your specter will never find me." She tilted her head and batted her eyelashes at Jen. "You said we could have whatever we wanted."

"Go on with you and your big blue eyes," said Jen. "Save those looks for some handsome young man."

"I don't want a man," said Clarissa. "I want your cookies."

"Cookies are certainly less troublesome than any man," said Maryn.

"Tis too true," said Jen. "Fine. I will teach you all how to make these cookies on the marrow."

"Oh, wonderful," said Nicolette. "That will be so much fun."

"Oh, aye," said Jen, "You too, my Lady?"

"None of that," said Nicolette. "You promised we'd leave everything from the world out beyond the walls. I am just another woman who wants sweets."

CHAPTER NINETEEN

Leave Taking

Prince Kevan sat on his golden horse the way only someone raised to ride from infancy could. The young man and the animal moved as one. Eryk, being so large, held some envy for the ease with which Prince Kevan waited in comfort on his mount while the King's men formed up and waited for Prince Henri, who dawdled just enough to assert some power over the group.

While Prince Henri held a higher rank than Prince Kevan, the King's nephew, half the age of the King's son, behaved with a confidence well beyond his age and position.

Eryk and Kellan would discuss this with Adam and their friends Jon and Stefan, who would accompany them to Verdun to meet with the King.

Eryk rolled his shoulders, settling Shadow's weight more evenly on his back. His father's sword vibrated with a low hum while he left it in his room. The servants refused to enter his chamber unless he was there to calm and silence the weapon.

Now that the princes were leaving, he could keep Shadow with him. They were both happier about this. While he had a knife hidden in each boot and another three strapped to his left hip, he only felt fully armed if he had Shadow with him.

Kellan nudged him in the arm.

"Heads up," said Kellan.

Prince Henri, mounted and cloaked, maneuvered his horse before him and Kellan.

Before he spoke, all the men on horses turned and faced the entrance to Hilltop Keep. Kellan and Eryk turned to follow their gazes.

Revena stood in the doorway, framed by darkness, accompanied by two of her ladies. Her red hair glowed in the sunlight.

Kellan left Eryk's side to meet his wife and accompany her to where the troop waited. He spoke in whispers to her. She patted his hand and smiled at him.

Kellan placed his wife between himself and Eryk, both men slightly in front of her, to block Henri's horse in case he accidentally lost control of his animal.

He was not riding Eryk's horse, Dirk. Warhorses made poor traveling animals. It stood off to the side, restless but harnessed and controlled by two stable hands and Kellan's horsemaster. These three would deliver Henri's new acquisition and then return home.

"Margravine Revena," said Henri, dipping his head. "It was unnecessary for you to bid me farewell."

"A hostess has duties," said Revena, "and this gives me an excuse for some fresh air."

"You have been more than hospitable during my stay here," said Henri. "I will speak highly of you to my father, the King."

Eryk almost snorted. No one believed these words.

"It was a pleasure to have you with us during these last two moons," she said. "They seemed to pass in the blink of an eye."

No one believed these words, either. They were all so civil, Eryk felt like gagging from the hypocrisy. But he could bullshit with the best of them, so he couldn't fault them. These little lies kept everyone alive.

"Feel free to visit at any time," said Kellan.

Prince Kevan moved alongside Henri.

"It is time to depart," he said. "We must move to arrive at our first campsite before dark."

Henri frowned.

"There are plenty of town and city burgers where we can lodge between here and Verdun. We need not sleep rough."

"But we must travel in a certain amount of stealth," said Kevan. "The King wishes to keep our movements unknown from observers that may pass on the information. So we avoid the settled places."

"Surely an inn or public house would not go amiss," said Henri.

"King Hugh wished me to tell you if you balked at the idea, the ground would stiffen your spine."

Prince Henri pulled on his horse's reins and spun about. The men in the party formed around him.

Prince Kevan smiled down at Revena.

"I am sorry we did not have time to meet properly," he said with a nod. "Legends seem to form around you, and I would have liked to compare the songs to the true stories from the source."

"Perhaps when your duties no longer demand your time," she said, "you will grace us with a leisurely visit."

Prince Kevan bent down and held out his hand. Revena placed her fingers in his palm, and he brushed his lips across them.

"I look forward to such a delightful interlude," he said.

"You flatter me, Your Grace," said Revena with a bright smile.

"Well deserved," said Kevan with a wink.

Eryk thought he heard his brother growl.

"He is but a boy," said Eryk in his brother's ear, followed by a chuckle.

"My husband does not find humor in our jests." Revena patted Kellan's arm.

"It is but a bit of courtly flirting," said Kevan. "Your wife is safe from me." He touched his fingers to his forehead in a brief salute. "Gentlemen, I look forward to seeing you in Verdun."

He spun his horse around and rode off with his men.

Kellan let out a woof of air.

"Finally," he said. "I am glad to see the back of them."

"As am I," said Revena. "We will finally return to peace and order in our household."

"Will you go back to your bed now?" Kellan looked at his wife as if she'd crumbled to the cobblestones at his feet.

"See how well your brother cares for me?" Revena reached up and stoked Kellan's jaw. She glanced at Eryk. "Maryn has raised the most amazing sons. There aren't any finer men in all these lands."

Eryk felt his cheeks get warm.

"It will please our mother that you are pleased, Margravine," said Eryk.

Revena swatted him.

"You always call me by my title when I embarrass you," she said. "Will you both walk with me once around the courtyard before I am regulated back to utter safety?" She pointed towards the hall. "As you can see, my ladies hover in case of any difficulty."

Kellan hooked her arm in his.

"Slowly," he said to her.

"Yes, my love," she said.

They walked silently for several moments, Revena tilting her head toward the sun.

A large red wolfhound trotted up to Revena and rubbed her head against Revena's blue dress.

Revena bent and stroked the dog's ear.

"That looks just like Ginger," said Eryk.

"That is Ginger," said Revena.

Eryk frowned.

"How old is she now?"

"Same age as me," she said. "Eighteen. Born on the night, I was born. The only one to survive from her mother's litters."

"That's highly unusual," said Eryk. "She looks to be in her prime."

"You are unusual, are you not, Ginger, my girl?"

The dog barked in assent.

"She acts as if she understands you," said Eryk.

"Yes, she does."

Revena twitched and looked at Eryk's back.

"Is something amiss?" Kellan stopped and looked at his wife closely.

"Not with me," she said. "My maids told me your sword sings. And just now, I thought I heard something. As I did the night I used my sword, Shadow, to serve justice." She shook her head. "Not the same song, but a music nonetheless."

"It is a noisy so-and-so," said Eryk. The blade vibrated its objection at his critique.

Eryk looked around to see if anyone was close enough to overhear them.

"We mustn't discuss the nonsense of longlived talking animals and musical swords," he said.

"Not to worry," said Kellan. "They built Hilltop to be a fortress to protect the unconventional."

"Tis well," said Eryk, "as I'm rather fond of the beauty of the uncommon."

They reached the entrance to the keep. One of Revena's ladies approached her and put a shawl around her shoulders.

"It is time for me to leave," said Eryk, "if I am to make it home before dark."

Revena's second lady handed Eryk a bundle and a drink pouch.

"For your journey, my Lord," she said, batting her eyelashes at him.

"Thank you," he said to her with a nod and a smile.

The young woman turned rose red and looked down. The other woman pulled on her sleeve, and they went inside.

"When will you wed?" Kellan nodded to the retreating women. "You certainly have a bevy to choose from, and you like them all well enough."

"Leave your brother alone," said Revena. "Eryk will know when the time and woman are right for him."

"Well," said Eryk, "on that note, I will be off. There is much to do."

A stable hand brought his horse forward and held him ready.

"If I bring my mother upon my return for us to proceed to the capital, will that be soon enough for you, my dear sister?"

"Yes," said Revena, "that will be perfect. I so look forward to having your mother with me."

"She will be honored and overjoyed to stay with you for your laying in," said Eryk. He kissed Revena on the cheek and grabbed his brother in a bear hug.

"Don't drive your wife to distraction with your worries," said Eryk.

The couple smiled at each other as if the rest of the world did not exist.

Eryk felt a stab in his heart that he would never experience that kind of love.

CHAPTER TWENTY

Homecoming

The afternoon wore on into the evening in pleasant, homey pursuits. The women and girls spent their time in the warm kitchen where spare tables held bits of cloth, ribbons, and thread.

Nicolette wanted a room like this one in her home. A fire always burned in the hearth, the warmth controlled by strategically placed windows with sheer coverings held in place with wooden poles in the bottom hems to prevent the wind from blowing too much into the room.

"Those are from a fine hemp linen with a more open weave," said Maryn. "They allow a breeze and light to enter," she said. "The tapestry you see pulled back there is to block drafts when fall and winter are upon us."

Thick woven cloths hung in the same way as the linen, but pulled back and tied to loops embedded in the walls.

"With the shutters closed and both curtains down, this room is the warmest in the manse during the coldest time of the year." Maryn showed Nicolette how the cloth panels hung and the items used to manipulate them. "Eryk moved the stores and staples to other, cooler and darker rooms as storage. That helps preserve the food longer and gives us more room for comfortable living space here."

The pride in Maryn's voice was clear to hear.

"He made many improvements when he became Count of Thornewood," she said, "and continues to do so. He works with never-ending energy from morning until night."

"This is quite clever," said Nicolette.

Maryn had taken Clarissa and her on a tour of the household, showing them the changes Eryk had made.

"You have given me so many good ideas to take home to improve my home," said Clarissa. "My departed husband and his forebears neglected their stewardship of the estate."

"I hope I will have a home for these changes," said Nicolette in a low voice.

Clarissa squeezed her hand.

"We will find a way to get you married to the right man," she said, glancing around Nicolette and catching Maryn's gaze.

"Oh, do you two plot against me?" Nicolette tried to pull away from her friend with a laugh.

"Never against," said Clarissa. She tied one of the red ribbons in Nicolette's left braid.

"Perhaps you both will allow me the pleasure of being your adoptive mother," said Maryn. "I have been so blessed with my sons and the life they have given me. I'd love to pass some of my good fortunes on to you young ladies."

Nicolette and Clarissa stilled.

Clarissa's eyes welled with tears. Nicolette's eyes grew large. They both moved towards the older woman and wrapped her in their arms. The three women stood together, swaying for several minutes until Clarissa sniffed.

They broke apart.

"I suppose wiping a runny nose on my sleeve would be unacceptable," she said.

Maryn handed her an embroidered cloth from the pocket of her apron.

They all wore shifts with over-the-head tabards open at the sides and pockets on the front as smocks.

"Cookie recipes," said Nicolette, "and home improvements and now a mother. We will leave here truly rich."

"I changed my mind. Can I call you mother?" Clarissa wiped her wet face.

"You honor me," said Maryn.

She took Nicolette's hand.

"I would like to write to your father about his plans for you," said

Maryn. "The times you and he visited in the past, he seemed a reasonable man, if inattentive to women's needs, as many men tend to be."

She reached for Clarissa's hand and pulled both women along as they went to the upper floors to view Eryk's current project, a system to haul water to the sleeping chambers so they could bathe in winter.

"We spoke several times," she said, "and he seemed to take my advice about you girls when you were younger."

They marveled at the rope and bucket system threaded through a hole in the floor in a room on the second floor. They looked down into the kitchen near the enormous cauldron, always full of water and a fire burning under it.

Libbe waved up at them.

"Come down," she said, raising her voice to be heard through the ceiling and floor. "Mother has the evening meal on the table, and the girls say they are starving." She laughed. "To be exact, Gisela says she will perish soon, if not fed."

They made their way back down to the kitchen.

Fronika sat with Betsey in her lap. The baby chewed on a crust of bread dipped in warm milk.

Ava, Ema, and Gisela sat at their places, hands folded in their laps, their feet dangling from the benches and moving back and forth.

"We helped set the table," said Ava.

"Mistress Jen, let us slice the bread," said Ema, "when we told her we knew how from working in the Hilltop kitchens. Since mother adopted us, we don't get to do it often anymore."

"Ema and Ava showed me," said Gisela, "so I could help."

"Such fine and industrious young ladies," said Jen as she placed platters of roast pork on the table, which already held mashed turnips, peas in a cream sauce, and stewed apples flavored with honey.

"The little misses have earned an extra cookie for all they've done to assist me this day."

The girls clapped in unison.

"I feel so much better," said Nicolette, "after these few days of your food, Mistress Jen."

"Oh, go on with you, my lady," said the cook.

"Come," said Maryn, "sit. Let us enjoy it all while it is still hot."

The women sat on the benches lined with cushions.

"I insist you join us this eve, Jen," said Maryn.

"Oh, yes," said Clarissa. "I want to hear more stories about your life before Thornewood."

The cook's apple-round cheeks grew red, but she joined them and seemed to relax as everyone filled their bread trenchers.

"Would you write to my father?" Nicolette took a bite of crisp pork skin. "I fear my sister may steer him in a direction that would not suit me best."

"Still no love lost between you both?" Maryn frowned.

"No," said Nicolette. "I had hoped that her pending wedding to Prince Henri would soften her, but it seems to have made her more strident and harsh."

"I will certainly send a missive to your father," said Maryn. "I will do it tomorrow and send it the same day. We can not be in too much haste over this matter."

"My future marriage weighs heavy upon me," said Nicolette.

"You are to be married?" Eryk stood in the kitchen doorway.

The man of the manor had returned.

CHAPTER TWENTY-ONE

WWW

Seven days passed since Eryk returned from Hilltop, and Nicolette hadn't seen him, but she thought about him every day, and thoughts of him kept her awake at night.

She meant her time at Thornewood to be restful. Instead, restlessness plagued her.

She dragged herself from bed on the morning of Beltane Eve and rubbed her sore eyes with her knuckles to wipe away unshed tears.

How dare he question her responsibility to marry?

He hadn't answered her. He turned his back on her and left the kitchens without another word.

No matter, she told herself. It would all be over soon. She would leave Thornewood in another two days, and the torture of Eryk being so close, yet forever out of her reach, would end.

She rose, pulled back the cloth covering her window, and let the rising sun raise her spirits. She breathed deep, held her breath, and let it out in one long intentional stream of air.

She could get through this. She had survived worse.

She dressed before Grite, and Kathe arrived with her morning repast and warm water for cleansing. She saved her hair for them to style.

"Church first thing," said Grite, "so one simple braid and a plain covering."

"How long will mass be?" Nicolette hoped she could stay awake through the service.

84

"Our priest prefers good works to the sound of his voice," said Kathe. "He performs the basic rituals and then sends us out to various homes to give comfort where needed." Kathe moved around Nicolette's room, shaking out the feather bedding and hanging the nightclothes to air.

"We take baskets of fresh bread and vegetables to some places," said Grite as she brushed Nicolette's hair.

"I will watch one family's children so the mother and father can spend the morning together without a care," said Kathe, examining a loose seam in one of Nicolette's shifts.

"I've never heard of such a thing," said Nicolette.

"Father Cysgod believes religion is about community," said Grite. "We must help one another. He said God prefers that over incense and chants."

"Interesting," said Nicolette. "Will he not be preaching on purging witches from this world?"

"Oh, no," said Kathe. She spoke in a whisper. "He comes from Cymru, the land of red dragons in the north, where they revered witches as wise women who heal sickness."

Kathe moved in front of Nicolette to show her two headscarves.

"He says we must blend in with the Church to save to old ways," she said. "So we celebrate Saint Walpurgis with bonfires to appease the ecclesiastics while keeping Beltane in our hearts."

"It's one reason the saint is so well loved here," said Grite, tying off Nicolette's braid. "Your hair is so thick and dark."

"My father says it's the same as my mother's, as is my dark skin. She was Berber and Basque from Hispania."

"Your skin is lovely," said Kathe. "I only have color if I spend time out of doors. Grite only has color when she blushes over a cute boy." She nudged her friend. They giggled.

"Where is Hispania?" Grite draped a sun-bleached white scarf over Nicolette's hair, tying it down with a heather-colored ribbon that matched Nicolette's new dress.

"I will look for a map in the library," said Nicolette, "and show you where we are in the world."

The girls clapped.

"That would be so amazing," said Grite. "I would love to see more of the world. Of course, that's not likely to happen."

"Serfs don't leave where they are born," said Kathe, all joy leaving her face.

"Unless sold or lost as a bounty of war."

"Surely, that's not likely to happen here," said Nicolette.

"I heard the men talking out by the stables," said Grite. "They said the war will be upon us soon. Count Eryk will head north to the King's capital with his brother to discuss a threat to the thrown."

Kathe gasped and wrung her hands.

Grite nodded and grasped her friend's wrist.

"When they saw me listening, they assured me no battles would come here. But they would go to foreign places to fight."

Nicolette stared at the young women. They knew more about the broader world than she did. She had spent too much time hiding in her private troubles.

"We would like to know the places they may go and never return from," said Kathe.

"Why must men and boys always go to war?" Grite wiped tears from her eyes.

"I do not know," said Nicolette. "I will ask questions and find a chart. We must not remain in the dark."

The girls nodded, hugging.

"Not knowing anything is worse than knowing the truth," she said. "Conjuring nightmares will help none of us."

She stood feeling the lethargy of the past week fall from her shoulders.

"Do you have other chores to do before church?"

They shook their heads.

"Perhaps you'd like to accompany me to Mass?"

They stared at her, eyes wide.

"If you have friends or family, you'd rather sit with...." She let her words trail off. What was she thinking?

"Inside the church?" Grite's voice squeaked.

"Sitting upfront?" Kathe spoke in a whisper.

"We've never sat at church before," said Grite.

"Dare we?" asked Kathe.

"Come, get out all of my ribbons," said Nicolette. "Pick out your favorite colors. This is a celebration. I want it to be special for all of us."

She brushed out their hair. They braided for each other, as they were more adept than she. Grite chose a red ribbon symbolizing the cardinals, and Kathe selected a deep blue for the blue jays.

Nicolette gifted them both white headscarves.

Kathe wanted to hide hers so it would never get soiled, but Nicolette and Grite insisted she wear hers, too.

They proceeded down the main stairs into the large hall, where people waited and chatted before going to the chapel in the woods.

The crowd hushed when they entered.

Grite hid her pink face in her hands. Kathe giggled.

CHAPTER TWENTY-TWO

BFFs

Hiding in a crowd was damn near impossible when you stood at least two heads taller than most people in the world. He never appreciated the massive posts that held up the hall's upper floor more than he did now. Made of entire tree trunks, they were at least wide enough for him to stand behind.

He stretched his aching back. He spent the last seven nights sleeping everywhere but in his bed and finally resorted to lying on floors, since most beds were too small for him.

Today was the first day he set foot in his hall in a week. He would have stayed away on this day, too, but as Count Thorne, he must play host to the Beltane celebrations. His mother would tan his hide if he shirked his duties. She wouldn't care how old or big he was. She'd take a switch to his butt, and she had a powerful arm.

Thank the gods, he had the excuse of the pending trip to Verdun to be away from the domestic bliss of a house full of women. The supplies needed for the journey waited, packed in oiled cloths. He sent and acknowledged messages to various people accompanying them to the King.

But today and tomorrow, he must be in the company of the people. Of course, only Nicolette nettled him under the collar.

There wasn't enough work on the entire estate to kill the thought of her marrying someone else.

His mother had tried to talk to him about it, first appealing to his usual good manners, but he met her with a wall of stubbornness that he rarely used with her or anyone he loved. Her rebukes got her nowhere.

Then she tried to appeal to his usual good nature. He barked at her.

His loud voice shocked them both. He got down on his knees in front of her to minimize his size. He hugged her. She hugged him.

"I'm so sorry," he said, choking on his words.

She stroked his hair and kissed his forehead. She wiped his cheeks.

"Go work it off," she said, her voice soft and soothing. "All will be well. You will see."

He shook his head and opened his mouth, but he couldn't utter any words.

"Go," said his mother, untangling his arms. "Work it out of your body, and your mind will eventually calm."

So, on her advice, he fled his house.

His body felt exhausted and worn out. That would help him control himself, or so he thought, until he saw her again.

His stomach twisted. He moved behind a column and groaned.

"Is all well, sir?"

He didn't know who spoke to him, but he nodded, eyes closed. You're a grown man, he said to himself. Get over it, for fuck's sake. He sucked in a lung full of air through his nose and stood up straight. He wasn't a coward and didn't run from his troubles. At least he was the only one who knew about this problem if he stopped acting like a mewling calf.

He stepped out into the crowd milling about the hall. He glanced at Nicolette. Their eyes met, and they smiled at one another for one brief moment, and he felt the way he felt when they were children and still friends.

All eyes turned to him.

He held his hand to his mother and led her to the main door. The rest of the room lined up behind them.

They walked down the lane, through the central courtyard, under the barbican, and turned right towards the woods that flanked the keep on the east.

They used the chapel in the woods for certain celebrations most closely linked to the old ways. It was smaller than the new church, but it had shutters on three sides that opened to allow the rituals inside to be seen by the people who had benches in the yard.

Before Father Cysgod arrived, it had been closed for two decades because of the new religion sweeping across the continent. The people paid lip service to the new rules.

The priest from Cymru arrived one day with a troupe of actors on one of their first market days. He traveled around the area, found the old chapel, and stayed. He integrated the old with the new, and the people flocked to him.

Eryk helped his mother sit at the front of the chapel where she and his father had married. He waited for his guests to join her, then moved off to the side, always conscious of his enormous size blocking anyone else's view.

He did not take part in the church rituals. Instead, he spent the next hour going over lists in his head.

When the priest began his procession from the altar to the door, Eryk gathered his mother, and they followed back to the keeps' courtyard. Tables and benches sat, spread with food and drink for all to enjoy by helping themselves. No one would serve anyone else for this meal.

Children ran among the adults, who relaxed in the sunshine. Eryk smiled. This was the way people should live. He felt satisfaction in helping make it so.

Several people brought out musical instruments and played. Those not too full of food danced.

Eryk got lost in the songs. He loved music.

A soft touch on his wrist startled him, and he jerked away. He looked down to see Nicolette fidgeting. He never remembered a time when she was nervous around him. You did that, he said to himself and felt a pinch in his heart.

He smiled at her. He couldn't stand that unsure look on her face.

"My lady," he said. He lifted her fingers to his lips, kissed, and squeezed them.

She shivered.

"Are you chilled?" He drew her out of his shady spot and into the sunshine.

"No, my lord," she said. "I worried you would not wish to speak to me." Her right cheek dimpled as her lips quirked up. "I fear our friendship is at an end."

He gazed into her eyes. Something broke in him. He took both her hands in his.

"We will always be friends," he said. "I will always be there for you, even when I am a complete and utter ass."

"I am glad to hear that," she said. "You are one of the most important people in the world to me." She gripped his hands as if willing her feelings into his body.

"I'm having difficulty reconciling our new adult responsibilities with our carefree childhood friendship," he said, "but I will manage."

Nicolette wrenched her hands from his, wrapped her arms around him, squeezed tight, released, turned, and ran away.

CHAPTER TWENTY-THREE

Plans

Maryn cornered Eryk in the kitchen before the rest of the household awoke the day after the celebrations. Not even Jen, the cook, was about.

"I hoped to be away without seeing anyone," he told his mother.

She caught him stuffing a sack with a loaf of dark rye bread, a hard, sharp cheese, and a couple of links of dried caraway sausage.

"I thought as much," she said, handing him a drink bladder filled with well water. "That's why I waited for you." She pulled on his sleeve, turning him to face her. "It's time you let us know what's going on."

He shook his head.

She raised an eyebrow.

He knew he couldn't win this struggle of wills, but he fought it anyway, being just as stubborn as his mother.

"Son," she said. "Eryk." She cupped his hairy cheek with one hand and dragged him to a bench with the other.

"Not knowing what's going on creates fear in the women and children." She sat across from him. "The truth, no matter how terrible, is nothing compared to what we conjure in our minds."

He stared into her eyes. She always answered his questions without evasion. And he knew her to be correct. Fighting make-believe battles in your head was infinitely more challenging than dealing with an actual target.

He sighed, letting go of the notion that women needed shielding from worldly troubles. They had never lived that way.

"Gather everyone who wishes to hear our doings in the great hall," he said. "Adam, Jon, and Stefan arrived during the night. I will set up the charts and maps and explain all to anyone who wishes to hear."

"Thank you," she said and smiled. "The burden will be less on all of us once shared."

The scullery maids and house porters clambered into the kitchen, laughing and chattering like children. They silenced when they saw Maryn and Eryk sitting at the table.

"Beg pardon, my lord, my lady," said one boy. They waited, bunched up in a group.

"Go about your business," said Eryk. "Pretend we aren't here."

"It will be a little while before the others stir," said Maryn.

A scullery maid placed a bowl of peppermint tea in front of Maryn and Eryk.

Maryn smiled at the girl. "Thank you, Thea," she said.

Eryk breathed in the brew's scent. He felt more alert, and it lifted his bad mood.

"Do I detect a hint of rosemary in this?" He took a long sip.

"Yes," said Maryn. She nodded to the girl, Thea, who placed buttered bread slices on the table. "Thea has a way with herbs. This is one of our favorite blends."

The girl blushed and turned away.

"This might be something we can add to the markets," said Eryk. "Would Thea have time in her day to work on teas for trade and barter?"

"If you think this is something worth doing," said Maryn, "Of course."

"She would receive part of the profits," said Eryk. "If she's interested."

A pot rattled on the floor.

Maryn and Eryk looked over to see Thea staring at them, her mouth open.

"Think on it," said Eryk to the girl. "As will I, and when I return from the north, we will make plans."

Thea nodded and bent to retrieve the pot from the floor.

After breaking his fast, Eryk gathered the scrolls he needed to explain the details of their future happenings. He laid it all out on the large table in the main hall.

Off to the sides, on additional tables, men, women, and children ate their morning repasts. They glanced in his direction and murmured to one another, but kept their voices low.

The room seemed fuller than usual. Maryn had gotten the word out that he would speak to them. Work halted for the morning as field hands, grooms, sculleries, porters, soldiers, milkmaids, brewers, weavers, seamstresses, washerwomen, ladies, and gentlemen crowded into the massive room.

Eryk did not know that so many people would be interested in what he had to say.

When it looked like those gathered ate all the food, the benches were full, and the walls lined with his people, he stood to his full height and surveyed the assembly.

He had known all these people his whole life; responsible for them and protected them. He felt the pressure of it on his neck and in his tightened muscles. He scowled.

"We woke the ogre," shouted Jon, waving his hands in mock horror. "Quick, someone, toss it a bone."

The crowd let out a collective gasp.

Eryk stared at Jon, who stared back, a huge grin splitting his handsome face.

Eryk laughed at his friend and threw an apple at him.

Jon bit into the fruit.

"Much sweeter than that look you gave us, Count Thorne," he said. "We are as we always were, as are you. Just speak plainly. We are all here as one people."

"Hear, hear," said Stefan and Adam.

Leave it to his oldest friends and Revena's brother to remind him not to take himself so seriously.

He grinned, his gaze passed from person to person, and let each of them know he saw them. It was the one quality that made everyone love and respect him.

He cleared his throat.

"You may have heard rumors," he said.

"Aye," the blacksmith shouted from the back of the room. "Lots of stories and tall tales, as always."

Laughter greeted this pronouncement.

"Too true," said Eryk. "This is not how we do things at Thornewood, and so I apologize for keeping you in the dark."

He breathed in deeply.

"While I visited Hilltop a few days back, Duke Kellan and I received a message from King Hugh."

"Eh?" The old tanner croaked from a corner.

"Come forward, Old Ben," said Eryk. "Clear a spot on that bench for him."

Eryk climbed up on a stool and waited for the old man to sit.

"While I don't have many specifics yet," he continued, "I know the King anticipates a threat to his lands."

He pointed to Jon, Stefan, and Adam.

"We have been called to Verdun, the King's capital. The wedding of Prince Henri and Lady Isuet, Lady Nicolette's sister, is our excuse for traveling and attendance."

"Once there, we expect to receive more information and specifics on the threat."

"We have placed sentries along our southern border and pulled people closer to the town. For now, we remain on alert, but don't expect an attack. Be aware of strangers and report any concerns to your local bailiffs."

"Anyone who wishes to see the maps may remain, and I will go over them, pointing out our town and Verdun. When I return, we will do this again."

"The bailiffs will show anyone interested how to use the tools to hand as weapons of defense and attack, and they will hold daily short drills. Anyone may attend these, not just the men."

"Lady Revena is with child."

The crowd cheered.

"Kellan is quite happy," he said. "And nervous." Nods and chuckles greeted this news.

"We will take my mother to Hilltop, as the Margravine has requested her presence during her pregnancy.

"We will also accompany the Ladies Nicolette and Clarissa on their journey north."

CHAPTER TWENTY-FOUR

Secret No More

Half of the people left after Eryk's brief review of coming events. Most of the older folks had seen war before and knew their lives went on the way the seasons moved one to another, with the occasional interruptions by other people's concerns. They would meet with their local community leaders, whether elders, priests, or bailiffs, for updates, but they would continue their daily routines.

Most people who stayed for more details were townsfolk, merchants, and younger people curious about new things.

Nicolette watched as Eryk answered questions, explained things in more detail, and pointed things out on his maps.

They left when they ran out of things to ask or felt the press of their business. By mid-afternoon, they were all gone.

Those leaving with Eryk were the only ones left. They gathered around the table where Eryk had his charts spread out.

Nicolette hadn't realized how many people would leave Thornewood. For some reason, she thought only Clarissa and her would go, but they would be a large party.

"The only wagon will be the one going to Hilltop," said Stefan. "So that portion of the journey will be the slowest."

Eryk nodded.

"We may need two wagons," he said. "One for the girls and my mother to travel in and the other to carry their belongings."

"We can manage with one," said Maryn. "Hilltop will have all that we need. I do not wish for us to slow you down, and it's best we make as little show of it as possible."

"I don't want you to be uncomfortable and cramped," said Eryk.

"Nonsense," said Maryn. "Even in a wagon, it will take less than a day. We can endure." She smiled at her son.

"As you wish, mother. Who will accompany you?"

"The three girls, the baby, and Fronika and Libbe," said Maryn.

"Will not Jen miss her daughters?"

"With all of us gone, she will have much less work, so she will not need them." Maryn brushed crumbs from the table. "And I promised them an adventure."

"Speaking of adventures," said Nicolette.

All eyes turned to her.

"I wanted to ask if I may bring Grite and Kathe with me," she said, watching Maryn. "I've grown fond of them, and they are eager to experience more of life." She flicked her eyes in Eryk's direction.

Ever since she hugged him on Beltane Eve, she found him watching her whenever she dared to glimpse him.

"I hadn't planned on taking a wagon to your father's estates or the capital," said Eryk.

"I'd hate for the girls to miss this opportunity," said Maryn. "We can fit them in with us to Hilltop. They aren't very big girls and won't occupy much space."

"They can ride behind Clarissa and me on our horses to Welf," said Nicolette. She watched Eryk. He didn't look upset over the change in plans.

"We can switch off as we go to Verdun," said Adam.

"It's settled then," said Eryk.

Grite and Kathe squealed behind Nicolette and clamped their lips together to keep their excitement contained. Nicolette reached behind her and patted their hands.

"Is there anyone else we need to include before we make our final plans?" Eryk scanned the people around the table. "We will leave in two days, as tomorrow is the Sabbath. This will give us a full day to reach Hilltop, a day to settle my mother and her party, and another day to collect Kellan and his troop." He inclined his head to Nicolette. "I understand your father expects you at Welf by the next full moon."

"Yes," she said. "He wishes a few days to discuss matters with me before we go to Verdun for Isuet's wedding."

"That gives us seven days of leisurely travel and plenty of time if unforeseen events occur."

He addressed Clarissa.

"Your men rested and make ready to take you home from Welf," he said to her. "We will add a group of men from Kellan's garrison headed by William, a veteran on the Marches."

"Surely that's unnecessary," said Clarissa. "We made it here safely with just my men."

"I would feel better having you out of my sight," said Nicolette, "if you had more people with you."

"And," said Eryk, "it's a good excuse for William to reconnoiter the borders in the east."

"Ah," said Clarissa, laughing. "The truth of it comes out."

"The truth is rarely just one thing," said Jon, who leaned forward on his elbows. "We've heard rumblings from out your way. Ever since the Marcher Lord's death, his foes have become braver without his vicious hand to curb him."

Clarissa sobered.

"Do you think my people are in danger?"

"We will see," said Eryk. "William served with Revena's father on the Eastern Marches. He will know the lay of the land and help you secure your estates if need be."

Nicolette reached a hand to her friend.

"Perhaps you should stay longer with me," she said. "I don't like the sound of this."

"I will not leave my people to fend for themselves," said Clarissa.

"All is not as dire as that," said Eryk. "When we know more, we can make better decisions." He locked eyes with each person around the table. "We will continue to meet as time goes on. Feel free to ask questions. Between Thornewood, Hilltop, and Beustel, we have the area covered and defended within a two-day ride in every direction."

He nodded in reassurance.

"Our castles sit atop hills; their walls are thick stone and manned by well-trained soldiers. Deep, fast-moving rivers surround us, and the mountains to the south are difficult to pass, especially unnoticed."

Eryk stood. Benches scrapped on the stone floors as the other rose with him.

"I ask that you gather your belongings. While we won't be leaving at first light, I do not wish to dawdle come Monday."

The room emptied, leaving Nicolette and Eryk alone.

"It would seem we will spend many more days together," said Nicolette. "I hope this will not be a burden to you."

"You could never be a burden," said Eryk. "I look forward to having more time with you while I can."

A housemaid passed from the kitchen to the stairs to the upper floors. She waggled her fingers at Eryk and giggled. Eryk raised a hand to her in greeting.

"You always know the perfect thing to say to the ladies," said Nicolette. She held her hands in fists at her sides.

"I only spoke the truth," Eryk said.

"The truth of the moment," she responded.

Eryk frowned.

"What are you on about?"

"How will you bear being away from all of your women?" She smirked. "Oh, I forgot. You'll just find new ones to keep you entertained. Is that why you won't marry? Too many to choose from? That doesn't stop other men."

"What has gotten into you?" He stood before her, a hand on each of her upper arms. "What women?"

Nicolette shook him off and waved a hand in the direction that the housemaid had gone.

"Women are always giggling around you," she said. "I can't stand the thought of you with all of them. Have you no self-control?" She pushed on his chest.

He fell back onto a bench.

"You're the one who will marry soon," he said.

She felt like sinking into his brown eyes.

"I have no other women," he said, his voice a whisper. "There is only you. There has only ever been you."

Tears welled up in her eyes. She shook her head in denial.

He reached for her, but she backed away from his hands.

"And I have never had a choice," she said as she turned and ran away from him.

CHAPTER TWENTY-FIVE

Sickness

The day broke clear and fresh with nary a cloud to mar the heavens' blue. The bright sun shone, sending stars dancing on the surface of the river Inn below Nicolette's bedchamber window.

Despite the apparent beauty and warmth of the day, she shivered and wrapped her woolen bedsheet tight around her shoulders. She felt a shadow pass across her vision. She blinked and watched as a murder of crows rose in a dark plumb from the gardens.

She inhaled sharply as the blackbirds chased a pair of doves. The air burst with panic, fear, and impending death.

Unable to turn away, willing the love birds speed to escape, she lost sight of the chase behind a copse of a tall oak surrounded by linden trees. The woods denied her the peace of knowing the outcome of the hunt. A portent of the days to come?

Nicolette turned from the window as Grite and Kathe entered her chamber to help her dress for the coming trip and finish her packing.

The girls braided her hair in a single, tight plait, wound it on the top of her head, covered it with a linen cloth, and tied it all into a package not likely to come loose on their travels.

She wore dark leggings of wool under her shift. A tunic covered these, split front and back up the middle, to allow riding atop a horse. A short tunic with wide sleeves to her wrists in her favorite green topped these. She would carry her cloak in case the air became chill.

She found a party of women and children in the great hall, breaking their fast. The girls barely contained themselves, fidgeting in their seats. The women paid them little mind as they were as excited by the prospect of the adventure.

Nicolette nibbled on a fruit tart, the bad feeling she experienced upon awakening still with her. She sipped on mint and chamomile tea, hoping it would settle her stomach.

Calm eluded her. She rose and approached Fronika, who held the squirming Betsey.

"Come, give her over," said Nicolette as she picked up the toddler.

"Thank you, miss," said Fronika. "I'll help Libbe finish packing the babe's belongings."

Nicolette cooed to Betsey. She nuzzled her face into the child's neck, inhaling the clean baby smell. She squeezed her tight.

It had been days since she spent any length of time with the girl. She tucked Betsey's hair under the cap she wore. They'd all be covering their heads as they ventured back into society to express their humility before God.

It had been difficult to distance herself from Betsey, but she knew she would need to give the child up to her new caretakers.

Today's trip to Hilltop would be the last of her time with the child she vowed to protect from all harm. She considered riding in the wagon with her, but it would be cramped enough without her.

She could take her on the horse for brief periods and let the sunshine wash over them in a kind of benediction.

"My Lady," came a voice behind her.

She turned in her seat to face the door to the courtyard. Betsey stood in her lap, trying to wave a rag doll she had clamped in her aching gums.

"The wagons be almost loaded," said the porter. "We be loading the ladies and girls momentarily."

Nicolette glanced around the room.

Kathe and Grite each hugged rugged men that looked like them. They were both motherless, but their fathers bid them Godspeed, one a farmer and the other a cow herder. The men looked uncomfortable, but proud of their daughters for being brave enough to venture out into the wider world.

Fronika and Libbe had come down from the nursery. Their mother, Jen, wrung her reddened hands in her apron as she wept.

"Ma," said Libbe. "We be but a day away at Hilltop."

"Do not fret so," said Fronika.

Jen swatted them.

"You let me be," she said. "Tis a mother's right to weep when her chicks leave the nest."

Jen's daughters burst into tears, and the three hugged as if they'd never see one another again.

Clarissa found Nicolette as they made their way out of the hall.

Clarissa handed Nicolette a small drinking pouch.

"From Jen," she said, "a willow bark extract for Betsey's teeth. In case the pain becomes too painful."

"I will miss her," said Nicolette. She glanced back at the cook. "We may never see her again."

"Never say never," said Clarissa. She hugged Nicolette's arm. "Do not despair so. Our stars are not so blackened by fate." She danced a jig, kicking up the hem of her dress with her heels.

"We ride again," she said. "We love riding horses. The weather is fine. We go adventuring." Clarissa's face shined with high color on her cheeks, and her eyes, wide and bright, held the promise of a better future.

Nicolette laughed and relaxed.

"Whatever will I do without your joy battling my despair each day?"

"Oh, poo," said Clarissa. "We ride." She pulled her dagger and stabbed it like a battle sword in the sky. "One day at a time, me dearest friend."

Betsey giggled in Nicolette's arms.

She handed the baby to Libbe in the cart setup for the women and girls. The men tied the curtains back to allow the sun to shine on the passengers.

Men helped Clarissa and Nicolette into the saddles of their horses. The wagons finished loading the travelers, and they were off with a shout to the garrison to make fast the gates once all passed through.

They were a party of twenty-two horses and two wagons.

Eryk and Adam rode behind the ranger, who watched the trail for dangers to the animals, like ruts, holes, and roots. Nicolette had not spoken to Eryk since their argument and his unbelievable confession two days ago.

"There is only you," he said. "There has only ever been you." She couldn't comprehend his words and obsessed over them during every moment, her mind was unoccupied by other pursuits.

She shook her head to dispel the intruding thoughts.

Two pairs of horses rode between her and Eryk's back. She saw his head above the four riders before her and Clarissa. They rode side-by-side.

Nicolette turned in her saddle.

Two soldiers took up behind them. The passenger wagon came next, two more soldiers, the supply wagon, and the last nine in their troop.

The morning passed in a peaceful and drowsy walk, interspersed with trots when the terrain allowed for a little more speed.

When the sun stood full overhead, they stopped in a valley pasture near a slow-moving brook with plenty of ash trees for shade.

Nicolette dismounted, throwing a leg over her saddle and sliding to the ground.

"Jealous," said Clarissa, who only took up riding in the past couple of years when it became clear her future husband expected it of her. She learned quickly, but still wanted to know more.

"Only requires practice," said Nicolette, positioning herself near her friend's mare. She held her hand up to steady Clarissa as a soldier steadied the horse with a tight grip on the reins.

"Gather up your skirts," said Nicolette. "Now, swing your right leg over. Pause to steady yourself. Deep breath. Slide down the side of the horse."

Clarissa's feet hit the ground. She balanced, straightened, and clapped her hands.

The friends walked over to the wagon, where all was quiet.

"Is everyone asleep?" Nicolette looked inside.

Maryn held Betsey in her arms. The baby's face was pink and shined with a thin layer of sweat.

"I fear she has a fever," said Maryn.

CHAPTER TWENTY-SIX

Change of Plans

Eryk expected the women and children in the wagon to disembark as soon as they stopped for their midday break. Instead, he found Nicolette climbing into the wagon.

Clarissa stood by the step, wringing her hands, her eyebrows drawn in, her mouth drawn down.

He hoped to make the trip to Hilltop and Welf with as brief contact with Nicolette as possible after his embarrassing outburst two days ago, but clearly, there was trouble, and he could not ignore it in good conscience.

He tied Smoke to a branch and asked one soldier to look after his horse as he strode off to the wagons.

"Do you think it her teeth?" Nicolette's voice was tight and low with worry.

"I've never felt a babe so heated while teething," said his mother. She sounded worried, too.

"We can not go into Hilltop if Betsey has a sickness," said Nicolette. "The danger to Revena would be too great." She sniffed. "And a fever in an enclosed fortress is dangerous. It could catch like a contagion and spread to all within." She paused.

"There is a secluded hunting lodge near Welf," said Nicolette. "Betsey and I can go on there. Do you think Eryk could spare a few men to escort us there?"

"No," he said.

The women jumped and faced him.

"If her fever heralds an illness or pestilence," said Nicolette, her voice rising.

"Hold," said Eryk. He held his hand up. "I only meant we would not let you go alone." He stepped back and held his hand up to his mother. She rose and disembarked.

"I think it best we rearrange the items in the wagons. We can put things on Clarissa and Nicolette's horses to make room."

He handed Grite, Kathe, Fronika, and Libbe out of the wagon. They helped Ava, Ema, and Gisela to the ground.

"We will camp here for a couple of hours," said Eryk. "I will send a soldier to Hilltop to tell them what has transpired."

The girls and young women went to a densely wooded area to relieve themselves.

"We can allow no one of our party to go to Hilltop," he said. "We do not yet know if this is an infection or if it has spread."

He turned to his mother.

"Take your ease," he said. "We can divert from here to Welf and arrive at the hunting lodge just before dark or near about, as does not matter."

Nicolette continued to sit in the wagon, cradling and rocking the sick child in her arms. Clarissa remained by her side, having climbed into the wagon bed once the others had left.

"I will bring a bucket of cool spring water and a cloth," he said to Nicolette. "You may wipe the babe's head and bring her some comfort."

Nicolette nodded to him, tears in her eyes.

"Fear not," he said to her. "I will not leave you."

"But what of your mission to the King?" She wiped her wet face on the shoulder of her tunic. "And Kellan?"

"Kellan knows the lodge as well as I," he said. "He can ride out and meet us there. He will appreciate your care for Revena and their people." As tall as he was, his eyes met hers as she sat in the dray. "We left plenty of time to meet all our obligations." His fingers stroked her wrist. "What else can I get you?"

"The cool water, please," she said. "Oh, Eryk, I am so feared for Betsey."

He squeezed her hand.

"We are all here for her and you," he said. "I promise to do all I can to keep you both healthy and safe."

She held his gaze for a long moment.

He smiled as he let her emotions sink into him. He determined not to keep himself from her again, no matter how much it hurt him.

"Water," he said, his voice a croak.

He brought back two buckets of clear, cool water and a soft cloth. While the others in the party ate apples, hard cheese, and dark bread, Nicolette and Clarissa undressed Betsey, bathed her fevered body, and looked for any other signs of disease. Once satisfied there were no lesions, blisters, or bumps, they wrapped her in clean garments and wool blankets.

Eryk waited by them in case they needed him to fetch anything, but it seemed all Nicolette needed from him was his presence. She looked at him periodically to assure herself he was still there.

He had not eaten and would only do so once he rearranged the wagons and Nicolette and Clarissa installed in the quarantine.

Maryn gave the two young women leave to see to their own needs, and when they returned, the wagon had enough room to hold all the women and children in comfort.

They pulled down the flaps of hide and tied them to the wagon loops to keep them in place and to prevent a draft on the child.

Betsey woke and screamed once, working her jaws together and chewing on her fists. Nicolette dipped her rag doll in willow bark extract and let her suck and chomp on the cloth. This seemed to settle her and gave them hope that only painful teeth plagued her, not an infection.

Eryk dispatched the messenger to Hilltop. He expected Kellan and his men to join them on the morrow at Grunwald.

He brought Nicolette and Clarissa a basket of food and drink.

"I know you are anxious," he said to them both, "but you must eat. At least the apples." He held one out to Nicolette, the skin of the fruit red and shiny. "Eat an apple before bed, and the doctor gets no bread." They stared at him. "It's something I heard." He shrugged. He waited until Nicolette took a bite.

"All of it," he said. "You, too, Clarissa."

He scanned the wagon interior.

"Do you have enough room?" He moved a sack. "I can get you more blankets."

106

"No," said Nicolette. "We are fine." She reached to him and clasped the sleeve of his shirt. "Thank you," she said.

He nodded.

"We will be off then," he said. "If you need to stop or you need me, call the soldiers behind you. Do not hesitate." He gave them a stern look. "I mean it. Have no fear of calling to me if anything goes amiss."

They nodded.

"Keep a keen eye out on them," he told the soldiers behind the wagon.

"Yes, Count Thorne," they said in unison.

He almost told them to use his given name, but realized he'd hear his title much more often now that they would be around strangers and acquaintances.

He strode to Smoke, mounted, and the party progressed.

They stopped once, for but half an hour in the late afternoon, to make water, stretch their legs, and check on Betsey.

Her condition seemed unchanged. Her skin shone bright red over her cheeks, but she did not cry out or cough. The women were so pale it appeared Betsey had stolen all of their color.

The water they used to bathe the child wet Nicolette and Clarissa's dresses, and both buckets needed refilling.

Once settled, they took off and did not stop until they rode into the front lawn of Grunwald Lodge. They arrived just after sunset.

The caretaker and his wife settled their unexpected guests. The soldiers unpacked and settled the horses.

Eryk, his mother, and Clarissa sat up with Nicolette all night as she attended Betsey.

CHAPTER TWENTY-SEVEN

Morning Has Broken

Nicolette woke with a start, knocking over a ceramic cup on the small table to her right hand. She blinked at the broken shards of pottery. She sat up straight, stretching her aching back.

Reality came back to her. Fever consumed Betsey, and the heat refused to leave her tiny body.

She jumped up in a panic. The last she remembered, the babe lay in the cradle before her chair. But the child's bed lay empty. She collapsed.

Betsey died during the night, and she slept through it. She gripped her throat, holding back a scream. No, a rational voice said inside her head. They would not let her sleep through that.

A whimper behind her broke through her panic. She turned.

Eryk slumped in a chair by a blazing fire in the hearth with Betsey in his arms. A feather comforter enveloped them both like a mummy's shroud.

His face was as red as newly spilled blood.

She rushed to his side and felt his face. Heat stung her fingers. He had a fever.

Betsey squirmed in his arms, eyes open, clear and bright. Her cheeks looked healthy. Testing the child's forehead, Nicolette found the high heat from yesterday gone.

She gently took the babe from Eryk's arms.

His eyes opened, and he gripped the child to his chest.

"Let go," said Nicolette.

He shook his head.

She pried his fingers loose.

"Betsey recovered," she said, "but you have caught the sickness."

Eryk let her have Betsey.

Nicolette placed her in the crib lined with fresh bed linens and a new rag doll. The child cooed, laughed, and granted her a grin showing off three teeth in redden gums.

Eryk came up beside her.

"You must get abed," she said to him. "You have caught Betsey's fever."

"No," he said. "Only heat from the fire and the quilts." He touched her wrist. "It seems having all those teeth raging to break free of her gums at once angered her body."

He directed Nicolette to sit.

He sat across from her.

Regular coloring washed his face.

"Twas no disease, after all?" She stared at him.

He shook his head.

She slumped back in her chair with a sigh.

"I feel adrift," she said.

"No wonder," said Eryk. "You refused to sleep or eat when we arrived. I sent the others away to their beds and promised not to leave. Only then did you succumb to sleep."

Nicolette studied him. His hair lay matted on the left side of his head, and vomit splattered the chest of his tunic. The index finger of his left hand was red, the skin broken.

She pointed at it.

"What happened to your finger?"

"During the night, Betsey took hold of my hand and shoved my finger in her mouth." He laughed. "She near gnawed it off. I felt the teeth break through her gums and into my flesh. After that, she calmed and fell asleep."

He rolled his shoulders, loosening tight muscles.

Betsey laughed, exposing her new teeth.

"Yes," said Eryk, "be proud of those weapons that caused us all such worry."

Nicolette glanced at the closed shutters.

"What day is it?"

109

"This is the second day since we arrived," said Eryk.

"You are truly not ill?"

"No, not ill," he said, "but dirty." He looked down at his clothing and pulled a corner of his tunic to his nose. "Ugh." He wrinkled his face.

Nicolette looked at herself. She wore the same clothing she had on for traveling.

"No more so than I," she said.

Eryk rose.

Nicolette placed her hands on the arms of her chair to leverage herself up. She was exhausted.

"No," he said. "Stay. I will call the girls to take Betsey and help you bathe and clean up your chambers."

He strode to the door, opened it, and called out.

"Mother?"

Maryn arrived. She rushed to Betsey, picked her up, and hugged her. She beamed at Nicolette.

"Oh, thank heavens," she said.

"Can you arrange for help for Nicolette?" He plastered himself back against the door as girls rushed into the room.

He chuckled.

Nicolette met his gaze.

"Thank you," she said, the words getting lost in the sounds of Nicolette's assistants.

He nodded and left.

Maryn organized her gang of helpers.

Nicolette scarcely lifted a finger except to feed herself warm bread chunks dipped in a light, warm chicken broth.

When she put her bowl aside after sipping the last of the savory liquid, Kathe and Grite manipulated her limbs to remove her clothing. She washed and donned a clean shift.

Since none required her to think or make any decisions, she watched for signs of illness and finding none. They all appeared healthy and happy.

They put the room to rights, opened the shutters to freshen the air and allow morning light to enter, banked the fire to embers, and ushered her to bed.

She thought she fought sleep, but the next thing she knew, it was night.

She sat up and stretched. Now that she conquered her exhaustion, she saw her favorite room in the lodge, lit with oil lamps.

She left the bed and peeked out the door into the great room.

Eryk was the first to see her. He stood. Maryn faced her.

"Finally," she said with a smile. "I had a devil of a time stopping Eryk from checking on you every few moments."

"Mother," he said.

"Don't you 'mother' me."

Kellan laughed.

"I did not know you had arrived," said Nicolette.

"Yesterday morn," he said. "I am glad all is well, and thank you for the consideration you showed my wife by diverting to this lodge."

Nicolette inclined her head.

Kellan's girls and Betsey sat on a bear rug before a low fire playing with wooden marbles.

Grite and Kathe pushed Nicolette back into her room with arms full of fresh clothing and a mug of warm milk flavored with honey and cinnamon.

They dressed her, brushed her hair, and she dutifully drank her milk. Her stomach rumbled.

"They saved you a plate from the evening meal," said Grite.

"Is it so late?" Nicolette held out an arm to Kathe as she tied the ribbons of her tunic at her wrist.

"Only a couple hours past the repast," said Kathe.

Nicolette left the girls in the room to tidy up.

As she entered the lodge's main hall, Eryk, Kellan, and Adam rose.

She gestured for them to be seated. She took the spot at the end of the couch occupied by Maryn.

She watched the girls play for a few moments.

Eryk cleared his throat.

She dragged her eyes from Betsey and met his; an eyebrow quirked up in question.

"We sent a message yesterday to Welf House," he said.

"Is my father home?"

"Yes," he said. "We told him we were here and not to approach until we were sure of the situation."

She nodded, but felt uneasy. Eryk seemed to hold himself stiff and tight.

"He bid us to keep him informed of your health." Eryk picked at an invisible loose string at the seam of his breeches. "He wanted to send his doctor and priest, but we convinced him it was best to keep all away."

"I don't think the men wanted to come," said Kellan, "so it was easy to sway them."

Adam snickered.

"Ha," he said. "Men of medicine and God are often easy to persuade."

"Some," said Eryk. "We were lucky it was so for them." His frown deepened.

"Is there some problem besides them?" She leaned forward, anticipating a blow.

"Isuet is in residence," said Eryk, a growl escaping his lips.

CHAPTER TWENTY-EIGHT

The Harpy Is Here

Based on the wane faces Eryk saw at the table the next morning, it looked as if he were not the only one who hadn't slept.

He had hoped he wouldn't see Isuet until they arrived at Verdun. She would be too busy with the wedding, and he'd be too busy on King's business.

The fates refused to smile upon him.

"How long do you think we can keep her at bay?" Adam, raised by his hedge witch mother in a swamp, ate his ham with the manners of one born in a palace.

The adults seated at breakfast in the dining room on the right wing of the lodge's main hall watched him with fascination.

At times, his rough, sharp humor erupted when most inconvenient, but always to shock and take the measure of those around him.

Now, surrounded by family and friends and with nothing to prove, his inborn elegance displayed care for those he loved.

A dimple appeared on his shaven face. He ran a hand across his shaven head. Not a bit of his red hair showed in either place.

"I know tis not a proper conversation for a pleasant meal," he said, "but it's best we have a plan as soon as possible." He speared a roasted turnip with more force than necessary. "Beg pardon," he said as his fork screeched on his pewter platter. "While I have not met your dear sister, Lady Nicolette, I have heard rumors."

He chuckled.

"She loves me not," said Nicolette. "The best we can do, without proof of sickness, throughout the lodge is another two days."

"What does she want with us?" Clarissa spooned some stewed pears onto her plate.

"Mischief, no doubt," said Eryk. He filled his plate a third time. Missing a day of meals made him ravenous.

"We'll send word for her to wait," he said, "for her safety. I think it best you sign the missive, Nicolette." He nodded at Kellan. "The previous messages went with Kellan's seal. We thought him best to appease her need for status and deference."

"Yes," she said, "I will consider the best words to keep her from rushing here."

They all turned towards the front of the lodge as the sounds of hooves and wagon wheels crunched on gravel.

The caretaker opened the front door and greeted the visitors on the lawn. They heard the muffled conversation.

A few moments later, he returned, hat in hand, and addressed the table.

"My wife," he said, twisting his cap between his gnarled fingers, "sent to the castle to inform the Lady Isuet that the danger has passed and there is no sickness here." His eyes fell to his boots. "I beg pardon," he said. "I did not know she did so."

"Who is out front?" Nicolette's voice came out in a whisper.

"Tis the Lady Isuet," he said, looking up at her. "She demands to be escorted into the lodge."

The half-dozen people rose at once, scrapping stools and benches across the stone floor. One seat fell over.

"It's barely past sunrise," said Kellan, anger making his voice rough. "It's unseemly and rude to visit unannounced at this time of day. The ladies have not even dressed yet."

"She wishes to make us uncomfortable," said Nicolette, "and put us at a disadvantage." She sighed. "I will go out and speak with her. I am used to her tricks and can most easily take her abuse."

Eryk shook his head.

"No, you ladies go dress," he said. "I will bid her welcome, flanked by Kellan and Adam for support until you are ready."

"Ugh," said Kellan and Adam in unison.

They grinned.

"I love you, brother," said Kellan, "but you ask too much."

114

"Brother-in-law," said Adam, pointing a thumb at his chest, "surely doesn't obligate me to such dangerous activities."

"Buck up." Eryk grabbed both of his brothers by their shirt sleeves. "Pain is good for the soul, and good works get you into heaven."

"Do I have to see her?" Clarissa whined like a ten-year-old.

"I thought you vowed to support me, come what may," said Nicolette, as the women left for their rooms to dress.

"Surely not, Isuet, though. That is too much to ask."

His mother laughed along with Nicolette and Clarissa but had made no comment that he could hear as the men went out into the yard to greet Henri's future wife.

She sat in a wagon driven by a man in Welf livery of green and black.

A woman sat beside her, holding a cloth shield over Isuet's head to keep the sun from her skin.

She could use some color, thought Eryk. Only her face and fingertips remained uncovered, and these shined like a sheet lit from behind by an unearthly blue light.

Expensive silk and linen, embroidered with gold threads and decorated with jewels, covered the rest of her. She wore at least five layers of dresses, the hems of each showing as if in steps. A white cowl wrapped around her hair and neck. A sheer veil held atop her head by a thin crown finished her ensemble.

He thought she must have been up all night dressing to arrive here so early.

"Lady Isuet," Eryk said as he held his hand out for her to help her from her conveyance.

She tried to ignore him, but no one else moved to assist her.

"Count Thorne," she said with a curl of her lip. Her fingers barely touched his hand as if afraid he'd contaminate her.

"You bless us with your presence," he said over her fingers. "We would have preferred to prepare properly for your visit. You find us in a state of disarray."

She did not respond to him, instead turning to his brother.

"Your Grace," she said to Kellan, holding out her hand.

He bent over her fingers and straightened.

"Honored," he said with a straight face." Let us get out of this hideous light," she said, brushing past Adam without acknowledging him.

Isuet floated before them, her woman hurrying to keep shade over her.

Adam grinned, a devilish look in his eye.

Eryk shook his head at the younger man.

"Behave," Eryk said to him.

"Of course," said Adam. He rushed in front of Isuet and held the door for her. He bowed, sweeping an arm and bending low.

Isuet's woman let out a short giggle, then clamped her jaws tight when Isuet scowled at her.

Eryk expected to entertain Isuet until Nicolette, Clarissa, and his mother joined them, but the ladies stood in the main hall as they entered.

"Sister," said Nicolette, coming forward. She hugged Isuet, who responded with what Eryk called her "cold, dead fish face."

"Come, be seated," Nicolette pulled Isuet to the best chair in the room, padded with abundant cushions, no doubt thinking of Isuet's fleshless bones.

"Would you care for a glass of wine?" This from Maryn.

Isuet glanced at Kellan and Eryk briefly. She knew from experience that while she could abuse them and they would remain cordial; they did not tolerate any disrespect to their mother.

"Yes, please," she said, her voice strained.

As with Adam, Isuet refused to acknowledge Clarissa, her gaze sliding over them as she looked around the room.

She accepted the glass of deep red wine Maryn handed her.

"Where is this child that has brought such chaos to our lives?"

She sipped the wine. It stained her pale lips like blood.

CHAPTER TWENTY-NINE

Princess Poison

Silence settled on the room, sucking the breath from its occupants. The lack of air forced everyone to collapse onto benches, stools, and chairs.

Nicolette closed her eyes. "Justice is the constant and perpetual wish to render each his due." The words of a long-dead Roman Emperor came to her mind. Dare she believe her sister receives what she deserves?

"I thought you would be in Verdun," she said to her older sibling. She settled back in her chair, observing the other woman. Isuet was cunning and had a way of forcing a danger into a tender and sore spot.

"Don't try to deflect my attention," said Isuet. She sat straight on the edge of her seat, her hands clamped together in her lap.

"I'm just curious why you are here and not there for the wedding," said Nicolette.

"If you must know," said Isuet, her eyes squinted at Nicolette, and she pulled back her lips, baring small, sharp teeth. She looked like a ferret.

"I escorted your future husband to Welf to meet father," she said.

Nicolette stared at her, mouth open in an oh.

"You do well to be surprised," said Isuet. "We intended to give you several days to get to know one another, but this mysterious child scotched our plans."

She stood and walked a couple of stiff steps to Nicolette, leaning towards her.

"So, I'd like to see the …. Cherub …. capable of ruining my plans."

Her cheeks flushed with circles of red staining her washed-out face. "Now, you and he will not meet until the wedding. He returned to Prince Henri's circle yesterday." She turned her head to Eryk and grinned. "Father considers him an excellent candidate for you, sister, and you will do as you are told. He is a legitimately born Duke." After a pause where she held Eryk's gaze, she returned her attention to Nicolette.

"So you see, I must know for whom you dared keep a peer of the realm at bay."

She returned to her chair, arranging the layers of her clothing in some order only she appreciated.

"Who is this person?" Nicolette choked on the words.

"I can keep a secret as well as you," said Isuet. "You'll find out in due time."

The caretaker's wife entered the room, approached Isuet, and waited behind and to the left. She made a low sound in her throat.

Isuet raised her hand and wiggled her fingers in a come-here gesture. The woman bent to Isuet's ear and whispered, sounding like a hissing snake.

Isuet nodded. The woman gave Nicolette a peek, her mouth tight and raised in one corner. She left.

"Your Grace brought your adopted foundlings," said Isuet. She gazed at Kellan. "Such a generous gesture, adopting children with no families." Her flat tone put the lie to her words.

Kellan did not respond.

Led by the caretaker's wife, Fronika ushered in Ava, Ema, and Gisela. She lined them up around Kellan's chair. He extended both arms and the girls, clearly frightened, clutched his hands.

Dressed in new tunics in the same shade of yellow, the girls appeared as miniature women, clean and neat, with their hair covered and hidden under snow-white silk wimples.

Fronika dressed them in their best for their first meeting with Lady Isuet.

"Aren't they adorable?" Isuet clapped her hands like a group of stage players entertained her. "They look presentable enough," she said. She leaned forward. "The twins are the kitchen serfs." She babbled. "Show your hands. Are they red from your labors?"

Kellan held their hands and kept them still.

"Lady Isuet," said Maryn, shock coloring her words.

Isuet threw Maryn a dirty look and opened her mouth.

"Isuet," said Eryk, "have a care."

"You may not use my given name," she said with a hiss, rising to her feet.

"Attend your words and tone," said Kellan. "The title, Princess, does not grace your name yet." He steered the girls to Fronika. "Please take the girls to their room." He kissed their hands as he released them, but this would not prevent the tears waiting to burst from the girls as soon as they were safely away.

"Do not spread your poison over innocent children," he said.

"Innocent? How are they innocent? Serfs and a foundling?" Isuet's voice rose and squeaked. "Who brings such persons into their household on purpose? Bad enough to have the base-born in your family. That, at least, was beyond your control."

Nicolette peeked at Eryk. His fingers gripped the arms of his chair, the wood creaking, his knuckles white.

"You ooze poison," said Nicolette, unable to control her anger. "What makes you so mean?"

Isuet glared at her sister, her arms straight at her sides, hands in fists. She took a deep breath, releasing the tension in her body. She smiled.

Nicolette shivered.

"You all," she let her eyes roam around the room, "will regret your behavior soon enough. In less than three weeks, I will be Prince Henri's wife with influence over all your lives."

She took her chair as if easing onto a throne.

"I have a long memory and an accurate balance sheet," said Isuet. "You do best not to forget this."

She brushed the skirt covering her lap.

"And I never turn from my target." She nodded to the caretaker's wife.

Nicolette couldn't remember the woman's name.

"Bring in the babe," said Isuet to the woman. "As I said, you can not dissuade me from my mark."

Nicolette started and ran her wet palms on the skirt of her dress. She leaned forward.

Libbe came in carrying Betsey. She looked at Nicolette for

instructions.

"Come here, girl," said Isuet.

Libbe hesitated.

"Now," said Isuet. She slapped her knee.

Libbe stood frozen in place, her eyes wide, her face pale.

Betsey squirmed in response to the tension. Her dark hair peeked out from under the cap covering her head, curling at the nape of her neck.

"You're scaring them," said Nicolette. She moved to go to Libbe and Betsey.

"Who does this child belong to?" Isuet squinted at her sister.

Nicolette turned towards Isuet, mouth open.

Clarissa jumped up and ran to Libbe, her arms out to receive Betsey.

"She's mine," said Clarissa. "My daughter." The words came out in a rush.

Nicolette turned to her friend.

"Yours?" Doubt washed over Isuet's face.

"Yes, mine." Clarissa hugged Betsey, who rubbed her face into Clarissa's neck.

"She has dark hair. I see it there, at her neck, under her cap," said Isuet. It sounded like an accusation. "Unlike yours." The word ended with sibilant contempt.

"Betsey takes after her father," said Clarissa. She stroked Betsey's cheek and handed her back to Libbe. "Go to the other girls," she said.

"Your husband had dark hair?" Isuet did not object to the child leaving.

"Yes," said Clarissa.

"You and he made quick work of the deed," said Isuet. "I had not heard you were with child. He did not care that you took his child on this journey with my sister."

"My husband is dead," said Clarissa. "You hadn't heard that?" She spoke with a sneer.

"No," said Isuet. "I hadn't heard that either."

"I am not important enough for such news to reach your ears."

"At least, that is true," said Isuet. She stared at Clarissa, who stared right back.

Isuet gained her feet.

Nicolette was the first to join her.

"What are your plans for them?" Isuet waved in the direction the girls had gone in.

The men stood. Clarissa and Maryn remained in their seats.

"I will send them back to Hilltop," said Kellan.

"And Clarissa and her baby?"

"We will go to Black Bear Lodge," said Clarissa.

Isuet watched Nicolette's face as Clarissa spoke. Her eyes reminded Nicolette of a falcon on the hunt.

"No," said Isuet, dragging the word out.

"Beg pardon," said Eryk.

Isuet turned her vicious mask to face him.

"I demand they all come to Verdun and attend my wedding," she said.

CHAPTER THIRTY

Duke Doom

They argued with Isuet about taking the children to the capital.

Eryk tried to remain the focus of her ire, but she spread her malice among them with exceptional uniform care.

In the end, Isuet threatened to send a message to Henri requesting he demand their presence. They gave up to save their energy—no point in fighting a losing battle.

Isuet left for the capital the next day. After sowing distress and fear, she went in good spirits and satisfaction.

Nicolette forced the caretaker's wife to leave the lodge. The woman tried to fight her, but Nicolette held her ground. Eryk had never seen her so uncharacteristically stubborn in the face of tears and distress.

"I can not have someone so untrustworthy around the children," she told the woman.

Once she saw Nicolette wouldn't budge, she tried to get her husband to abandon his duties. He refused and sent his wife to stay with her sister in the town.

The occupants of the Grunwald Lodge required a couple of days to recover. They spent some time out of doors in the spring sunshine during the day and played games in the evenings.

Eryk told them tales as they sat in the great room around the hearth. One of their favorites, The Smith and Death, had them all shivering with fear and chased away the terrible memory of Isuet's visit.

On the Sabbath, they dressed in their best and ventured to the church at Welf for mass. The girls enjoyed the service's pageantry and the women from the nunnery singing.

Afterward, they joined Tomas, Nicolette's father and Count of Welf, at his castle.

Eryk had forgotten how much he liked the man. Spending time with Isuet tended to wipe away wonderful memories. She was so different from Tomas and Nicolette.

Since attendance at Mass required them not to eat before the service, even the children, Tomas provided them with an afternoon repast to chase away their hunger.

"Oh, thank you, Father," said Nicolette. She kissed his cheek.

He had wasted no time on formal greetings. Instead, he ushered them into the dining hall.

Once the children had food in front of them, Tomas took his seat at the head of the table.

"Sit, sit," he said, waving his hand at the chairs.

"Sir," Eryk began.

"No, no," said Tomas. He liked to say certain words in doubles. "Eat something first. Once you've slaked your hunger and thirst, we can address all the rest."

Eryk smiled at him.

The party ate.

In a quarter hour, they felt their ravenous appetite quelled. The mood of the girls improved with full bellies.

Libbe and Fronika collected them and took them to the nursery.

"Lovely children," said Tomas as he watched them go. "You and your wife have done well by them. And now, the Margravine is with child." He raised his wineglass to Kellan. "May your blessings be many," he said.

"Hear, hear," the rest of the table occupants joined in the toast.

Kellan inclined his head.

"I thank you, sir," said Kellan. "We were hoping you could convince Isuet to change her mind about them attending her wedding."

Tomas frowned.

"Unfortunately, she already warned me not to try," he said. "She insists. I did try to make her see reason, and I don't know why she's doing this. She doesn't like children. It makes no sense." He held his cup out for a refill by a servant behind him.

"She has been flexing her newfound authority as Prince Henri's future wife," said Tomas. "By the time we get there, I'm sure she will have forgotten all about them, and you can hide them out of the way."

Clarissa snorted.

"Beg pardon, Lord Tomas," she said.

"Tsk, tsk," he said. "She garners that sort of response." He shook his head. "I've never understood her." He reached out a hand and covered one of Nicolette's. "I understand she has insisted you divert your return home to accommodate her." He faced Clarissa. "And demanded you bring your babe, who recently recovered from a fever."

"Growing teeth afflicted Betsy, not a true disease," said Clarissa.

"Still, still," he said, "she is young for so much travel. You've had so much trouble upon your young, delicate shoulders. A new marriage, widowhood, the death of your parents, a child. You've weathered these tribulations well."

"Nicolette's presence made all the difference," said Clarissa. "Her generous heart and genuine care deserve her future happiness."

"Who is this Duke Isuet mentioned as a prospective husband for Nicolette?" Maryn nibbled on a slice of cheese.

All eyes turned to Tomas.

"Yes, yes," said Tomas with a smile. "Now that's a boon. A shame he couldn't stay for you to meet him. Isuet wanted me to keep it a secret, but I disagreed. That would be too much."

"But who is he?" Eryk's voice was louder than he intended.

Tomas blinked.

"Well." Tomas cleared his throat. "Well, Duke Ramnlf." He let go of Nicolette's hand.

"You can't be serious," said Eryk.

Nicolette looked from her father to Eryk.

"Who is he?" She turned back to her father.

"He's the Duke of Nantes," said Tomas, not meeting Nicolette's eyes.

"He's old," said Eryk.

"He's got three grown sons," said Kellan.

"And he's fat." Kellan bent the pewter spoon in his left hand. "With a lame leg."

"He's a Duke," said Tomas, "a Duke with deep coffers." He grumbled.

"Did you receive my letter?" Maryn broke through the men's

tensions.

Tomas blinked.

"Yes, yes," he said. "I've done nothing but meet the man. He is quite interested. Henri has been singing Nicolette's praises to him."

Nicolette knocked over her glass of wine, spilling the contents over her dress.

A servant offered a cloth to help her clean up. Nicolette waved the man away.

"So, you did not come to any agreements?"

"Of course not," he said. "The choice is entirely yours, but I encourage you to consider him. He has the ear of the future king."

Tomas retook her hand.

"He will be at the wedding," said Tomas. "Just meet him. Allow him to woo you."

Eryk grunted.

Tomas caught his eyes.

"You. You'll understand someday when you have children," said Tomas to him.

Eryk shook his head.

"I have no other family than my two girls. I must be sure they are safe when I am no longer around to care for them. I can not leave them to the vagaries of the world."

Eryk pursed his lips. He felt hot and cold at once. The thought of Duke Ramnlf touching Nicolette made him ill. The food he had just eaten rose sour in his throat.

"You'd be a Duchess," said Tomas. "Your future would be secure."

"We would never leave Nicolette on her own," said Maryn.

"We appreciate your friendship," said Tomas. "But that's not enough to secure her future. I can not trust my Nicolette to the vagaries of affection."

Tomas breathed deeply.

"I must have her protected by a legal contract before I die," he said.

"Father, what is all of this talk about you dying?"

Eryk looked at Tomas closely. He looked thin and wane.

Oh shit, he thought. Tomas was dying. Eryk saw the realization strike Nicolette.

She would grant his dying wish. He saw the truth of it in the way she looked at her father.

Eryk clamped his teeth together to prevent bile from leaving his mouth and embarrassing him.

CHAPTER THIRTY-ONE

Love or Security

The last few days before the trip north to the King's capital involved finishing touches to wedding finery, anticipating the children's needs in the unexpected circumstances of an unprecedented journey, and making memories with Count Tomas.

Nicolette tried to see to her father's comfort. She played for him in the evenings, surrounded by their friends. Her father enjoyed the time spent with Eryk, Kellan, and Adam. They reminisced about Tomas' old friend, Allan, Eryk's father.

Tomas enjoyed the antics of Kellan's girls and Betsey's attempts to stand and walk. He used an hour each afternoon to read to them, Betsey on his lap. After his time with the children, he napped until the evening meal.

They had but two days at home.

The trip to Verdun required five days for them to arrive before the Sabbath ahead of the wedding day.

Nicolette supervised the packing and organization of the wagons and pack animals.

"Be sure to include the cushions," said Nicolette to the household steward. "I want as much comfort as possible for my father on this journey."

"Yes, my lady," said the steward. "Rest assured, Count Tomas' man followed your instructions completely. His Lordship will have every comfort."

"I could not convince my father to ride in one of the wagons," she said. "He insists on riding with the men."

"Certainly, the Lords will be good company for His Lordship," said the steward as he checked his list. He handed a sheet to Nicolette.

"The scribe drew up an itinerary," said the steward. His finger traced a line on the map. "He marked off the inns along the way in case his Lordship tires during the day."

Nicolette nodded.

"Thank you." She smiled at the man. "I see you have done well."

The leave-taking day dawned on the twelfth of May, warm and bright with sunshine. The weather did not improve her mood.

Her father was dying, and she'd marry an old man to make her father's last days peaceful. She shivered despite the warmth of the sun.

She shook herself, determined to make this trip an adventure to distract her father from his ailments and make his last days pleasurable.

Before mounting his horse, Count Tomas kneeled on the ground, bent forward, and kissed the earth of Welf. He rose, shaking, his eyes roaming over his estates.

His people gathered around the Count, solemn but smiling. He raised his right hand as if bestowing benediction with his goodbye wave. Tears filled the eyes of more than the women who ranged around him.

He nodded, took a deep breath, turned on his heel, and mounted his horse with the help of his old groom.

He sat straight in the saddle, and Nicolette turned away lest her father saw her tears.

The rest of the party filled the wagons and mounted their horses, and they were off.

They rode leisurely, taking many breaks to accommodate her father and the children.

The men distracted Count Tomas with japes and tall tales. He seemed more robust in their company, the wane color he had while at home replaced by a healthy flush in his cheeks.

The soldiers with them seemed wary and alert, though, and Eryk, Kellan, and Adam took turns riding forward and back to the scouts that watched the trails and roads upon which they traversed.

Despite the unease she sensed in the men, the first three days passed without incident. They spent their nights in inns and their daytime breaks in picnics, lingering in play and naps while the weather allowed.

On the fourth day, they woke to a cold, all-encompassing rain.

"We must go on," said Kellan, "if we are to arrive in a timely fashion."

"This rain will slow us down," said Adam, looking at the gray sky, then glancing at Count Tomas, who sat in the inn's main room surrounded by the children and women as they broke the fasts.

"I will tell him he must ride in a wagon," said Nicolette. She did not relish wounding his pride. She stiffened her spine and approached her father.

She touched his shoulder. He looked up at her, and she tilted her head toward a room to the left.

He followed her.

When they were alone, she sighed.

"The weather tis foul this day," she said.

"I saw," he replied, glancing at a shuttered window.

"We can not stay here until the rain ceases if we are to make it to Verdun on time." She took his hand and squeezed it. "I need you to ride in a wagon so that we may continue with as few stops as possible."

He took up her other hand and held them both in his. He shook them in reassurance.

"Fear not, my daughter," he said. "I do not wish to slow us down. And truth be told, I find my arse is a bit weary of the saddle. It has been many a year since I needed to travel so far and for so long. I fear I am no longer up to the task." He kissed her cheek. "You have always been a wonderful daughter," he said. "So like your mother in appearance and temperament. My first marriage was for duty's sake. My second for my heart. I loved her so."

Her father brushed her hair from her face.

"I can not leave you alone to the vagaries of a fickle and cruel world," he said.

"Father," said Nicolette, "do not trouble yourself over me." She wanted to ease his mind. "I will marry as you see fit if it gives you peace."

"Peace," he said with a hint of bitterness. "That is not the best I wanted for you." He spoke in a whisper to himself, she thought. He closed his eyes and shook his head. "We conceived you in love, made for love. That is what I wanted for you, but alas, time is not on our side."

"All will be well," she said. She felt her responses as weak as watered-down tea.

"He seems a kind man," said Tomas. "And war is on the horizon. Perhaps he will die in battle and leave you a merry widow like your friend Clarissa."

"Father," she said in mock outrage.

"You might get lucky," said her father.

She laughed.

Eryk's laughter from the other room floated to them. They both looked through the doorway and saw him tickling Betsey under the chin as the child tugged on his beard.

Nicolette caught Tomas' glance. She shook her head as she realized her father saw into her heart.

"That is not a path I may take," she said. "He deserves a different kind of woman."

Her father squinted at her but said nothing.

He linked his arm through hers.

"Come," he said. "Let us be off on this gloriously wet day to splash like children through puddles and mud."

They purchased some bags of thick beer and fresh pasties filled with pork, carrots, and peas from the innkeeper. The food and drink would keep them warm and full and induce dozing in the occupants of the wagons, thus keeping them moving with fewer stops.

They mounted up. Those on horseback wrapped themselves in woolen cloaks. The continuous drizzle beaded on the fabric and rolled off, but the wetness lingered on faces and hands.

The fourth day of their journey ended with them uncomfortable and tired.

CHAPTER THIRTY-TWO

Encroaching War

The rain ceased during the night of the fourth day of travel. Eryk convinced the party to go to Luxembourg, which had a large inn as fortified as a fortress.

They had encountered patrols on a fourth day that alerted them to German troops massing in the east and Viking ships teasing the coastline along the North Sea.

"Do you think the King knew of these invaders when he sent his message to us?" Adam frowned. He took a dim view of the machinations of important folk.

"His message only mentioned dangers from the south," said Kellan.

Adam's lip curled up in a sneer. He spit on the corral ground where they striped the horses for the night. Grooms from the inn would brush them down and feed them, thank the gods, thought Eryk.

He felt weary from the trip, the damp and chill making his joints ache.

He glanced at the wagons where Nicolette helped his mother and her father from a wagon and handed them off to serfs from the inn.

Count Tomas stretched his back and limped towards the inn and the warm yellow light glowing in the doorway. The spicy scent of a northern stew wafted on the air, and Eryk's mouth watered.

He turned back as he missed something his brother had said.

"Beg pardon," he said to Kellan. "My mind drifted."

"We need a good night's sleep," said Kellan, "And warm food."

"I need a beer," said Adam. He rubbed the top of his head with the palm of his hand. "A shave, too."

Eryk peered at the red stubble on Adam's head. He always forgot how bright his hair was because he kept himself hairless, and Adam's skin was not fair like most red-headed people's. His skin never burned when he stayed out of doors all day.

"Do you think he'll expect us to bring troops north?" Kellan draped his saddlebags over his shoulder.

Eryk and Adam had theirs. Goodnight, they bid their men, who would bed down in a separate building closer to the inn's walls. Their soldiers would help the inn's guards protect the compound while they stayed the night and part of the morning.

"I doubt it," said Kellan. "That would leave him vulnerable on too many fronts."

Eryk nodded.

"I suspect he will want us to keep a path open for him if he must flee south to evade captured," said Eryk. "Although if he leaves Verdun, he opens up the way to the capture of Paris, and that would be fatal for his monarchy."

They ceased their discussion of war and invasions for the rest of the evening so as not to be overheard by the children.

Once in dry clothes and a warm meal of thick stew in rye bread trenchers, they all went gladly to their beds despite the raucous laughter of the other guests who remained in the large tavern room.

During the night, soldiers ranged along the palisades of the wall surrounding the inn and shouted an alarm that woke everyone.

Eryk jumped out of bed, grabbed his sword, and dashed down the stairs and into the yard. He had slept fully clothed as the previous day's news had made him uneasy.

He climbed the stairs to the wall facing east. Off in the distance, he saw the glow of fires.

"How far away do you think them?" He spoke his question to no one in particular.

A man half his height and twice his age looked up at him and blinked.

"Findel," said the man. "They are burning the logs."

"They mean to frighten us," said a tall, thin man with long, thin blond hair. "But Fort Kirchberg has never fallen."

"Aye," said the first man. "With the Alzette River betwixt us and them and our walls, we always stand firm."

The tall blond man nodded down below them.

"We just burn the Red Bridge down when we see them coming, and they back off," he said. "The Alzette is too deep and too long for them to go around and come back. It wears them out."

"But they take the surrounding lands," said the old man. "It's why we all speak French and German. Helps us get along with whoever sits on the throne." He snorted.

"So we aren't in any real danger for the moment?" Kellan had joined him on the wall.

"No, my lord," said the old man. "But we must be watchful never-the-less." He spat next to his boot. "These raiding parties do like to destroy the small farms around us. It depends on who is attacking. Some are more interested in destruction for its own sake."

"Which do you think these?" Eryk frowned as the distant fires flared up.

"We have had rumors that the Germans and the Vikings work in league to defeat King Hugh," said the old man. "There may be more than a little truth to the tale, no matter how unlikely it seems." He pointed towards the fires. "There you see King Hugh's shipbuilding lumber go up in flames."

There was silence as the orange glow in the east mesmerized them.

The tall blond coughed as if he had inhaled some smoke.

"Makes no matter," he said. "We have no hope of defeating the Vikings at sea. Much better to fortify the coasts and the fortresses at the river mouths. But as travelers from the north have told us, he has left it too late."

A man down the line along the wall laughed without humor. Eryk couldn't make out his features as he stood in shadow.

"We'll be speaking whatever barbaric language the Northmen speak in a few months," said the disembodied voice.

"As needs must," said the old man, all practicality. "They'll never make it down our river, and they are more interested in the church's gold and gems. As long as we supply them with mutton and ale, we will survive as always."

"But you might put a bug in the King's ear," said the blond. "He has unmarried sons and daughters. Better to marry the enemy than have them swallow the whole."

"Tis wise advice," said Kellan.

"Best be back in your beds for what little rest ye can get this night," said the old man.

Eryk turned towards the stairs to go back to the inn. His mother, Nicolette, and Clarissa waited in the yard below.

The women were in their night shifts and wrapped in quilts.

None of the three wailed in distress or cried in fear, and each carried a knife, ready to do battle.

He laughed, then cut it off in mid-sound as he saw the indignation on their faces.

"What news?" Maryn narrowed her eyes at him.

"Tis naught for us this night," said Eryk. He motioned for them to go back to the inn.

"Do not hide the truth from us," said Nicolette. She rooted to the spot, and he would have to knock her over if he kept moving.

"Eryk speaks the truth," said Kellan.

"Then why was the alarm raised?" Clarissa joined ranks with Maryn and Nicolette.

"The Germans are burning timber," said Adam. "King Hugh's future ships are no more."

"We are safe for the time being," said Eryk. "I promise," he said as the three women scowled at him.

"You will not need your weapons this night," said Kellan. "Tis a warning. A threat."

"Aye," said Eryk. "The King's enemies are surrounding him and tightening their ranks." He narrowed his eyebrows and frowned. "If we had known how dire the situation, we would have defied Isuet's demand that we bring you all to Verdun."

CHAPTER THIRTY-THREE

Inherited Gifts

The day before the Sabbath remained damp, with periods of light but soaking rain. Nicolette still felt wet from the day before. Her woolen cloak had not dried overnight. As their band of not-so-merry travelers rode on to Verdun, they swerved around pockmarked roads but could not avoid splashing mud.

They rose before the sun and left the inn at Luxembourg as the sky lightened, clattering over the Red Bridge toward the capital. They were eager to arrive at the city, despite what awaited them.

Nicolette convinced her father to ride with Maryn in her wagon. He agreed without complaint. His illness killed his pride and made him easier to manage. Tears sprang to her eyes whenever she looked at her once robust father. She didn't think he'd live much longer.

"If I could just see you married," he said as she helped him to his cushioned seat, "I could die in peace."

"I promised you I would," she said, patting his frail wrist.

They stopped only to relieve themselves and stretch. They reached Verdun by midafternoon, miserable and exhausted.

Château Foix sat on a slight rise surrounded by forests of old-growth aspens. A long white gravel drive with thick, close-cropped lawns on either side approached the three-story manor house.

King Hugh prided himself on living in an unfortified castle. As he was fond of saying,

"God smiles upon me and keeps me safe as his appointed representative on this good Earth."

The coming conflicts would test his theory, Nicolette thought.

They lined up in front of the main entrance, the wagons with Maryn, Tomas, and the children the first emptied and ushered into the dry hall.

Servants swarmed and bundled them off to their respective suites, where fires burned and food awaited them.

Nicolette and Clarissa followed their caretakers in a daze up the broad stairs opposite the main doors and down a long, straight hallway on the right. Nicolette tried counting the doors they passed, but gave up after a dozen on each side of her.

They installed her and Clarissa in a set of rooms connected to Maryn's suite that she shared with the children as a nursery.

They had their own sleeping chambers but shared a lounge with a large ceramic tiled fireplace. Teal and pink colored the woven fabrics on the walls and curtains, with gold and silver threads highlighting the stems of flowers in the decorations.

Layers of Oriental rugs covered the oaken floors, and it felt like walking on mattresses. Nicolette wanted to fall over and sleep where she fell. The opulence enticed her.

She hoped the King could fend off war and invaders. She couldn't imagine the loss of such dazzling wealth. The only place she had ever seen something like it was in churches.

"I'm off to bed," said Clarissa as she hugged Nicolette. "I'm not sure I'll ever be dry and warm again." She gave a half-hearted laugh that contained no humor as she went into her sleeping chamber, followed by the lady's maid assigned to her.

Nicolette entered her bedroom decorated in shades of soft, dusty rose.

"I'll change into a dry shift," she said to her maid, "and then check on the children."

The young girl who helped her change toweled her hair, brushed it, and left it loose so it would dry completely. She wrapped a soft woolen shawl around Nicolette's shoulders, then went to unpack Nicolette's belongings while Nicolette went to Maryn's room.

She found Eryk's mother and the three young girls uncharacteristically out of sorts, bickering amongst each other. Grite, Kathe, Fronika, and Libbe left to wash and rest before resuming their duties, but under the palace's household customs.

"I don't like these cakes," said Ema as she poked a small dainty on a large platter.

"Don't touch the food if you aren't going to eat it," said Maryn in a typical parenting response.

"The milk smells funny," said Gisela, sniffing her cup.

"It has the essence of rosehip in it," said Maryn. "It prevents sniffles. You don't want a red, runny nose, do you?"

"What is that?" Ava pointed at a dish of black roe.

"Fish eggs," said Maryn as she collapsed on a Roman-style lounging couch. She and Ava groaned at the same time, but for very different reasons.

Betsey sat on the floor in the middle of the chaos. When she saw Nicolette, she began crying.

Nicolette scooped her up and rested the child on her hip.

"Maryn," she said to Eryk's mother, "be off with ye to bed. I'll settle this hoard down with the help of these fine women."

"Oh, thank you," said Maryn as she levered herself upright. "I am done in." She hurried to her bedroom and closed the door behind her with a firm thunk, shutting out the maid who would have helped her.

"Nevermind," Nicolette said in French to the confused woman. "She'll need you on the morn once she's had a good night's sleep. It has been a long and winding road to get here."

The maid nodded and left.

"Let's get the girls fed and to bed," she told the nursery maids, assigning one child per girl.

Nicolette ate with the girls, supervised their cleaning, and changed them into dry night dresses. All four shared one sleeping chamber, and the maids took turns watching over them during the night so they wouldn't wander off and get lost in the vast palace.

While the servants played with Ema, Ava, and Gisela, settling them in their beds with fairy tale stories, Nicolette took Betsey to the sofa before the fire in her sitting room.

Betsey fussed until Nicolette gave her some willow bark tea to ease the pain in her gums.

She cradled the child in her arms and cherished this quiet moment alone. She hadn't had any peaceful time with Betsey since leaving Clarissa's home.

"Will you remember any of this?" She whispered to the girl, whose eyelids fluttered lower. The patch of white in her dark hair stood, so she tucked her bangs back under Betsey's sleeping cap,

Betsey fell asleep in her lap. Nicolette untied the chord around her neck. The two-sided silver pendant glowed in the firelight, flames dancing on the Berber infinity circle on one side and the Basque four-armed leaf lauburu symbol on the flip side. She placed the necklace around Betsey's neck.

"This was my mother's," said Nicolette to the sleeping child. "I didn't know my mother, either, but I always had this to remind me of her."

"Where is Clarissa?"

Nicolette jumped, startling Betsey, who whimpered.

"Isuet," said Nicolette. "You startled me." She took a deep breath, settling her heart.

"I just wanted to be sure my dear sister had all she needed," said Isuet, approaching Nicolette's seat, "and here I find you attending to ...." she paused and narrowed her gaze at Nicolette, " .... Another woman's child." Isuet's voice rose as if in question.

Nicolette folded Betsey's blanket around her and covered up the necklace. Had Isuet heard and seen?

"I will hand her back to the maids shortly," said Nicolette. "I have been with Betsey since her birth, as with Clarissa. Like a dedicated aunt."

"Yes, well," said Isuet. "Don't be too dedicated." She waved her fingers at Nicolette. "I will need you rested and ready to join in the special service at church tomorrow. It is, after all, all about me."

CHAPTER THIRTY-FOUR

Keep In Line

Eryk, Kellan, Adam, and Tomas housed in rooms in the left wing of Château Foix. Before going to their suite, they waited until the servants placed their belongings in the rooms. Then, with only one servant to show them the way, the three younger men helped Tomas up the stairs and down the long passage, sometimes carrying Nicolette's sick and exhausted father.

"I never imagined I'd be so much trouble," said Tomas, his voice a whispered croak.

"Nonsense," said Eryk as he linked hands and arms with Adam in a makeshift chair.

Bright pink dotted Tomas' wane cheeks. He kept his eyes closed as if he could keep his embarrassment encased in his rapidly failing body.

Eryk called for a physician once Tomas was abed. He paced the floor of the main room of their suite, his damp travel clothing drying on his body. He refused to eat, worried that Nicolette's father would die before she could see him again.

When the physician didn't come quickly enough for his stressed nerves, he searched for the man. A servant took him in hand, steering Eryk to Henri's rooms, where the physician who served as barber groomed the prince.

Eryk waited to be noticed by the prince and barber as the two men joked and told each other ribald stories. Eryk lost his patience after ten minutes.

"I beg your pardon, Your Highness," he said, the sneer clear in his voice.

Prince Henri cocked an eyebrow in Eryk's direction as he reclined on the barber couch.

"The audacity," said the physician. He looked down at the prince. "This barbarian dares address you without your leave? Would you like me to inform the guards?"

"This bastard," said Henri, "my pardon, this newly minted Count is one of the King's pets."

The prince and the physician laughed as Eryk stiffened.

He needed to keep his head if he was to be of any help to Tomas. He sucked in a deep breath and waited, as it was clear the men were not inclined to hasten their activities.

Another long ten minutes later, Prince Henri, freshly shaved, combed, and brushed, sat up and addressed Eryk.

"To what do I owe the grand honor of your visit? I know it's not for my sake that you invade my rooms like a Saxon raider."

The physician snickered as he packed his belongings into a wooden box ornate with gold and glistening gems, totally at odds with his monastic robes.

"Tomas, Isuet's father," Eryk added since he didn't think Henri could be bothered to keep that information to mind, "is ill and in need of attention and a sleeping draft." Eryk had not moved from the wall next to the door.

"I see," said Henri. "And you think some haste would prevent his timely demise?"

Eryk clenched his hands into fists by his sides.

Henri noticed and smiled.

The physician, barber, and monk, all in one as they were in France, waited beside Prince Henri, clearly comfortable in the royal's presence, and waited for Henri to determine what he should do next.

"While it might not save his life," said Eryk, throat tight, "the physician might bring the man some comfort."

Henri waved a hand towards the monk.

"I've enlisted Dom Aimoin to barber my groomsmen," said Henri. "For my wedding in a few days."

Eryk nodded. He envisioned striding over to Henri, pounding him into the floor, couch and all, and then tossing Dom Aimoin in after him. He hoped it didn't show on his face.

"I understand," said Eryk, getting that lie out between his lips. "But perhaps he can spare an hour to treat Isuet's father. I'm sure your bride would appreciate the kindness of ensuring her father can attend the wedding."

"Hmmm," said Henri, plucking a fat red grape from a bunch on a silver platter next to him. "Keeping one's future bride happy is important." He chewed the fruit in his mouth, thinking. "Although I'm not sure how much she cares. What do you think, Aimoin?"

"Might be best to keep up appearances for now," said the monk.

"I suppose you are correct," said the prince, distracted by a slice of cheese. "Off you go then."

"Get my box," said Dom Aimoin to Eryk without address, as if he were a servant.

Eryk considered setting the cleric straight, but feared another delay.

He hefted the box over his shoulder by the leather strap used to carry the physician's tools.

As they left the Prince's chambers, he heard Henri speak to some unknown person in the room, or maybe just to himself, although he doubted the prince was alone.

"I'll need to do something about him."

Eryk knew Henri spoke of him. He'd love for the prince to attack him and allow Eryk to retaliate. Not that Eryk would survive such an encounter.

"You there," Eryk said to a passing servant. "Please show us to my rooms. I no longer know where I am in this labyrinth."

When Eryk returned to Tomas' bedside with the physician, sweat covered Nicolette's father, and he tossed in the tangled blankets.

Kellan cleared off the table near the bed, and Eryk placed the physician's box on it.

The monk began working by examining Tomas' body. He searched for lesions and sores. He prodded Tomas' body and discovered a large, painful tumor in the Count's stomach.

He pulled pouches of herbs out of his medicine box.

"Fetch me a bowl of hot water," he said to the room, "and get a servant to put a pot to boil over the fire. We need to steam up the air."

Dom Aimoin placed a pinch of this and a handful of that into a cup of hot water. He covered it to steep and instructed a servant to use a bucket of cool water and a cloth to wipe Tomas' body. He tossed twigs and dried leaves into the pot simmering on the fire — the room filled with pungent steam that made all of their lungs easier.

He strained the tea.

"Sit him up," he said to no one in particular.

Eryk sat behind Tomas and held him up like a young child. Dom Aimoin held the ceramic cup to Tomas's lips and encouraged him to drink. It took time and patience. The monk surprised Eryk by using both with Tomas. When all the liquid was in the tired old man, the monk packed up his wares.

"That's all I can do for him," he said. "It will dull the pain and help him sleep. I will make up more tea between my other duties and send it to you." He shook his head. "He has a tumor in his stomach that is quite large, and it is eating away at the rest of his body."

Now that he was away from Henri, the monk seemed more in line with his physician's code.

"I could do some bloodletting the day after the Sabbath, but I don't think it would do much good now."

"Thank you, Dom Aimoin," said Eryk, cradling the now dozing Tomas. "I appreciate your attendance."

"We do what we can," he said, turning to leave, "and we do what we must." He pulled two of their servants away to carry his box off to barber Henri's friends.

"That was cryptic," said Adam, pacing Tomas' sleeping chamber.

The men didn't want to leave Tomas just yet.

"I found him grooming Henri," said Eryk, "and nearly incited the prince to violence to dare disturb such important work."

A sigh escaped Tomas' lips as his eyes fluttered open, and he looked up at Eryk. He patted Eryk's wrist.

"Ah, if only I had a son like you."

He fell asleep wrapped in Eryk's arms.

CHAPTER THIRTY-FIVE

Sunday Best

The morning of the Sabbath saw them all in much better moods after a good night's sleep.

Nicolette rose to the sounds of laughing girls and giggling maids. With all the help from the servants of the royal household, she was last to get out of bed and had little to do.

She found the children, Maryn and Clarissa, lounging in their communal room, waiting to dress for Mass. Platters of food, most of it gone now, covered several tables: fresh apples, grapes, and berries, a square of the famous soft rind-washed Maroilles Craquegnon cheese, small rolls of bread, a pot of smooth, thick cream, sliced sausages, and one-bite pies.

"Look," said Clarissa, sipping tea, "sleepyhead is awake."

Nicolette laughed with the others.

"Quite a feast for a Sunday morning," said Nicolette. "Does the Royal household not fast before they attend Mass?"

"The Bishop gave a dispensation in honor of the wedding," said a maid. "They expect many donations because of all the guests."

Nicolette smiled at the cheerful faces as she took a fruit tart from the breakfast table.

"But now you must hurry," said Maryn. "They have informed us that the procession to the church will begin at nine. They've moved Mass to eleven instead of the normal ten."

"We get to go," said Ema, dressing a cloth doll in reds and

blues.

"Oma says we are to behave," said Gisela, peeking at Maryn from under her long lashes.

"Act like grownups," said Ava, who sorted through beaded necklaces.

"I think you can manage for an hour and a half," said Maryn as she hopped Betsey on her knees, dropping her between her legs at surprise intervals. The baby laughed while the maid sat idly by.

Clarissa handed another maid a fruit pasty. Her friends have added more girls to their informal family, thought Nicolette.

"I think we will make a fine presentation," she said. "I'll go wash and dress so we are not late for the celebration."

Two young girls helped her braid her hair into four plaits, wrap them around her head like a garland, and tie them into place with green ribbons that matched her overgrown.

A tunic in rosy wool topped her white shift. An overtunic in deep green with elbow-length sleeves and a hem at mid-calf topped these. Woven bands in yellow and red threads and semiprecious beads decorated the moss-colored dress.

She ran her hands down the finery covering her body.

"You look beautiful," said one maid.

"You'll put the bride to shame," said the other maid, who widened her eyes and covered her mouth after speaking.

The other maid gasped.

"Fear not," said Nicolette, as the two girls stammered, trying to apologize. "Tis but a slip. No harm done." She took a deep breath to dispel a sudden feeling of pending doom. It was bad luck to speak ill of a bride before her wedding. She shook herself.

"Let's go. The others must be ready and waiting by now."

Revena's three daughters wore tunics in the Margravine's bright red, the bumble bee symbol Kellan's wife chose as her signet embroidered on their dresses. Their hair sat upon their heads, braided and wrapped in matching ribbons, like crowns. She had never seen them stand so still, trying not to disturb their finery.

Clarissa decked herself in the Black Bear house color, a dark brown, almost black. Her blond hair and cornflower blue eyes shone like heavenly bodies at night. She held Betsey, who wore the same colors, the baby's head cap edged in a sheer white fabric that must irritate her as she tried to pull it off.

Clarissa giggled as she struggled with the wiggling little girl.

"We should give Betsey a dolly to keep her occupied," said Clarissa.

Nicolette searched for the baby's favorite toy. One maid found it in the girls' nursery. Her plaything distracted her enough to get her to leave her cap alone.

"We have special prayer books," said Ava, holding up a small, thin packet of vellum.

"We may read them in church," said Gisela, holding her book close to her heart.

"We will be pious," said Ema, her brown eyes soft and serious.

"You are lovely young ladies," said Maryn. "Your mother will be so proud when I tell her how well you behaved."

"Thank you," the three girls chorused and curtsied, as if they had practiced for perfection.

Maryn wore the deep green of the Thornewood estate, and Nicolette realized she had chosen the same color as Eryk's mother. Luckily, their undertunics and trims did not match.

The color suited the older woman well, highlighting the auburn of her hair and her body's tall, slim lines. She seemed young just then to Nicolette, and she wondered if Maryn were lonely for someone her age.

She realized she did not know how old Maryn was. Did this pending wedding make Maryn think of romance?

Eryk had told Nicolette how Maryn loved Kellan's mother as a sister. And Maryn's love story with Eryk's father was like a fairy tale worthy of the songs of the bards.

Perhaps spending so much time with Eryk and pondering what might have been between them caused her to wonder about the lost loves of all those closest to her.

She shivered as she remembered the old duke that awaited her as a possible groom.

A servant came to escort them down to the main hall.

As the bride's sister, Nicolette, headed the procession,

followed by Maryn and the three girls. Clarissa carried Betsey at the end of the line.

They would meet Eryk, Adam, Kellan, and Tomas in the massive foyer filled with guests in their Sunday best.

CHAPTER THIRTY-SIX

Dead Duke

Duke Ramnlf, the old Duke of Nantes, and Isuet's choice of a husband for Nicolette, died on the way to Verdun.

It seemed the trip to the Prince's wedding was weeding out the old guard, thought Eryk. A happy thought since the idea of Nicolette married to a man forty years her senior and in ill health made Eryk sick.

He received the news as gossip overheard between two servants who lit the morning fires. The old Duke rested in a cold storage room until after the wedding, so as not to dampen the festivities. The new Duke, the eldest son of the former, rode into town with a big grin, his two younger brothers flanking him.

It took some time to get Tomas, their family elder, ready for church. They tried to convince him not to go to Mass, but he insisted.

Dressed in simple clothing, unadorned by jewelry, Eryk and the other men in his party went down to the main hall to wait for his mother and the other women and children.

Tomas leaned heavily on Eryk as Kellan searched for a chair or stool for Nicolette's father.

"I heard that Duke Ramnlf died en route to the wedding," said Adam.

"I heard the same," said Eryk.

"I suppose fate meant Nicolette to have a different husband," said Tomas, gritting his teeth as he clutched his belly.

"Oh, thank goodness," said Eryk as Kellan returned with servants carrying a stool. He lowered Tomas onto it.

"Just as well," said Tomas with a sigh. "I didn't relish the thought even if he was a duke."

"Are you Count Welf?" asked a grinning man of around thirty, dressed in bright red from head to toe. The color of his clothing made his hair and complexion appear as orange as carrots. Two younger men with the same coloring in body and clothing stood on either side of him.

"Yes," said Tomas, glancing up at the man.

Nicolette interrupted them, approaching her father with concern.

Tomas stood and leaned on Eryk. Nicolette took his hand.

"You should have stayed abed," she said to her father. "You don't look well. Surely you may skip Mass today." She linked his arm in hers on one side of him. Eryk had his other side and held her father's weight, keeping him upright. Nicolette smiled at Eryk.

"I can manage," said Tomas, his voice a whisper and almost lost in the crowd's noise.

She leaned into him to hear him better.

"They promised me a bench and cushions." He patted her wrist. "It has been too long since I had my girls in one place. I do not wish to miss it." He kissed her cheek. "I will rest in bed right after, I promise."

Nicolette glanced at Eryk over her father's head.

"Ah," said the man in red. "This must be my poor dead father's former betrothed." The man bowed to Nicolette.

"Not engaged," said Eryk.

The new Duke looked up and blinked, then narrowed his eyes.

He bowed to Tomas and Nicolette.

"Francois, Duke of Nantes," he said, "and my brothers, Peter and Montfor."

Nicolette and Tomas nodded politely.

"My father was doubly unlucky to have died and missed out on such a fine morsel for a wife," said the duke. He winked at his brothers, and they chuckled.

"Some things just aren't meant to be," said Eryk.

"You are not this maiden's family, are you, Count Thorne?" He didn't look at Eryk, but at Tomas.

"I'd be willing to go through with the contract," said the Duke, as he gave Nicolette the once over, head to toe and back again, lingering at certain places along the way.

Nicolette shivered, her reaction not lost on any of them.

"There was no formal agreement," said Tomas, squeezing his daughter's fingers.

"Henri's soon-to-be wife hinted otherwise," said Montfor.

"I expected someone more like Isuet," said Francois, the Duke. "You are a fine surprise."

"This isn't the time or place," said Eryk, gritting his teeth.

"You keep talking when it's not your place," said the duke's brother, Peter.

"Count Thorne is an old and dear friend," said Nicolette.

"Like a son," said Tomas, short of breath.

"But not a son," said Montfor, the Duke's other brother.

"There is no better time than at one wedding to discuss and plan another nuptial." The Duke tried to take Nicolette's hand, but her father kept a firm grip on her.

"As you can see," she said pointedly to Francois and his brothers, "My father is not well, and this conversation distresses him."

"Yes, he doesn't look well at all," said Peter.

"More's the reason to talk about the future while we can," said Montfor.

"You gentlemen forget yourselves," said Kellan.

"The Margrave of Bavaria speaks up," said Francois. He turned his head to the left. "At least he's someone's proper son," he said in a stage whisper.

Adam stepped into the Duke's personal space.

The Duke and his brothers touched their daggers tucked into the belts around their waists.

Kellan pulled Adam back.

"Have a care," said the Duke with a scowl. "Wedding or not, I will end you."

"Sirs, please," said Nicolette. "I beg of you. Another time and place. Have a care for my father."

"As Lady Nicolette wishes," said the Duke with a smile. "I guess I have to get used to pleasing her." He snickered. "At least until she has to get used to pleasing me."

Tomas stood straight and tall, stiff in his outrage.

"Sir, you are speaking about my daughter and a lady," he said to the Duke. "Your manners do not do your rank justice."

"Ah, I see the Duke is spreading joy wherever he goes," said Prince Kevan, coming up behind the three red-haired men who scowled in perfect imitation of one another.

"I have a sudden thirst," said Duke Francois to the group. "Let us find something to quench my dry throat."

He bowed to Nicolette.

"Until we meet again," he said to her with a wink.

He turned and left the hall, followed by his brothers. The other guests parted to allow them plenty of room.

Prince Kevan leaned into Nicolette and her father.

"Do your best to avoid him over the next few days," he said. "Our newest Duke does not have the King's favor. He and his brothers have made questionable alliances in direct conflict with their father's wishes."

He bowed to their party and waved as he disappeared into the growing crowd.

"Thank God we are well out of that family," said Tomas. "What could your sister have been thinking? She spoke so highly of the sons." He shook his head. "Perhaps I misunderstood her, or they hid their real selves from Isuet."

She knows exactly who they are, thought Eryk, but leave it to Tomas to have the best opinion of his eldest daughter, as always.

Eryk glanced over at Nicolette. She seemed shocked by the encounter, and who could blame her? She must be thinking about what life would have been like with those devils around her.

"Better unmarried than shackled to a man like him," she said under her breath.

"Eh?" Tomas leaned into her. "Did you speak, daughter?"

"No, no," she said.

"I don't want you to be alone," said Tomas.

"She will always have us," said Maryn to Tomas. "Remember? As we talked about in the wagon. I promised you we will always care for her. Always."

Maryn and Nicolette looked at Eryk at the same time. He nodded and smiled at both of them.

"Sir," Kellan told Tomas, "Your daughter will always be a part of our family. I swear this to you." He nodded and smiled. "The scribe we spoke of will join us this evening. He has the documents ready for your signature."

"What documents?" Nicolette asked.

"Maryn has agreed to adopt you," said Tomas.

That would make Nicolette Eryk's sister. Eryk cringed inside.

CHAPTER THIRTY-SEVEN

Black Sabbath

The room stilled.

Nicolette turned along with everyone else to face the main staircase. At the top stood Isuet on Henri's arm. They glowed in a ray of sunshine and paused to allow everyone a good look.

Isuet gleamed in the morning light, her pale skin white as alabaster, her blond hair, unbound, hung around her like spun silk. She wore a dress of the deepest blue that must have required multiple dyes to get so dark. Gold thread sparkled in the weave. She wore no jewelry.

Nicolette hoped this wedding made all of Isuet's dreams come true. Her sister desperately wanted distinction and status, validating her position in life as first above all others. By marrying Prince Henri, King Hugh's named successor, she stood to be Queen of Franconia one day. Isuet beamed with a victorious smile.

Henri wore gold from head to toe. A gold circlet crowned his dark hair, the white patch on his forehead the only other color. His short tunic, leggings, gloves, and soft boots shone like a warm summer afternoon. He stood triumphant, like a Roman god high on Mount Olympus, surveying those he held with life and death, his predatory gaze more pronounced than usual.

There was a collective sigh from the waiting guests. Struck by awe and dazzled with unprecedented spectacle, they gawked like prey, stunned into paralysis.

Nicolette did not know the three women who followed Isuet and carried the train of her gossamer cloak. Dressed in plain, undyed frocks, they formed a blank canvas to highlight Isuet. They left considerable room between themselves, Francois, Duke Ramnlf, of Nantes, and his two brothers.

The men, looking demonic with fiery hair, leered at the women. One, maybe Montfor, Nicolette thought, waggled his eyebrows like a character in a jester's play.

Duke Ramnlf scanned the crowd below them, snagged on Nicolette, and he leered. He leaned into Henri and spoke to the Prince, whose smile broadened as he nodded. The Duke laughed and blew Nicolette a kiss.

Nicolette shivered despite the morning's warmth and the crowd's press. She dragged her eyes from the smirking Duke and focused on Isuet. She wanted her sister to be happy.

Isuet beamed as Henri escorted her down the stairs, through the crowd, and into the morning sunshine, where they blazed on their way to Sunday Mass.

Guests covered their eyes as they followed behind the dazzling couple. This day the entire city celebrated, the towns' people looking forward to the free food and drink supplied by their monarch.

A troop of musicians playing flutes and lutes serenaded the couple through the streets. The troubadours sang a popular and bawdy love song, L'autrier Just'una Sebissa, about a knight's not-so-courtly love for a shepherdess. The lyrics brought laughter to the listeners. Nicolette felt the author knew Henri well.

"Girl, I am completely sure you're chaste of heart, oh so pure. I am true to my own nature, so no need to put it off until later. In a small shed by this field, you'll feel safe and sweetly yield."

Isuet would do well to take the words as a warning, but she did not know the lyrics sung in Provençal, the southern language of Franconia, and no one was likely to break the news to her of her husband's true nature if she didn't already know it.

Servants, serfs, and townsfolk lined the pathway, bending, bowing, and curtsying as the resplendent couple nodded and waved in benediction. Freshly scrubbed children tossed fragrant sprigs of lavender, rosemary, and mint leaves that sweetened the air when trod upon.

When they arrived at the heavily carved oaken doors of the cathedral, the Bishop and his attendants entered the church first, followed by Isuet and Henri.

Deacons in plain white robes anointed the air with the incense of myrrh and frankincense. Altar boys carried candles, and a priest held the golden crucifix. They took their places in the sanctuary and at the altar.

Once the priest blessed the attendants, those with chairs took their seats.

The engaged couple sat in unique chairs, like mini thrones. Tomas had a stool, but everyone else stood where they could find room.

The Royal family occupied their benches on the left side of the altar.

The priest performed the service in Latin as usual. Because of the special occasion, the Bishop offered Communion, extending the service length as he distributed the sacred bread and wine. The monks from the local monastery chanted songs in Latin from their alcove on the right, directly across from the Royal family's box.

Always in tune with his flock, the attending priest felt the restlessness of his parishioners, guests, and, most significantly, the King and Queen and ended the service before he lost the goodwill of his audience.

"May the Lord bless this happy couple," he said, addressing Isuet and Henri, "bidding them good fortune and prosperity."

The priest invoked the sign of the cross.

"Go forward in peace. The Mass is ended."

CHAPTER THIRTY-EIGHT

Do As I Say

When they returned to the château after the services, they entered the long, vast gallery with its high ceilings, where a buffet and music awaited the guests.

Eryk positioned himself as far in the gallery's rear as possible without being rude. The mural-painted wall behind him depicted hunting scenes with men seated on massive steeds and dressed in the royal colors of red and indigo spearing deer with twelve-pointed golden antlers. He did his best not to lean against the art, but the press of women made it difficult.

At that moment, three women held him captive. They competed for his attention. He looked down at them with a smile plastered on his face. He did not know what they were saying, but they expressed themselves with vigor and emotion. Nodding, he hoped he didn't agree to anything that would get him in trouble and wished someone would save him.

"...tiny, even stitches..." said the blond as she touched the hem of his tunic. "Much finer than these."

He liked his shirt, made by his mother. He fought down a frown.

"People from around my father's estate rave over my beer," said the brunette.

He had never tasted beer in his life. He stifled a groan.

"I have seven brothers," said the tall woman with black hair. "No sisters. Bodes well for me having lots of sons." She glanced up at him and fluttered her eyelashes.

Good for you, but not with me.

He looked across the room and saw Nicolette staring at his little group. He smiled at her. She didn't return the smile, but frowned and turned her back on him.

He'd exchange this bevy of admirers for the friendship of just one woman. Oh, well. He always knew she wasn't for him.

A steward in King's livery approached him.

"Count Thorne," said the man with a bow of his head.

"Yes?" Thank goodness, a polite excuse to ignore these women.

"His Highness wishes a word." The man turned, expecting Eryk would follow.

"Ladies," he said in farewell as he fell in step with the servant.

The steward left him in a line progressing to the King and Queen's seats placed on a dais. He didn't care if he had to wait. At least those looking for matrimony would leave him in peace.

He glanced over his shoulder and found Nicolette's eyes upon him again as he stepped into his place before the monarchs.

"Eryk, Count Thorne, of Thornewood," announced a page.

Eryk bowed to the King, pivoted, and bowed to the Queen.

King Hugh beckoned him forward with his bejeweled fingers.

Even though the King sat on a throne elevated on a raised platform, Eryk met the King's eyes on a level.

"This fine celebration of my eldest son's upcoming wedding has me in a romantic frame of mind," said the King. "I understand you are yet unmarried yourself."

"Tis true, Your Highness," said Eryk, his stomach tightening. He didn't want the King's attention on him, especially not regarding this subject.

"You hold an important expanse of properties on my southern border," said the King, "and I rely on your loyalty to my crown to keep us all safe." The King drummed his fingers on the arm of his chair, the rubies in his rings throwing red lights dancing upon the walls.

"I do, Your Highness, and gladly so," said Eryk, "with all my heart."

"Speaking of hearts," said Queen Adelaide, sipping from a ruby-encrusted golden goblet.

These two loved red and gold, thought Eryk. He waited for her to continue.

The Queen inspected him.

He had allowed the menservants to tame his long hair by brushing it smooth and braiding it to keep it under control. They had wanted to shave his beard and mustache, as was the current fashion, but he refused.

He wore his favorite tunic, a deep forest green embroidered in yellow thread along the collar, cuffs, and hem. He only wore it for special occasions, as his mother had made it for him for his eighteenth birthday and to celebrate his being made Count Thorne.

"You are a fine-looking man," said the Queen, her cheeks dimpling. "Why have you not married?"

"The right woman has not agreed to marry me," he said, as close to the truth as he dared.

"So, you have asked for a maiden?" The Queen leaned forward.

"No, Your Highness."

"Hmmm," she sat back and spoke to one of her women.

"Surely you can find someone," said the King. "We saw you surrounded by our kingdom's best."

"There are many lovely and fine maidens, Your Highness," said Eryk, as he chose his words carefully, "but I am still settling into my new duties and do not wish to move on such an important decision in haste."

"Yes, fine," said the King, a touch of exasperation and encroaching boredom in his voice and posture. "Heed well, Count Thorne," he said, meeting Eryk's gaze. "I require loyal subjects, and if we don't get them by capturing people during war, I must get them with future generations."

The King sat up straight and pointed a finger at Eryk.

"Therefore," he said, "you must marry and have children." He took a breath. "Soon."

"Yes, Your Highness."

"Within the coming year." He focused on Eryk. "Since you have no father, I, as your King, take that prerogative, and I will choose a bride for you if you do not." The King turned to the scribe seated on his left. "Make note that we wish to follow up in one year." He slapped the palm of his hand on his thigh. "Make it a decree. Send our dear Count Thorne a vellum, with the Royal seal upon it."

He turned back to Eryk.

157

"Have we made our wishes clear, Count Thorne?"

"Yes, Your Highness."

King Hugh waved Eryk off.

Eryk bowed, stepped back out of line, and immediately caught Nicolette's eyes. She looked sad.

He shrugged and approached her, but women who heard the King's proclamation immediately swallowed him up.

Save me, Eryk mouthed to Nicolette.

She laughed out loud and with a snort that she attempted to smother behind her hand.

She placed her hand in his and pulled on him.

"Come, Count Thorne," she said, loud enough for all his admirers to hear. "My sister, the future bride, wishes our presence." She dragged him through the crowd of guests.

"Your sister?" He moaned. "I'm not sure which is worse."

"I'm sure you will regret your audience with Isuet," said Nicolette, "but that will be the punishment for your tomcatting ways."

"You wound me, Nicolette," he said, his fingers sending pleasure throughout his body from hers, glad to touch any part of her.

They joined their party at a table near the bride and groom's chairs. Henri disappeared. Eryk looked around the room and did not see him, and he would have stood out in his golden finery.

Eryk bent down to Nicolette and whispered so only she could hear him.

"Why do you always accuse me of having a bevy of women?"

"I'm not blind," she said. "I see your hangers-on and the smiles you have for each and everyone."

"I only try to be polite," he said. "Truly, Nicolette, there is no place in my heart for any of them."

"You may keep your heart free, as most men do, but you seem quite free with the rest of you, too."

He turned her to face him, his hands on her upper arms, heat in his voice.

"I was born a bastard," he said to her, the tendons in his neck standing out. "Because of this, I vowed never to have a child out of wedlock, and there is only one way to make sure of that outcome."

CHAPTER THIRTY-NINE

Forced Out

Henri's family occupied tables on the left of the hall, his brothers and sisters as blond as the King and Queen. The princes and princesses laughed and talked as if they enjoyed one another's company. They numbered an even dozen. Nicolette did not see Henri among their group.

Isuet's family sat on the right of the room, an even two. Nicolette's friends filled out their party.

"You promised to rest," said Nicolette to her father as she and Eryk joined their table.

"Soon," said Tomas, his bright face red.

"Leave him be," said Isuet to Nicolette from her throne-like perch between the two families. She sneered, her lip curling up, her countenance unapproachable and miserable.

The guests ignored Isuet, fearing their future princess's foul mood. The servants did not have the luxury of avoiding her. She snapped her fingers for their attention and barked orders at them, dissatisfied with their every effort to comply with her demands.

Once the Mass finished and the greetings at the church entrance finished, Henri left Isuet alone. She walked back to the château with her attendants in tow, stomping and grumbling displeasure.

Nicolette couldn't blame her sister. To be so treated by one's fiancé, in so public a display of neglect would cause anyone great pain and heartache. Isuet's misery would burst forth as destruction for anyone unlucky enough to cross her path. Nicolette was Isuet's favorite target and took the brunt of Isuet's displeasure since early childhood.

Nicolette felt uneasy as Isuet's smile widened when Betsey toddled over to Nicolette, tugged on her dress, then held her arms out.

Nicolette picked Betsey up, adjusted the child's cap, and wiped a smudge of fruit from her cheek.

Betsey wrapped her arms around Nicolette's neck and nestled her face into Nicolette's neck, closed her eyes, and sighed. Even though it was only an hour past noon, it had been a long day for the children.

"Perhaps we should take the girls to our rooms," said Nicolette to Clarissa.

"They have eaten from the buffet," said Clarissa, glancing at Kellan's daughters, "And tasted the cakes.".

Ema rested her head on her arm, elbow propped on the table. Gisela leaned on Maryn's arm, eyes fluttering. Ava yawned.

"I'll take them up," said Maryn. "I could use a rest. You two stay and enjoy the afternoon." She touched Tomas on the arm. "Perhaps you'd like to retire also, Tomas?"

Isuet narrowed her eyes and bared her teeth.

"Father," said Isuet. Her voice held a growl and a strange lilt, as if a new happy thought had occurred to her.

Eryk and Adam paused in helping Tomas to his feet. The older man gripped each of them as his attention fastened on his eldest daughter.

"Isuet," he said, his voice a wisp among the clatter of the other guests.

"Did Nicolette introduce you properly to your granddaughter?" Her voice carried, and people turned to see what she was talking about.

Nicolette shook her head as she hugged Betsey closer, hoping to protect the child.

"Look," said Isuet, pointing, "look at your precious, perfect daughter and her bastard."

Deafening silence washed out in waves across the gallery.

Tomas groaned.

Nicolette stared at her sister.

"Why?" Tears threatened to fall from Nicolette's brimming eyes— pressure built in her forehead.

"Because our father should know you're not flawless," said Isuet into the quiet. "Everyone should know exactly who and what you are." Her chest heaved, and her hands fisted.

The sisters locked eyes. Nicolette's ears popped. Sound rushed into her head. She glanced around her.

Tomas slumped in a chair after Eryk, and Adam lowered him into it. The three men stared at her with identical shocked expressions.

"What say you?" Tomas rubbed his brow as if the gesture would help him understand. "The baby belongs to Clarissa," said Tomas with a weak croak.

"Not so," said Isuet. "Lying is not the worst of Nicolette's deeds, it would seem." Isuet sat forward, stiff with righteousness. "What think you now of your precious baby girl?"

"I ..." Tomas looked around in confusion.

"He is not well," said Nicolette. "How could you do this to him now?"

"I'm not doing anything," Isuet shouted, rising and pointing at Nicolette. "You are a wanton whore, and he should know who you are before he dies. How you have deceived him your whole life."

The two hundred guests gasped as one.

"Isuet, that's just cruel," said Eryk.

"How dare you speak to me?" Isuet's voice shrilled. She looked around the room.

"Where is Henri? Why isn't he here to defend and support me?" She grabbed a passing servant and shoved her. The girl spilled wine from the jug she carried.

"Find my betrothed," said Isuet with a shriek loud enough to kill. She looked around, wild-eyed.

The maid scurried off, ducking out of Isuet's reach.

Tomas turned towards Nicolette.

"You were with child?" He shook his head. "When? How were you able to hide this from me?"

He tried to rise, but his legs would not hold him.

"Is this true? Is this child yours?" His eyes swelled with tears. "You lied to me all this time?"

"I'm sorry," said Nicolette. "I wanted to tell you. Please try to understand."

Nicolette kneeled beside her father, holding out her child to him.

"This is your granddaughter," she said, her throat tight.

He reached out and stroked Betsey's rosy cheek with one hand and Nicolette's tear-stained cheek with the other. He stared at them for many moments, then granted them a small smile.

"No," said Isuet. "You can't be happy." She stomped over to Nicolette.

"Who is the father?" She pulled at Nicolette's sleeve, tearing her dress.

Nicolette shook her head.

"I will not say," said Nicolette.

Eryk stepped forward.

"I am," he said.

"What?" Tomas and Isuet asked at the same time, each in a different tone.

CHAPTER FORTY

Kiss the Bride

"The child is mine," said Eryk, again only louder than before.

Nicolette shook her head.

He turned to Tomas.

"I beg your pardon, Sir," he said to Nicolette's father. "I have done you and especially your daughter a great disservice by my deeds."

Tomas slumped in his chair, staring at Betsey, Nicolette, and Eryk. He frowned, glanced at Maryn, and nodded.

"There is naught for it but that you two must marry immediately."

Maryn returned his assent.

"No," said Isuet, her voice rising to a painful pitch. "No, she can't get married. She's a wanton whore."

"What goes on here?" Henri had returned, followed by Duke Ramnlf and his brothers.

Isuet ran up to him, pointing at her sister.

"That child is her bastard," said Isuet, "and they want to cover up her sin by marrying her off to him." She flung her hand towards Eryk.

Duke Ramnlf snickered.

"Dodged a good one there, brother," said Peter.

"Told you she was only good for one thing, Francois," said Montfor.

Isuet laughed.

Henri narrowed his eyes at Nicolette and opened his mouth, but got nothing out as the King and Queen's approach interrupted him.

"So, Count Thorne," said the King, "I see you took my demand to heart. I like a subject that makes haste to give me what I want."

163

Duke Ramnlf snickered again.

The King glanced at him without moving his head.

Francois and his brothers slinked off before the King paid them any more direct attention.

"It is not unusual for things to happen out of order," said the King. "Your families have known each other for many years. Is that not so?"

Tomas tried to stand.

"No," said the King, "stay seated, Tomas. Be at ease."

"Thank you, Your Highness," said Tomas. "I was close friends with Kellan and Eryk's father, Allan."

"Then all will be well," said the King.

Isuet growled.

"You are not my daughter yet," said the King to her quietly.

"I have decided." The King took Nicolette's fingers in his hand.

"It is best to put this situation right," said the King.

She shook her head.

"Now, now, I know how young women like to be wooed and courted, but we are beyond that. You have a child to consider."

"My dear," said the Queen. "Think about how romantic this is. Marrying at the château. Few people can claim such a distinction."

"Here? Now?" Nicolette croaked.

"Yes, of course," said the Queen. "Have done with it and enjoy this party as your celebration. I'm sure your sister won't mind."

They all turned towards Isuet.

She stood with eyes wide and mouth hanging open.

Henri nudged her.

She nodded.

The Queen clapped.

"Where's the Priest?" The King placed Nicolette's hand in Eryk's.

"Ah, here is the cleric," said the King. "Marry these two, here and now."

"Yes, of course, Your Highness," said the Priest. "As you wish."

"Wait," said Eryk.

The room became still as everyone held their breath.

"Count, your sovereign is waiting." The King frowned at him.

"May I speak with Nicolette alone for a minute?"

"No," said King Hugh. "No more alone time until you officially wed."

The King and Queen took over Isuet and Henri's seats.

Isuet's skin pulled tight on her face, giving her the look of a death mask. Her fists clenched at her sides; her body vibrated with tension. She exuded anger from her ridged posture, her lips compressed to invisibility.

Henri waited beside her, his body relaxed, a smirk on his face.

His attitude made Eryk nervous, as if Henri had a surprise to spring upon them, but his father, the King, compelled him to stillness.

Nicolette refused to meet Eryk's eyes and respond to him.

"I'll tell them to stop," said Eryk. "If you want."

She kept her eyes upon her father, who held Betsey in his lap with help from Maryn. Tomas rocked the toddler and cooed to her.

"This is but a mere formality," Eryk whispered. "This will protect you and Betsey, as you wished all along."

She ignored him.

The priest placed the large, gold crucifix upon a table and consecrated the space as a makeshift altar.

His attendants lit candles, burned incense, and sprinkled the area with holy water.

He cleared his throat, and the gallery quieted. The guests pressed in at their backs, trying for better views and listening posts.

Scandal makes the world go round, thought Eryk.

The priest beckoned Nicolette and Eryk to stand before him.

"Are your parents present?"

Maryn came forward beside Eryk. Kellan and Adam helped Tomas stand beside Nicolette. Her father would not give up holding Betsey in his arms.

Isuet screeched, shook her head, and wedged a fist in her mouth. Her eyes shot daggers at her sister. Heads turned in her direction.

"Get on with it," said the King. "The tension seems a bit much for some."

"Yes, Your Highness," said the priest.

"Hold each other's hands," he instructed Nicolette and Eryk.

Eryk held his hand out to Nicolette, palm up.

She stared at his hand for many heartbeats before she looked up at him.

"Do you promise to always treat Betsey as your own?"

"Eh?" The priest leaned forward. "I didn't hear you."

Eryk nodded.

"Yes," he said. "I promise."

Nicolette rested her fingers in his palm.

"You may proceed," she said to the priest.

"Of course I may," said the cleric in a snit. "Kneel so that we may begin."

Eryk helped Nicolette to the floor. They had no cushions here as they would have in the church.

Eryk felt ill. He could only imagine how Nicolette must feel, forced to marry a bastard to protect her own bastard, but at least she and her baby would be safe, under his protection, and she could openly love and mother her child.

Nothing much would change for him, although maybe the gaggle of girls would leave him be. That was a plus.

Of course, having Nicolette living with him and yet unable to touch her would be agony, but one he was used to.

He blinked. The priest wanted him to repeat something.

"I, groom, take thee, bride to be my wedded wife...." He took a deep breath, studied Nicolette's delicate fingers resting in his big hand. He could die happy knowing he kept her safe. At least she would be somewhere familiar and with friends instead of living with that perverted red devil, Duke Ramnlf. He could grant her certain freedoms she'd get nowhere else.

He'd settle that.

"....and thereunto I plight thee my troth." He finished his portion of the vows.

The priest turned to Nicolette.

"Repeat after me," he said.

He assumed she'd say the same little speech he said, so he stopped listening and concentrated on controlling his emotions and schooling his face to hide his inner turmoil.

"....to be bonny and buxom at bed and at board...."

He startled and glanced down at her.

She watched his face, squeezed his hand, and quirked the corner of her mouth, highlighting a dimple.

He kept his eyes on her as she finished speaking her vows.

He told himself she was copying the priest, repeating words as instructed.

"I now pronounce you man and wife," said the priest.

The gallery erupted in applause.

"You may kiss your bride," said the priest as the noise died.

Nicolette held his gaze.

Eryk bent down, meaning to kiss her on the cheek, but she moved her head so their lips met, and they lingered.

CHAPTER FORTY-ONE

Wedding Night

An hour passed before the King and Queen wandered off, searching for new entertainment. Thank goodness for the quick boredom of the royals.

Nicolette's nerves felt like old zither strings ready to pop from being wound too tight for many years.

"You think you've won again," said Isuet, hissing in her ear and digging her fingernails into Nicolette's arm.

"Won?" Nicolette wrenched her arm from her sister's claws. "This isn't a footrace at a fair."

"You stole my moment in the sun." Spittle from Isuet's mouth fell on Nicolette's clothing.

"You created this mess," said Nicolette. "As always, you make things worse instead of better."

"Worse? You are married and not punished for your wanton ways. How are things worse for you?"

"You exposed our father and me to public ridicule," said Nicolette. Isuet flung her hands in her father's direction.

"Look at him," she said. "Once again, you have made him happy. You gave him a grandchild. You always come out the better."

"You forced me to marry in a social spectacle." She wrung her hands. "And trapped a good man into something he didn't want."

"Hah," said Isuet, her white face a mask of hatred. "Good man? He got you with child and did nothing to set it to rights."

"You know nothing of what you speak," said Nicolette. "There is no finer man in all the world than Eryk. I will not have you speak ill of him."

"You may think you have the upper hand," said Isuet, froth foaming her bloodless lips, "but I will make you pay; see you get what you deserve. I will be a princess soon. You will see."

Eryk came up beside Nicolette. He frowned at Isuet.

"Your father tires," he said to them both, hoping to release some of the energy in their words. "Perhaps we should all retire."

"Just because you wed my sister, do not think that gives you leave to speak to me," said Isuet.

"My dear," said Henri, taking Isuet's elbow. "Calm yourself. You will have the wedding of the century in three days and not some hasty farce to cover one's misdeeds."

Henri smiled at Eryk, his eyes twinkling with mischief.

"Let us bid the new couple our best wishes," he said as he lifted Isuet's fingers to his lips.

Isuet leaned into Henri, pink patches high on her cheeks.

"Count Thorne," said Henri formally, "I guarantee you robust fun with your ... new ... bride."

Nicolette blanched and felt faint.

Eryk took her hand.

Henri laughed and pulled Isuet behind him as he went off searching for other entertainment.

Nicolette and Eryk sighed at the same time.

"Such a family you married into," she said. "I fear you will regret it mightily."

"Come, let us leave this place," said Eryk. "My mother has returned from rearranging our accommodations as befits our new status."

"Oh," said Nicolette, startled. "I hadn't thought."

"We have all moved together in an enormous suite," said Eryk. "Our marriage has allowed us to house as a family since we no longer have any unmarried maids in the company." He lifted Betsey into his arms, freeing Tomas to walk with the aid of Kellan and Adam on either side.

Maryn and Clarissa ushered the three girls together, and they progressed as a cohesive unit to their new rooms.

"You can keep an eye on your father," said Eryk, wincing as Betsy tugged his beard. "He seems happy with today's outcome."

Nicolette peeked at her father. His color seemed better, and he could walk on his own. At least she'd be able to make his last days more pleasant.

"And how do you feel about our pairing?" Erik removed his belt and gave it to Betsey for play so she'd stop ripping out the hair from his face. "I heard what you said to Isuet. I promise not to make any impositions on you. You are your own woman."

"The entire enterprise surprised me," said Nicolette. "Now that I've had time to think about it, I see this arrangement is best for Betsey and me. I worry about you, though. More responsibility traps you. I will do my best to be as small a burden as possible."

"You are never a burden," he said. "I am happy with this arrangement."

"I promise not to make any impositions on you," she said. "You are free to live your life as you always have."

Nicolette remembered their brief kiss at the hastily erected altar. Keeping her promise would take a lot of work. Eryk's mouth, soft yet firm, filled her with excitement. She shook her thoughts away as heat rose in her face. She looked at her feet to hide her reaction.

She cleared her throat.

"Father says the King agreed to my dowry," said Nicolette, "so I may pay for our upkeep. While Welf will go to the crown when Isuet and Henri marry, the settlement is generous."

"The gold means nothing to me," said Eryk.

"Still," said Nicolette, "I'm glad I could add to Thornewood's coffers."

They fell into silence.

The sitting room of their new quarters felt as large as the great room at Thornewood. Eight doors pocketed the walls. Would Eryk expect to share a bed with her? A thrill rushed through her body.

Her father stumbled, drawing her attention. Kellan and Adam helped him to a chair piled with pillows.

He clutched his belly, leaned over, and retched. Luckily, Maryn knew the signs, held a pot out for him, and caught the poison before he soiled himself or the rugs.

He groaned.

"Come," said Maryn, wiping Tomas' face with a cool, damp cloth. "Too much excitement for one day. Let us get you to bed."

170

Tomas was too weak to respond.

Eryk lifted him gently and carried her father to his room.

They shooed the servants out and attended to Tomas, surrounding him with family and friends.

Nicolette sent a maid to Isuet to let her know their father was gravely ill. She did not respond or attend to his bedside.

"Can the little one sit next to me?" Tomas patted the quilt beside his pillow. He seemed calmer after being changed into loose, comfortable bedclothes and with a cup of the monk's tea to calm his belly and ease his pain.

Betsey climbed up on her grandfather's bed and nestled into his arms. Tomas smiled. He looked around the room. His daughter and her new family sat arrayed around him.

He nodded and closed his eyes.

Nicolette pulled her chair beside her father and held his thin hand.

"I bet," said Adam, "in all the excitement of the day, you missed the jester at the celebration."

They had missed that entertainment.

"He told me a riddle," said Adam. "Would you like to hear it?"

Tomas opened his eyes, watching Kellan's brother-in-law with a hint of mirth.

"What hangs at a man's thigh and wants to poke the hole it's often poked before?"

"Adam, the children," exclaimed Maryn with a grin.

"It's a key, you naughty minx," he said.

Tomas let out a breath.

"My life is good," he said before falling asleep.

Nicolette spent the rest of her wedding night watching vigil over her father with her new family.

CHAPTER FORTY-TWO

Death & Heaven

Nicolette woke when Eryk touched her shoulder. She rubbed her eyes and smiled at him, remembering her dream of them laying in a Thornewood field of wildflowers, the sun warming their naked skin.

His eyes held sadness.

Her heart pinched in her chest.

"Your father passed on during the night," he said.

She realized her father's hand lay stiff and cold in hers, but his face seemed peaceful, his lips upturned.

She leaned back in her chair, allowing herself time to absorb the loss of her parent.

Eryk squatted beside her, quiet and waiting. She took his hand, and they remained so for many minutes.

Tears rolled down her cheeks at her loss, but she wasn't truly sad. He was no longer in pain. He had been a good man, and so she knew he'd be in the heaven he believed in, perhaps reunited with his wives.

"Where are the others?"

"I chased them out before I woke you," said Eryk. "Maryn and Clarissa took the children to their beds and are also sleeping."

She nodded.

"Good," she said. "They all need a well-earned rest. What of Kellan and Adam?"

"They are resting, too."

"And what of you? Have you slept?" She glanced at him.

"I am fresh as the morning dew," he said and laughed.

She laughed with him.

"Come with me," he said. "You should rest."

Eryk pulled her to her feet.

"My father...."

"I have asked the monks to prepare him and lay him out in the small chapel in the south meadow," said Eryk. "They will do their best for him as I paid them well for his entrance into heaven."

"Thank you," she said. "I'm not tired, though. There must be something for me to do."

She looked around the sitting room as if a task would present itself.

"Come," he said. "You don't have to sleep, but you should rest comfortably. You spent the night twisted in that chair."

He escorted her to her new room. Her belongings covered various surfaces.

"Are you hungry?" He pulled over a small table set with platters of fruits, cheeses, and yeast pastries. "Or perhaps some wine to help you sleep?"

He kept his eyes on the food as she pulled her dresses over her head and uncharacteristically let them fall to the floor.

Dressed only in her shift, she crawled under the blankets and pulled them up to her chin.

Eryk sat on the edge of the bed and handed her a cup of wine.

"None for you?"

"You know I don't drink," he said.

"Not even in celebration of our nuptials?" She sipped from her cup and offered it to him.

"Not even for that," he said.

He reached around her and plumped her pillows, helping her to sit up more comfortably.

"We are friends," said Eryk, staring at the sun dancing patterns across the oaken floor.

Nicolette nodded.

"I want us always to be friends," he said.

She frowned.

"But we are also man and wife," she said.

"In name only," he said. "I have no intention of taking advantage of the situation you find yourself in. I will take care of you and Betsey, but I will not abuse that position."

He held up his hand to stop her words.

"Let me get this out, please," he said. "You must have loved Betsey's father dearly. I understand how that is. And to keep his name a secret when it put you and her in danger. Love is a powerful thing."

Nicolette shook her head.

"You are not to worry about that matter," Eryk continued. "I will never begrudge you your love or hold it against you. I can only assume there is a really good reason he could not be in your life, and your secrets are yours to keep or share as you see fit."

This man.

"I know none of this has happened in the best way possible or at the best of times, but I wanted you to rest assured that we are friends, and I value that for us."

Friends, she thought. The idiot wants us to be friends. She needed to fix this, but didn't have the energy right now. There would be time later.

Her eyes drooped.

Eryk took the wine goblet from her hand.

"We have always been best friends," she said sleepily, "even when we misunderstood one another."

She clutched his hand.

"I am glad I married you," she said. "Friends can have a satisfying marriage."

Nicolette patted the space beside her on the bed.

Eryk smiled at her, but there was sadness in his eyes. Why was he sad?

Betsey cried out.

Nicolette and Eryk jumped.

"Stay," said Eryk. "I'll get her and bring her to you."

He returned with her daughter in his arms, the little girl's head resting in the crook of his neck. He was such a natural with children that he should have a herd of babies, she thought, making herself giggle.

Eryk lowered Betsey onto the bed next to Nicolette, helped her under the covers, and tucked her in.

Nicolette adjusted her baby's nightcap and snuggled her next to her body. She sighed in pleasure. She had missed this since leaving Clarissa's home.

Eryk stood over them, smiling.

"A beautiful picture," he said.

"Thank you for giving me this," said Nicolette.

"My pleasure. Glad I could be of service." He turned to leave.

"Will you not stay with me for a bit?" She scrunched down under the quilts. "It would help me fall asleep."

"Of course," said Eryk as he pulled a chair near the bed and the food table. "I'll eat up all your goodies since you don't want them."

They laughed, remembering all the times he devoured any leftovers. He popped a cube of cheese and a grape into his mouth.

Nicolette watched him from under her lashes. The chair wasn't where she wanted him, but at least they were in the same room together.

She'd have to work on the rest when she was less tired, her father laid to rest, and this blasted wedding of her sister was over.

Once they were back home, in familiar surroundings and comfort and without strangers watching their every move, she would tell him how much she wanted him.

Perhaps the Fates were kinder than she first thought. Left to their own devices, she and Eryk would never have married. But now that they were, she would have to be brave enough to make it a genuine marriage.

She never dared think of it before, as it wasn't even a possibility in her mind. Now that it was a reality, she couldn't think of them together any other way.

She opened her eyes and found him watching her with an intensity that he was not quick enough to hide.

This may be easy. Nicolette had to let Eryk know they could do this. They belonged together. She saw it so clearly now. She just needed to get him to see it, too. He could be stubborn and have ridiculous ideas about gallantry. Well, too bad, she thought and giggled. I am determined, too. And he said he'd take care of me. She giggled again.

"You know I love you, right?" She asked him as she fell asleep.

CHAPTER FORTY-THREE

Princess Banshee

She said she loved him, then fell asleep.

Loved him as a friend? As a brother? As something more?

They needed to get home. Once back at Thornewood, they could sort this out. He needed to know what exactly she wanted from him, but wouldn't get his hopes up. He was still a bastard born.

He stayed in her sleeping chamber a few minutes after she closed her eyes. She was so beautiful, she and her child.

Could he survive on this? Years of just watching her sleep? The culmination of his dreams fulfilled so close and out of reach.

Quiet settled over the suite. His friends and family, his new family, asleep safe in their beds.

He felt agitated. His nerves zinged, his arms and legs like bowstrings pulled tight to fire arrows. He'd never sleep the way things stood.

He wound his way through the château, never encountering another guest. Only servants were up and about, doing their chores an hour after sunrise.

He followed his nose to the kitchens. His easy, friendly manner and common jokes endeared him to the serfs who packed up some victuals in a sack and a pouch of well-water to keep him full on his explorations of the grounds.

He found the chapel where Tomas, Count Welf, the last of his male line, lay in state. A tapestry showing his coat of arms, a blue lion, rampant on a yellow background surrounded by red hearts, covered his body.

The monks completed their task of washing and anointing the Count's body, dressing him in his finest, and then laying him on an oaken table in the cool stone chapel. His sword formed a cross as it lay on his chest, pointing towards his feet, hands clasped on the pommel.

One monk kneeled on the floor on the other side of Tomas' head, reciting prayers for the dead.

Eryk stood at Tomas' feet. He would miss Nicolette's father. Tomas' death brought back memories of the loss of his father. He knew Nicolette felt her sorrow as much as he felt his own.

They would take Tomas' body back to Thornewood and bury him next to Allan so they'd always have their fathers nearby.

He pulled his sword, Shade, from its sheath and raised it in salute, and recited his farewell from memory.

"O Sun of Righteousness, in all unclouded glory, supreme dispenser of justice, in that great day when Thou shalt strictly judge all nations, we earnestly beseech Thee, upon This Thy people, who here stand before Thy presence, in Thy pity, Lord, then have mercy upon us. Amen."

The monk raised his head and blinked at Eryk.

"You've read Dunstan of Canterbury," said the monk, bobbing his shaven head.

"Some," said Eryk. "I find his writing intelligent and not unkind. His defeat of those who lied about him inspires me."

"We model our monastery upon his guidelines," said the monk.

"What are you doing here?" Isuet's high-pitched voice vibrated around the thick stone walls.

"Speaking of enemies and personal attacks," said Eryk in a whisper to the monk, who hunched down to remain unseen by Isuet.

She approached her father's head and ignored the monk. Her eyes shot daggers at Eryk. They appeared feverish and bright, like a frozen lake struck by sunlight.

"Paying my last respects," said Eryk, "and ensuring his proper care."

"I don't need you to do that," she hissed, her hands clenched tight in pale leather gloves.

"I wasn't doing it for you." Eryk placed his sword away before he felt tempted to use it on this shrew. "I'm doing it for Tomas and

Nicolette."

"I'll make you pay," said Isuet.

"For what exactly?" Eryk shook his head. "What have I done to you that you hate me so?"

"You exist," she said, "and dare be in the same room as me." She glanced down at her dead father and frowned. "I could never convince him you were unfit company for us. And you proved me right. Yet, he still didn't see you for what you are." She sucked in a deep, shuddering breath. "You are a bastard and always will be. Born to a serf who whored her way into her master's bed to elevate her status."

The monk gasped and scurried out of the chapel on his hands and knees.

Eryk gripped the table Tomas lay upon. It creaked in his hands.

"Say what you will about me," said Eryk through clenched teeth, "and you may very well be right, but you will never speak of my mother again." The table moved towards Isuet as Eryk struggled to maintain his temper.

Isuet stepped back, startled.

"I will be a princess soon," she said as she approached the door. "Queen someday. I will put the injustice of your elevation to Count to rights." She screamed at him, her face red, eyes bulging. "I will have my sister sent to a nunnery for her sins and her bastard child dealt with properly."

The doorway to the chapel outlined Isuet, rays of the sun piercing Eryk's eyes as he tried to understand her. She paused there, chest heaving, her breath loud and ragged.

"I can understand your hatred of me," said Eryk, "But why do you hate your sister so? She has done nothing to you."

"She was born, and my father loved her more than he loved me. I knew it right away. I've always known it. And he pined for Nicolette's mother. Everyone realized he married her out of love, unlike my mother."

Isuet stomped back to her father's side. She lifted his right hand, tugged his signet ring off, and held it to Eryk's view.

"Mine," she dared him. "I will have Welf through Henri, and then I will have him take Thornewood from you. I will use my last breath to see you and my sister get what you deserve."

Isuet cackled.

Eryk shivered as if a ghost passed through him. He watched Isuet leave. Was that Tomas' spirit following his daughter? He squeezed his eyes tight and rubbed his forehead.

How could he keep Nicolette and Betsey safe from such poison and hatred?

He opened his eyes to see the monk had returned with two of his fellows.

"How long were you here?" Eryk leaned on the wall near him, exhausted.

"Long enough," said the monk. "We will pray for you." He handed Eryk a small book wrapped in silver wire and encrusted with an epidote, the cabochon smooth and polished. "Dunstan created this Classbook when he stayed at our Abbey during his troubles. The dark green stone came from the Alps near your home."

"This is beautiful," said Eryk. "But it belongs with you." He tried to hand back the book.

"We have other copies," said the monk. "One such as you, with an interest and perhaps love for our brother's word, might spread the good news. We give it to you as a blessing, for protection. Tomorrow is Dunstan's feast day. Serendipity."

Lord knew he'd need all the help he could get.

"Thank you," he said. "I will leave a donation with the Abbey."

"We prefer you keep the relic safe. We know war is coming, and you tasked with our defense. There may be other reasons to flee from here." He glanced at the doorway. "We may move south and look for a new haven."

"You will be welcome," said Eryk.

"Dunstan knew how to defeat the Devil," said the monk.

"I need some of that power," said Eryk.

CHAPTER FORTY-FOUR

Pork & Berries

Betsey bounced on the bed.

Nicolette peered at her daughter out of one eye. Her daughter; it was safe to say it now.

"My daughter," she said out loud.

Betsey laughed and fell over onto Nicolette's stomach.

She had avoided even thinking of Betsey as her daughter because she knew she'd have to give her up and not take any chances with strangers finding out Betsey's parentage.

She heard voices coming from the main sitting room of the suite.

"Time we got our lazy bones out of bed," said Nicolette. She washed them both and changed her daughter's nappy and shift and her clothes. She brushed her daughter's dark hair and covered her head with her cap, tucking the white patch under it, keeping it hidden.

Nicolette wore a simple undyed tunic as they would spend the day in their rooms, except for an hour to attend prayers in her father's honor in the chapel.

She entered the sitting room to find it full of games and laughter until they noticed her and immediately quieted.

"Please," she said. "Don't stop your revelries. Laughter brought my father joy."

She held Betsey on her lap to feed her. Betsey squirmed until Nicolette put her on the floor. The baby crawled over to Ava, Ema, and Gisela, who sat on the floor playing dice with Adam.

"Adam, are you teaching the girls to gamble?" She laughed as four sets of eyes, wide and innocent, stared at her.

"They need to know how to avoid the vices of the world," said Adam, the picture of innocence.

She shook her head. Maryn and Kellan appeared unconcerned.

"Where's Clarissa?" Her friend appeared to be absent from the little party.

"Here," chirped Clarissa as she entered the room from the hall. "I needed a particular color thread to fix Adam's tunic that he plans to wear at the wedding. How he tore out this part of the design is beyond me, as he claims he has yet to wear the item."

He smiled at Clarissa, and he transformed into a beautifully angelic man. That's one dangerous trick, thought Nicolette.

Clarissa stumbled a step as she looked at Adam.

He jumped up with the grace of an acrobat, took Clarissa's hand to steady her, and showed her to her seat.

She kept her eyes down as her cheeks turned rosy.

Well, well, thought Nicolette. She could keep her friend around longer or forever, if lucky.

Maryn sighed.

Nicolette glanced in her direction and found Eryk's mother smiling at her.

"I have another daughter," said Maryn. "Do you mind if I think of you so?"

Nicolette kneeled at Maryn's feet and held her hands.

"I am honored to have you as my mother," she said, tears in her eyes. She sat on the floor and rested her head on Maryn's knees. Maryn stroked her hair, and Nicolette felt comforted and calmed.

"Is Eryk still asleep?" Nicolette chuckled. "I never knew him to be such a slugabed."

"He's not here," said Kellan, not lifting his head from the parchment he read. "I believe he left several hours ago. His bed's unslept in."

"No word from him?" She straightened. "This is not the safest place to wander around alone."

"I asked one servant when I discovered Eryk's absence," said Kellan. "He visited the chapel, then took Smoke out for a ride. He had Shade with him, so I'm not too worried. If he doesn't return by mid-day, Adam and I will search for him."

"Could you not go now?" asked Nicolette.

"Look at you," said Adam with a laugh, "the hen-pecking wife already. Shall I fetch you a pot from the kitchens so you may treat the wayward lad to a proper lesson in his husbandly obedience?"

Nicolette threw a carved wooden horse at Adam.

"I am more worried about Isuet, Henri, and their cohorts trapping him in some sort of mischief," said Nicolette. "Isuet is angry and vindictive. Henri is cruel and devious. I trust neither of them."

The door to the suite banged open, startling cries from the girls and women within. Kellan and Adam rose to their feet.

Eryk filled the doorway, heaving great breaths.

His hair was loose, twigs and leaves stuck in his whiskers and beard, and dirt covered his tunic and leggings, a boot missing from one foot. He held Shade, drenched in blood, in his left hand and a bulging sack in his right.

Nicolette ran to him.

"What in all God's good Heaven has happened to you?" He stepped back.

"I'm filthy," he said, "don't touch me."

"You're hurt," she said.

"Am not," he said through gasps. "Invigorated." He bellowed out a laugh. "I brought a treat."

He handed the sack to Nicolette.

"Berries, fresh from the bush."

The girls clapped.

"And we will have fresh boar for our evening meal."

Kellan and Adam pulled a plain pine bench near Eryk. He collapsed on it, laid his sword across his knees, and toed off his remaining boot.

Nicolette stood before him, fists on her hips, shaking her head.

"Some water would not go amiss," he said to her, "if I may ask such a boon from my wife." His whiskers trembled as he chuckled.

She sighed as if he were so unmanageable.

He quenched his thirst.

"Let me wash and change," he said, "then I will tell you of my adventure."

He returned several moments later, his hair damp, wearing a fresh tunic and hose, and carrying oil and cloth to clean Shade.

They gathered around him.

"We are waiting, dear husband," said Nicolette, hoping the title would speed his storytelling.

He winked at her.

Her heart fluttered.

Oh, to be home and alone with him.

"Sleep eluded me," he said. "I ventured to the chapel to see to the proper preparation of your father. The monks did well by him." He wiped Shade with a damp cloth, removing the rusty, dried blood, paying particular attention to the fuller. The grove in the blade's center often held onto dirt and stains.

"Isuet appeared," he said with a grimace. "I can not say she paid her respects. She has well-honed cursing abilities."

"What did she say?" asked Nicolette.

Eryk shook his head.

"I will tell you in private," he said. "No need to distress the children with her ravings."

Nicolette agreed.

Eryk rubbed oil on his clean blade.

"I thought a ride might calm me," he continued. "I found a patch of ripe strawberries, so I left Shadow to graze as I filled my bag." He gestured to the now empty sack on the floor and the juice-smeared faces of the girls.

"Did you at least share with the adults in the room?" He laughed as he saw they, too, had pink smudged lips.

"Well, unbeknownst to me, a mad boar plagued the countryside of late and it decided I presented him with a perfect target for his rage."

"Seems to be a theme for you," said Kellan.

"Tis true," said Eryk. "Shade and I had the better of the beast, though. And since I defeated the monster, we can choose the best portion of his rump." His eyes twinkled.

"Perhaps you may rest now," said Nicolette.

"Nonsense," rejoined Eryk. "I am refreshed, restored, and revived."

"May this day's event portent your victory in all future encounters with such fierce enemies," said Nicolette.

CHAPTER FORTY-FIVE

Dark Night

The afternoon spent with his family and friends was pleasant. His new wife laughed along with everyone else. He'd have to keep reminding himself; she was his wife in name only. Still, their time together was relaxed and easy.

Nicolette smiled and joined in the games. He believed she did it for the children, but he noticed the sadness in her eyes.

"Perhaps you'd care to go to the chapel for evening prayers over your father's spirit," he said as he watched Nicolette put Betsey in a crib for a nap.

"I would," she said, tucking a blanket around the sleeping babe. She kissed the girl's forehead and lingered there for a few moments.

She must have truly loved Betsey's father deeply, he thought, curiosity about the man gnawing at his insides. Not his business unless someday she chose to tell him. Although, he was pretty sure he didn't want to know.

The man who stole her heart from him was just a ghost. He preferred to think of him as dead, but he could be wrong.

He shook his head to dispel these thoughts that twisted his belly and took away his appetite.

He chose freely to marry her and keep her safe from the evil words of her sister and gossiping folks and promised to be her friend. He could give her that and be the best of friends to her, as this day proved. As they always were.

His heart was no worse for his decision. A true marriage with her was never meant for him, anyway.

"Eryk?" She faced him.

He realized she had said his name several times.

"Beg pardon," he said. "It must be the lack of sleep."

"Oh, then you must go to bed and rest." She wrapped a cloak around her. "I can have a servant accompany me."

"Nonsense," he said, letting her leave the nursery first. "I don't want you to have to grieve alone."

"I appreciate your kindness," she said as she tucked her hands in the folds of her cloak.

He noticed. She must not want to touch him, he thought. Just as well. Less temptation that way.

He clasped his hands behind his back. They walked down the halls of the château side by side and out into the dusk. The setting sun colored the sky a dusky pink.

"Tomorrow will be a beautiful day," said Nicolette, nodding to the west.

"We should take the children out for a picnic," said Eryk. "I saw a lovely pasture near a shallow brook."

They reached the door of the chapel, and Nicolette paused before entering.

"Would you mind if I go in alone?" She peered into the dark interior of the small church.

"Of course not," he said. "If that is what you wish. Sometimes it is easier to grieve alone."

She left him standing just outside, like a sentinel guarding a crypt.

It would have been best if Maryn had adopted her instead of creating this sham of a marriage. Could they change things now? Of course not. He had announced to the world that he was Betsey's father.

What must that world think of him?

He was sure Nicolette had time to think of the mess they were in and realize her mistake in agreeing to this.

What possible good excuse was there for him not marrying her on his own before being forced into it? There was none. He was a cad, no doubt about it.

The world would know her reasons for not wanting to marry him. He had taken advantage of her. He was a bastard and clearly beneath her in rank and birth.

Such a fool as he had never been born before.

At least her father was no longer around to grieve over his favorite daughter's plight.

Eryk heard Nicolette's sobs as he stood guard beside the entrance. She cried as if the world were at its end. She suffered so much grief, and despite his best intentions, he was part of the reason for her heartache and regret.

He wanted to return to the woods to find another wild boar to kill, to vent his anger, frustration, and uselessness. He felt the urge to pull the door off its hinges.

He kicked at the ground, and his toe struck a rock used to line the path.

"Fuck," he said, none-too-quietly.

He hopped on one foot and rubbed the other.

"What are you doing?" Nicolette peeked at him from the doorway.

"Nothing," he mumbled.

"Come inside and sit with me while they finish the evening prayers."

"Are you sure you want me there?" He frowned, but she couldn't see his expression because the sun had fully set.

"Yes. I asked you, didn't I?" She sounded amused. "Perhaps you should have taken a nap. You are cranky."

Benches beside the table where Tomas' body rested let mourners contemplate his life at ease. Right now, only the one monk Eryk had met early was the only other person with them.

He recited the prayers for the dead as he and Nicolette sat, heads bowed and hands folded.

The candles flickered and danced off Nicolette's dark brown hair, tiny curlers escaping her braids. The glow warmed her dark skin. Eryk did his best to ignore her beauty and keep his thoughts chaste and pious, but his mind ran away with inappropriate visions.

He dug his fingernails into his palms, the piercing pain returning him to some calm. This time alone with Nicolette caused him pain and pleasure that felt like it lasted a lifetime.

Finally, the monk stopped his chanting.

Nicolette offered the man her thanks.

Eryk offered him a coin for the poor.

He escorted her back to their rooms, the exact reverse of their walk down, without speaking.

He waited while she checked on Betsey, then escorted her to her bedroom door, unsure why he felt the need to do so.

"Thank you for everything," said Nicolette, holding her door between them. "Good night, and sleep well." She closed her door.

He stared at it for a moment, alone in the sitting room.

"Sleep well." He snickered at himself. "Not likely."

He padded to his room, undressed, and fell into bed, face first in his pillows.

Maybe he'd suffocate during the night. That would solve all their problems.

CHAPTER FORTY-SIX

Love & Enemies

Eryk woke up with renewed resolve. His marriage to Nicolette had changed nothing. He decided life would go on as it always had. Nicolette and Betsey were new aspects of his responsibilities. He was just the caretaker of Thornewood and those who lived within its borders until Kellan's sons took over the stewardship. He felt better confirming his role in life.

He broke his fast in the sitting room with his family and friends. He liked this casual communal setting. They could continue this relaxed kind of morning at home.

"Nicolette mentioned a picnic you two spoke of last night," said Maryn. His mother handed him a slice of bread slathered with butter and blackberry jam. "Unfortunately, we cannot go out with you this day." She sipped a bowl of tea mixed with cream and honey.

"Queen Adelaide requested," Clarissa snorted from her spot on the floor amongst Kellan's girls, "that we attend a party for the bride." She watched as a maid braided Gisela's hair.

"Tis called a French braid," said the maid, "because we created it." The girls giggled.

"You have to spend the day in Isuet's presence?" Eryk grimaced. "How's that going to work?"

"The event will be in the Queen's solar. The rooms divided into sections of small seating groups," Clarissa continued as the maid taught her the new hairstyle.

"The Queen's maid who brought her invitation assured us the

Queen has Isuet under control today," said Maryn. "But she said Nicolette must attend, and we will not leave her to jump this fence alone."

Nicolette slumped back in her chair. Betsey crawled on the floor at her feet, occasionally trying to pull herself up using Nicolette's skirts.

"Only two more days," she said. "I keep repeating that in my head. Two more days, and then we can leave."

"We must meet with the King today, anyway," said Kellan. "The real reason we all agreed to this trip."

"When is that?" asked Adam, looking over the fresh fruit.

"Soon," said Kellan. "I expect one of his aids to knock on our door in moments."

"What of the children?" asked Kellan, rubbing his temples.

"The maids will keep them occupied in the nursery," said Nicolette as she added some of Betsey's willow bark extract to a cup of water and handed it to Eryk.

"This will ease your head," she said.

He smiled his thanks and down the contents.

"The girls saw plenty of excitement in the gallery." Nicolette picked Betsey up, but a maid scooped the child out of her arms.

"She needs a nappy change," said the girl. "We'll be back soon."

"The battlefield will be easier for all of us to negotiate if they aren't with us," said Clarissa.

A knock on the door.

"This will be for us," said Kellan. "I believe the ladies have a bit more time."

"May we all survive our skirmishes," said Adam with a wink.

"Farewell," said Eryk, "we will see you on the other side of hell." He held his hands over his heart. "May we all come out of this alive."

They left for their meeting with the King, with the women laughing at them.

They met with King Hugh in his war room. A table large enough for thirty people filled the center, a map of the known world painted on its surface. Carved wooden pieces representing troops dotted the landmasses, and boats filled the seas.

The King sat at the head of the table, flanked by his advisers. He waved at Kellan, Adam, and Eryk to take seats.

"This is how things stand," said the King pointing at his map. "You will find your estates marked with your colors and crests."

Eryk looked around at the men and raised an eyebrow.

"The King wishes to speak to you southern nobles without the others present," said Prince Kevan, standing at the King's right hand. "He'll talk to the other nobles later. And Prince Henri has...wedding tasks to attend."

"Your borders are secure to the south according to my scouts," said the King. "I may need you to take refugees if war breaks out here."

"Of course," said Kellan. "We will do all we can, as you wish."

"Hilltop is a might fortress," said a man on the left, "and large enough to hold many people."

"The waterways allow for swift travel north and south," said another.

"Mostly, the King requires that you prepare for any eventuality," said Kevan.

"Of course," said Kellan, speaking for Eryk and Adam as their elder.

"I am negotiating with the Saxon King Otto, who sits on our northeastern border. He is not eager for war at this time, so I invited him to attend Henri's wedding feast after the marriage ceremony."

The King stretched his legs.

"King Otto was a childhood friend of our Queen Adelaide. Few people know she was a Saxon princess before our marriage. We hope that the relationship will act as an inducement to peace. I will meet with him the next day to bargain a treaty of more permanence."

Kevan filled the King's golden chalice with a deep red wine.

His Highness lifted his cup, swirled the liquid inside, and sipped.

"Mmmmm," he said in approval. "From your father's vineyards?"

"Yes, Sire," said Kevan.

"Lovely," said the King. "Send my brother my compliments for another fine vintage."

"Of course, Uncle," said the Prince.

The King sighed.

"We need peace with the Saxons right now," said King Hugh. "I am experiencing some strife with some young people in the court. It requires due diligence to resolve."

The King slapped his fingers on the table.

"So, be prepared," he said, toying with his goblet.

"Baron Beust, how fare you in your duties?"

"I believe your generous gift of the baronacy has not gone amiss," said Adam. "The fields and forests prosper once again. His Highness should come hunting when more pressing matters clear up."

The King nodded.

"Your reports regularly reach me," he said. "I'm glad I listened to your sister."

"As am I, Your Highness. Revena is rarely wrong, I've found."

"Women rarely are," said the King, and the men laughed with him at his joke.

"Count Thorne," said the King, directing his attention to Eryk. "Allow me to convey my condolences to your wife at the loss of Count Tomas."

"I will tell her your kind words, Sire," said Eryk.

"Do you enjoy your wedded bliss?" The King waggled his eyebrows. "The beginning of the marriage is the best of times."

"Beyond happiness," said Eryk.

"Of course," said the King. "I expect you to work hard on getting me those new subjects I need."

These words met hearty laughter all around.

Eryk groaned inside.

"Be prepared," the King repeated, waving them away.

Prince Kevan showed them to the door.

"Be alert the rest of your time here," he said. "Danger lurks close to the King. You are sober folk. We expect faith and diligence from you."

They were silent on their walk back to their rooms, not wanting any discussions overheard by unfriendly ears.

"I didn't expect to see you ladies back before us," said Eryk as he entered their suite.

"It turns out Isuet was beyond the Queen's control after all," said Nicolette with absolute exhaustion. "Isuet refused mollification or separation from us. She expressed no joy until she threw us out."

"We left gladly," said Clarissa. "I still don't understand how she got the Prince. Did you ever say?" She looked at Nicolette.

"The King wanted Welf," said Nicolette. "A marriage was the easiest way to get the land."

"Ah," said Clarissa. "Even so ... Isuet? Can Henri be happy?"

"What care he?" Nicolette stared out the window as she spoke. "He spends little time with her and takes other women as he wants."

Clarissa took her friend's hand and sat at Nicolette's feet.

"Let's not think about either of them anymore," she said. "We will be done with them soon enough."

"Yes," said Nicolette. "Let's do something enjoyable since the rest of the afternoon is free."

"Let's go to that spot I mentioned," said Eryk. "It's still early, and the day is sunny and warm."

"Yes, let's do it," said Nicolette, clapping.

Eryk spent the rest of the afternoon with his family playing ball toss, wading in the creek, resting in the sunshine, and eating.

It felt like the calm before the storm with Isuet's wedding on the morrow and an enemy Saxon King invited to celebrate.

CHAPTER FORTY-SEVEN

Surprise

The Basilica of Saint Saintin featured a nave, a wide aisle stretching from the entrance to the altar and crossed by two transepts, side aisles at right angles from the main walkway. Two bell towers flanked two opposing apses, semicircular and with vaulted ceilings.

The morning of Isuet's and Henri's wedding began with the continuous clanging of the four bells from sunrise until the third hour.

The ornate church, just finished this year, displayed painted statues of the saints, carved pillars adorned with roses and gargoyles, and twelve-branched candelabras in every side aisle, along the arcade, and in the small chapels off of the nave approaching the high alter.

Guests filled the interior leaving the center open for the Bishop, several priests, deacons, and alter boys to process to the front, splashing congregants with holy water from the silver asperge bucket and sprinkler, fumigating the air with incense from the brass thurible swung from a chain.

King Hugh and Queen Adelaide followed the religious parade to their thrones to the left of the altar.

A choir of monks in the balcony over the entrance hall sang a cappella as the bride and groom walked down the aisle together.

Both wore pale shades of blue shot through with silver threads and clear crystals.

Isuet looked like a specter shining in the candlelight, gossamer shimmers that distorted her body from head to toe. She floated beside Henri.

The Prince looked sharp as a knife next to his soon-to-be wife. His clothing fit as if sewn onto his body. Nicolette had no name for this new style of close-fitting tunic, short so that his muscular thighs stood out under the hem.

The couple kneeled before the bishop, and the wedding Mass began.

"Blessings, lords, and ladies. As their bans have been posted and witnessed, we are here to join the Lady Isuet of Welf and Henri, Prince of Franconia, in holy matrimony," said the Bishop.

"Take one another's hands," he said.

He turned to Henri and gave him the groom's vows.

"I, Henri, take thee Isuet as my wedded wife, for better or worse, fair or foul, till death us do part. I plight thee my promise."

Isuet's vows followed. Her voice rang in the eves and rattled the windows.

"I, Isuet, take thee, Henri, to my wedded husband, to obey from this day forward, to be bonny and buxom at bed and at board, to love and to cherish, till death us do part. I plight thee my promise."

"As you are now man and wife," said the Bishop, "You may kiss your bride."

Isuet closed her eyes and tilted her pursed lips up to Henri. He kissed Isuet on the cheek. She blinked her eyes and frowned.

Henri signaled the Bishop to finish.

"Go in peace and greet the new couple."

Isuet grinned, her teeth sharp, as she left the church on Prince Henri's arm. Her eyes caught and held Nicolette's eyes.

"Princess," she mouthed to her sister.

The bright white of the royal family filled the dais at the back of the reception hall. Isuet fit in, but her new husband, Prince Henri, stood out like a black x on a treasure map.

Guests came forward to pay their respects to Princess Isuet and announce their gifts to the newly married couple.

Nicolette stood off to the side with her family and friends. Since her father's death, her sister required only her presence to witness Isuet's newfound splendor and elevation. She was grateful for the respite.

Eryk explained the political purpose of the event to their small party the day before. King Hugh of Franconia and Otto, the Duke of Saxony, acting King of Germania, intended to solidify their rulerships through various marriages with their relatives.

King Hugh intended to show off his daughters to Otto the Illustrious at today's ceremony, and thus prevent a war with the Saxon King.

The crowd of lesser nobility waited with curiosity and tension and held their breath to see the man who menaced their eastern borders.

With the press of people, Nicolette would not see the man until he reached the area right in front of the King and Queen, but she knew when he entered the room and had no need of the herald's announcement.

"Otto the First, the Illustrious, Duke of Saxony, King of the Germans."

It seemed as if a storm approached. First, there was a silence so heavy it pressed upon your lungs and stole your breath. Then came a rush of sound, low and all-consuming, crushing thought and vision.

Nicolette's ears popped. Eryk took her hand and squeezed her fingers. He saw everything, his eyes well above the tallest head in the room.

She looked up at him. Eyes wide, mouth open, he stared at the procession. She pulled on his arm and stood on tiptoes, trying to get a look at what could have shocked him so.

Queen Adelaide gasped.

Nicolette turned to see the Queen slump on her throne, the blood draining from her face. The Queen glanced at King Hugh, who sat straight as a board, facing the approaching enemy, eyebrows narrowed and mouth down-turned.

Henri moved forward in his seat, hands gripping the armrests. He sat on the Queen's left, half a step below her. Her son's movement caught her attention, and she watched him, shaking her head.

Nicolette felt the Saxon King's movement as waves of reaction rippled through the crowd, and Eryk's head followed.

Queen Adelaide rose.

"How could you, without telling me?" She addressed her question to King Hugh. "You never told me King Otto was my Otto."

"How could you?" The King's face flushed red.

Henri stood, his hand gripping the hilt of his sword.

Isuet whispered something to him. He scowled at her. She flinched and slid back into her seat, eyes fixed on the aisle to the dais as if it were a poisonous snake.

The King and his children stood as one on his right.

Otto, the ruler of the Saxons, stood before the royal family of Franconia, and Nicolette understood the agitation of all parties.

He had an identical swipe of white at the front of his black hair that matched Henri's. Their bright violet eyes clashed, Henri with anger, Otto with amusement.

"It's good to see you again, Adelaide," said Otto, "although it seems you failed to mention something important."

The Queen turned and fled with her ladies trailing like frightened ducklings.

Duke Ramnlf ran his hand through his red hair. He whispered into Henri's ear as he watched Otto. Henri nodded and exited with the brothers from Nantes, leaving Isuet alone like a lost feral cat.

"Leave," said King Hugh.

The guests stampeded from the hall and left with an entire afternoon to contemplate the morning's spectacles.

Nicolette felt numb.

"What do you think will happen now?" Clarissa reclined on a sofa after changing into a more comfortable dress and removing her jewelry.

"It is clear that Henri is Otto's son," said Kellan, twirling a wineglass between his fingers. "Henri has a host of bastards, and they all have his black hair with the white mark." He sipped from his cup. "The question I want answered is whether King Hugh knew."

"He mentioned Queen Adelaide and Otto were childhood friends," said Adam.

"Henri can no longer be King Hugh's successor," said Eryk. "I doubt he can even remain at the palace."

"Should we check on Isuet?" Maryn looked at Nicolette.

"I've sent a message by the maid," said Nicolette, "but knowing my sister, she will not want me or us anywhere near her." She shook her head. "I feel adrift and conflicted. This revelation feels like the earth is cracking and will swallow us whole."

"I'm glad the children remained behind," said Maryn. "Where are they now?"

"The nannies took them to an enclosed park at the back of the estate," said Nicolette. "The château boasts a menagerie, and they will share a picnic, alfresco, as they say here." She giggled and covered her mouth. "My nerves are strung a bit too tight."

She felt sympathy from Clarissa and Maryn. Her closeness to them comforted her.

Kellan and Adam discussed repercussions of today's events to the country and the King's plan to have the Franconian and Saxon kingdoms join by marriage.

Eryk watched Nicolette. She couldn't read his expression.

She felt guilt, shame, and fear. If Eryk ever found out the truth, how would he react?

The door to their suite opened and banged against the wall. A disheveled maid stood in its frame, chest heaving.

Kellan's three girls rushed past her, talking at once.

"They took Betsey," said Ema as she pulled on Nicolette's arm.

CHAPTER FORTY-EIGHT

Kidnapping

The maid had a bruise on her face.

Kellan's girls collapsed in Maryn's arms, sobbing.

The other servants responsible for watching the children huddled together, fear painted on their expressions.

"Come sit, Sissy," said Eryk, "take a deep breath. Tell us what happened." He squatted by her seat. He wouldn't look at Nicolette, afraid of what he'd see. He must concentrate on practical matters to get her child back.

"We sat on a blanket for our picnic," said Sissy, the maid squeezing her apron in her hands. "The baby slept. She were tired from watching the animals. The young misses ate their luncheon."

She breathed deep and reached out to Eryk, clutching his arm.

"We didn't know," she said, a sob escaping in a hiccup. "She's a princess and the Countess's sister. How could we know?"

"You couldn't know," said Eryk, keeping his voice low and calm. "Just tell us. It's not your fault. We do not blame you for anything."

Sissy nodded and looked at Nicolette.

"She said you asked her to fetch the baby, but it didn't feel right to me. I picked Betsey up and said I'd bring her to you."

Tears rolled down her damaged cheek.

"Prince Henri hit me. Said I was to do as I was told. The Princess grabbed the baby from me, pulled off Betsey's cap, and shrieked."

Sissy got lost in her tale, pantomiming the voices and actions of the people involved.

"I knew," says the Princess. "She has your hair, like all your other bastards."

"That haughty bitch," says the redheaded Duke. He winked at Henri. "And you kept that morsel to yourself."

"You catch her, she's all yours," says the Prince. "Once was enough for me. Her knife left a deep gash in my thigh when I thought her cowed."

"You raped my sister?" The Princess held the baby as if she'd never seen one before.

"She wouldn't give herself to me willingly, so I had no choice. Shut that kid up," says the Prince. "Do something useful."

"The Prince grabbed the Princess's arm and dragged her holding Betsey from the menagerie through the back gate, followed by the red brothers." Sissy gasped. "Oh, I forgot, I heard the Prince say he would beg sanctuary from the Saxon King, his father."

Clarissa handed the maid a cup of ale.

"Anything else?"

Sissy shook her head.

"Let my mother clean your cheek and put a soothing ointment on it," said Eryk as he stood. "Mother, please go to the nursery with the girls, and all of you rest. Clarissa, Adam, will you stay with them?"

"Yes," said Clarissa, her voice hoarse.

"We will not leave them," Adam said beside Clarissa. "What will you do?"

Eryk met Nicolette's eyes.

"We will beg the King for an audience and ask him to intercede with the Saxon King for us." He strapped Shade to his hip. "That is, if the man still resides within these walls." He turned to Kellan. "Can you organize a search party?"

Kellan slid Shadow, Revena's sword, into the sheath at his waist, his face grim.

"Of course," he said. "I will check out the menagerie and ask for witnesses and information. They make a group that will not go unnoticed in the region."

Eryk and Nicolette stood at opposite ends of the suite's sitting room, staring at one another.

"Eryk," said Nicolette. "You must hate me." The light in her amber eyes dimmed.

"This is not the time," he said. "We must concentrate on getting your daughter back. There will be plenty of time to talk once we've done that and made that son-of-a-bitch pay for all the misery he's caused."

He crossed the room, took her hands, and kissed her fingers.

"I will never hate you," he said, and his smile went to his eyes.

"Go put on something more practical and less...." He rolled his hand at her. She still wore her finery from the wedding. "We will be on the run and need to ride, I am sure. I do not envision any of them escaping on foot."

They waited in the antechamber of the King's quarters for almost an hour.

Eryk paced from one end of the room to another, eating up his excess energy.

Nicolette sat on a stool, back straight, hands clasped to knees, feet together. She stared at the door to the King's inner sanctum as if she could burn a hole in the wood.

She jumped up when the door opened, and His Highness joined them with his advisers trailing, Prince Kevan on his left.

"Sit," said the King as he took his chair. He examined the floor for several minutes, took a deep breath, and looked at them.

"This day has gone awry, askew, amiss," he said with a laugh of derision.

"Your Highness," said Nicolette, leaning forward.

The King held up his hand, palm facing her.

She clamped her lips together.

"I know you are anxious," he said. "I have mustered my troops, and they are helping Kellan gather information and search the grounds."

The King hung his head. Prince Kevan placed a hand on his shoulder.

"I'll take over, Uncle," he said. He looked at Eryk and Nicolette.

"We knew of a faction of young nobility intent upon usurping the throne. Henri headed this group with the support of the New Duke Ramnlf and his brothers. Henri intended to overthrow his father and steal his crown.

"Today's revelations laid waste to their plans, as Henri can no longer stand in line for the throne based on heredity."

The King grimaced.

"The Queen retires to a nunnery," said Kevan. "The King does not wish to punish or humiliate her for decisions, not her own. He spoke with both Queen Adelaide and Otto. They were young, and their future originally meant for them to be together."

"Still, she should have known and warned me," said the King, primarily to himself.

"While the King met with Otto, the Saxon King received a message from Henri asking for his rightful place in that King's family. After my uncle informed Otto of the intended coup, Otto sent word to Henri, denying his request."

"We heard rumors of the child's appearance," said the King glancing up at Nicolette. "Are they true?"

Nicolette nodded, her eyes on her knees.

"Did you know, Count Thorne?"

"I know Betsey is Nicolette's daughter," he said. "That is all I need to know, and that is all that matters to me."

"They make fine men in Bavaria, do they not, Kevan?"

"Yes, Uncle." Kevan sighed.

A knock on the chamber door: a soldier entered and stood at attention.

"You have some news," said Kevan.

"Yes, your highness." He held his helmet in the crook of his elbow, one hand on the hilt of his sword.

"Nine horses are missing from the stables," said the soldier, "those belonging to Henri, his wife, and the men from Nantes. We assume some followers joined them. The Queen's ladies report missing gold, silver, and precious stones. Small jewelry that can be hidden and broken into pieces."

"Anything else?" Eryk approached the man. "Any sign of where they've gone? A direction? Something for us to follow?"

The soldier, a big man in his own right, still had to look up at Eryk, but he did not flinch when meeting his eyes.

"We found tracks from a party of horses through the woods at the back behind the animal gardens. Your brother is with a scouting party."

"With your leave," Eryk said to the King.

"Of course." The King stood. "Hold," he said. "I tasked you previously with watching my back, Count Thorne. That directive has not changed, although its current look is unexpected."

"I understand," said Eryk as he took Nicolette by the hand, and they followed the soldier from the King's presence.

CHAPTER FORTY-NINE

Fun in the Dark

The dark night hindered the hunt for the kidnappers. Cloud cover made it impossible to see without a torch. The flickering of torchlight made movement over fields and through forests dangerous.

Eryk consoled himself, knowing that Henri and his party must also stay in place until morning. While he had supplies and extra horses supplied by the King, Henri's newest circumstances limited his resources.

Eryk rested with little sleep. Kellan returned with the setting sun. His scouting produced a direction and plan for them when daylight broke.

The night saw them gathered in their suite, keeping each other from the brink of despair.

"Come from the window and rest," he said to Nicolette. "I will wake you as soon as dawn breaks. You will need your energy."

She checked their saddle bags, prepared hours ago. She wore thick woolen leggings and a short tunic. Her feet rested in boots procured from a boy in the King's household. A short sword lay ready near a traveling cloak.

"All is ready," said Eryk. "We will move at the first possible moment, but you must at least sit and close your eyes."

He pulled her to a chair next to his and held her hand.

She looked dazed and far away.

"We will get her back," he said, stroking her fingers.

She took a shuddering breath and looked at him, her eyes sparkling in the candlelight. She nodded.

"I want to kill them all," she said.

"As do I," he said.

She closed her eyes and laid her head on his biceps, exhaustion taking control of her body and forcing her to sleep.

He alternated between watching Nicolette sleep and checking for the first signs of morning through their room's east-facing window.

He had spent four days awake before and could do so again. Kellan could do the same. He let the anger he felt fuel his body and attention.

The color in the rectangular opening of the window went from black to gray, tinged with pink.

"Nicolette," he said, shaking her shoulder. "It is time."

She sat up straight, fully awake.

Clarissa and Maryn hugged Nicolette.

"May the gods speed your success," said Maryn to Eryk and Kellan as she kissed them.

Nicolette, Kellan, and Eryk gathered their traveling packs and dressed for the open road.

Adam said nothing for once, but his face held a fierce expression. He held his sword unsheathed at his side. He simply nodded to them as he ushered them out the door and locked it behind them.

The King's men assigned to them waited in the yard, their horses saddled and ready to ride.

Prince Kevan approached them before they mounted.

"A bird arrived a moment ago, confirming the destination of Henri and his band of traitors," said Kevan. He handed Eryk a scroll of vellum. "This is a writ from King Hugh charging you to do what is necessary to correct this injustice upon yourselves and the crown."

Eryk tucked the document into his shirt.

He clutched Kevan's forearm, and they shook in the Roman style.

"May fate see you successful," said Kevan as he stepped back, allowing Eryk to help Nicolette on her horse.

He and Kellan mounted, and the troop trotted out of the courtyard and headed east towards the rising sun and the King's treacherous former son.

They rode hard, and by the end of the day, their scouts returned with news that the kidnappers camped within a mile of their current location. Several of their horses were lame and their supplies were low.

"We'll stop here," said Eryk, "And approach them with stealth. We don't want them to do anything more drastic or deadly."

"We'd want to negotiate with them, if possible," said Kellan. "Our priority is to get Betsey back. She is their greatest bargaining chip and our weakest point."

"I can talk to Isuet," said Nicolette. "There must be something I can say to her to stop this madness." She wrung her hand as she spoke.

"If it were anyone else," said Eryk, his voice soft to weaken the blow, "I might agree, but your sister aims to hurt you with her every word and deed. If she sees you, she may do something even more horrendous than taking your child."

Nicolette nodded, a tear rolling down her cheek.

They made camp while they still had light, attending to their horses and their own needs. They made no fire to avoid alerting their quarry, eating jerky and black bread.

In the middle of the night, Eryk, a scout, and a couple of soldiers left for the enemy campsite.

Despite his size, Eryk moved as quiet as a lynx on the prowl. They reached their destination and hid behind trees and bushes, close enough for a good view.

Eryk watched the group around the fire. He did not see or hear Betsey. Where was the child? His stomach tightened and cramped. He felt ill and shook himself, dispelling his fear. He told himself to concentrate on what is real and not succumb to the unknown.

He counted Henri, Isuet, Peter, Montfor, and three others around the fire. Francois and one other were missing from the nine they knew to be in the group. Perhaps they were off seeing to personal needs or posted as guards.

He sensed no one nearby, but remained alert to any disturbance.

Isuet rose from her log and approached Henri.

"I want to go home," she said.

He ignored her as he stared into the fire.

"Did you hear me?" Her voice shook the leaves.

"Shut up," said Henri.

"How dare you?" Isuet pushed Henri's shoulder. "I am the daughter of a Count."

"And I am a King's bastard. Do you think I give a shit about you? I only married you for Welf." He continued to speak without raising his voice or his eyes to Isuet. "You're nothing but a washed-out bag of bones. I can't bear looking at you and the thought of touching you...." He shivered. "Your only value to me is to care for my brat. Do that, or I have no use for you."

Isuet stood with her mouth and eyes wide. She shimmered like a wraith, her body's outlines wavering in the dark.

"I curse you," said Isuet.

"Do your best," said Henri with a chuckle. "My life can't get much worse."

Isuet spit on the ground over her left shoulder.

Betsey must be alive and still with them, Eryk thought.

Isuet walked away from Henri and the fire to a tree trunk, plopped on the ground, and lifted a bundle to her arms.

The bushes off to her right rustled. Eryk heard a grunt, flesh hitting flesh, and a woman's cry.

Francois tripped into the small clearing with Nicolette clutched in his arms. He limped, and blood ran down his right cheek.

"Lookie what I found," he said as he threw Nicolette to the ground at Henri's side.

"Well," said Henri, lacing his fingers into Nicolette's hair. "This should be fun."

CHAPTER FIFTY

Death Becomes You

Nicolette clawed Henri's face.

As he stood, he yanked on her hair and pulled her to her knees.

She rammed her shoulder into his legs. He staggered, but kept his grip.

"I see why you like that one," said Francois. "She has some life to her."

"Did she fight like that when you took her maidenhead?" Montfor joined his brother.

"Aye," said Henri. "She was the least cooperative of all my conquests. A scar reminds me of our last romp." Henri tilted Nicolette's face up. "This," he said, touching the fingernail marks she just gave him, "will be the last time you mark me."

He slapped her, and she fell back into the dirt.

She tasted blood and spit it at him.

"You Welf women sure like to spew your venom at me," said Henri.

"Where's my daughter?" Nicolette stood and looked around the camp.

"You mean our daughter," said Henri.

"No, never. She will never be your child."

"Matters not to me," he said. "They litter the ground."

"I say we quit with the talking," said Francois, "and garner some enjoyment from what was a hideous night."

Nicolette saw Isuet holding Betsey, who was tied and gagged. Nicolette gagged on her anger and fear.

"Sister, what are you doing to my baby?" Nicolette moved towards Isuet, but Francois grabbed her wrist and pulled her to him. "Have a heart, Isuet. She's just a babe, your niece."

Nicolette kicked at the Duke, her legs unhindered by a long dress. Her boot struck his shin.

"Help me hold her," said Francois.

His brothers clasped her legs and forced her to the ground, lying on her writhing body.

"Stop," said Henri. "We don't have time for this now."

He stood over Nicolette and the redheaded brothers.

"If she is here," he said, "you can be assured that Eryk and others are nearby. Tie her up, and we'll take her with us."

He gestured to the other men of their party that Nicolette did not know.

"Search the woods for others."

He tossed a rope to Francois.

"Pack up the brat, Isuet." He looked to where Isuet had been. She was gone, along with the child.

"Shit," he said. "She's run off." He stuck a branch in the fire pit. It flamed. He handed the torch to Peter. "Take your brother and find her. My whelp is the only thing giving us a bit of safety."

"Let go of me," said Nicolette. "There will be no mercy if you hurt or kill us."

Henri watched the flames in the pit as if they could tell his future.

"There will be no mercy, regardless," he said.

Francois grunted as Nicolette landed a blow.

"Can't you deal with one woman?" Henri turned to the fighting couple.

Nicolette stared at Francois as he clutched her knife in his belly. He staggered back, eyes wide, mouth open, blood dribbling down his chin.

She glanced at Henri. Shock stunned him. He blinked and took two long strides toward her.

She jumped to Francois, pulled her short sword from his body, and pointed it at Henri, who stopped just beyond her reach.

"You always were a fool, Francois," said Henri, shaking his head.

Francois gurgled and fell face-first to the ground. His feet drummed the earth, and he slumped dead.

"Well," said Henri as Nicolette backed away from him. "It's just you and me now." He drew his sword. "The last time I came at you with my weapon drawn, you did not fare so well." He laughed at his sick joke.

Nicolette stepped back and into a tree trunk.

"Cornered," said Henri. "I have nothing much to lose now. Not a prince. No home. Can't go back to Franconia because Hugh learned about my plot to overthrow his rule and take his throne. My "real" father doesn't want me, despite having no other living children. Seems he, too, knows about my machinations and says I can't be trusted. They cloistered my dear mother." He sighed as if reciting minor inconveniences.

"That leaves me with the here and now," he said, "and you."

"No," said Eryk, coming out of the black foliage behind them.

Henri stepped sideways to keep Nicolette and Eryk in sight.

Nicolette looked at Eryk and smiled until she saw his blood-soaked tunic. He approached, favoring his wounded right side.

"You don't look so good," said Henri with a snicker. "Did you cut yourself?"

"You're not as amusing as you think," said Eryk. He raised Shade in Henri's direction.

"I only need to entertain myself," said Henri, returning Eryk's salute.

The men circled one another.

Nicolette ensured she stayed out of their way, not wanting to cause Eryk to falter and Henri to take a hostage against Eryk.

"It is only fitting that the end comes down to the two of us," said Henri. "You've been a thorn in my side for as long as I've known you."

"You have always talked too much," said Eryk. "Words without substance. Shut up and do something."

Henri lunged.

Nicolette knew Henri to be a superb swordsman, trained by the King's best military men, and despite his pampered ways, he was big, strong, and capable. And Eryk was injured.

She chewed on her lower lip to prevent crying out and distracting Eryk.

The men clashed swords, blade pounding on blade, as they danced around the fire pit.

Nicolette caught sight of men on the edge of the clearing as they came out of the woods and ringed the area to watch. Their men, she noticed. They did not interfere.

Henri hit Eryk over his wound with the flat of his weapon. Eryk grunted and staggered back, stumbled, and his movements awkward.

Henri laughed as if demon-possessed.

He pounded into Eryk with blow after blow, bending Eryk and forcing him to his knees.

"I had expected more of a challenge from you," said Henri between strikes. "So, so disappointed. This is what you ended up with," he said, glancing at Nicolette.

At that moment, with Henri's attention directed at her, Eryk twisted the point of Shade up and left, surged up like a geyser, and thrust his sword into Henri's heart. Shade vibrated as if in victory and flashed bright white.

Nicolette thought she heard that organ pop into the stillness of that moment. All movement slowed, and sound disappeared.

Henri's bright violet eyes flashed; he dropped his sword, placed both hands on Shade, and smiled. He blew Nicolette a kiss, then leaned into Eryk.

"I had her first," he whispered, and shoved against Eryk, dislodging himself from Eryk's weapon.

"No," said Eryk. "You never touched who she is."

Henri fell back, arms and legs spread wide as if he fell back into a lake to float, dead eyes on the star-studded sky.

Eryk collapsed on his ass and fell back onto his back, his sword falling from his fingers. He groaned.

Nicolette ran to him, kneeled, and kissed him on the mouth.

Eryk reached up, laced his fingers in her hair, around the back of her head, and held her in place.

Kellan cleared his throat. "While I can understand you wanting to celebrate your victory in this battle," he said, standing over his brother and sister-in-law, "The war is not over."

Eryk broke the seal of his lips on hers and kissed her forehead.

She sat back on her heels.

"Let me see your wound," she said.

"A lucky, from his point of view, hit by that pissant Montfor," said Eryk. "His last."

"Did anyone find Isuet?" Nicolette bound Eryk's wound tight with strips of cloth ripped from a dead man's cloak to stop the blood loss, which seemed to be the worst part of Eryk's wound.

"She ran off with Betsey." Nicolette pointed in the direction she thought her sister had gone.

"She is the only one of the nine we have not captured," said Kellan. "All the others are dead."

Eryk held his hand out to Nicolette. She pulled, and he stood.

"Isuet has Betsey bound, so she can not move or cry out," said Nicolette.

She walked into the trees, leaving the men to follow.

CHAPTER FIFTY-ONE

Doofus

"Nicolette, wait," said Eryk, catching up to her in the woods.

"If Isuet can escape through the trees, I can follow." She held onto the trunk of a larch, peering into the dark.

"Fear fueled her flight," said Eryk, "and not attempting to follow another's path. One of the King's men is a woodsman and can track Isuet come morning."

Eryk walked around Nicolette to face her.

"We don't want to stumble around in the dark or follow with torches," he said. "It might make her do something even more desperate."

Nicolette punched the tree with the side of her fist.

"I hate you," she yelled into the night, then leaned her forehead on his chest.

Eryk wrapped his arms around Nicolette and held her stiff body. He rubbed his hands on her back in soft, smooth circles. She relaxed into him and wrapped her arms around his waist.

They stayed entwined for several minutes, listening to the night, the scurrying of small animals, the wind through the branches, and the whispered voices of the men in their group.

Leaves crunched behind them.

"We've cleaned up the campsite," said Kellan. "There's tea on the fire and fruit and cheese to eat."

Eryk walked back to the camp with his arm over Nicolette's shoulder. She sat next to him on a log and leaned against him. He kept his movements slow and easy so as not to startle her.

He enjoyed having her next to him and enjoyed giving her what comfort he could.

Nicolette ate an apple and drank some rosehip tea.

"Does anyone know where we are?" She sat up and glanced around the area. "Where are Henri and the others?"

"We moved them into the underbrush," said Kellan. "We'll use this as our base until we can find Isuet. We think she ran off with no supplies." He shook his head. "She can't get far, alone, with nothing to eat or drink and carrying a child." Kellan nodded to a short, stocky man to his left.

"Claude believes he will have found her by the time the sun is at its midday peak." Kellan poked an ember with a stick.

"Aye," said Claude.

"There are a few cottages in the direction Isuet went, so we think she will look for help from them."

"We will try to convince her to return with us," said Eryk. "I can't imagine her living in the rough."

"I no longer want to know anything about her," said Nicolette. "Her anger, hatred, and resentment make no sense to me." Nicolette yawned. "I'm going to try to rest," she said. She closed her eyes.

Eryk pulled her closer and draped his cloak around her. He snagged his brother's eyes.

"We will find her on the morrow," said Kellan. "She fled in haste and will leave a trail easy to follow."

"She's not much for physical activity, either," said Eryk. "That will be in our favor." He brushed the hair from Nicolette's face. "Go get some sleep, brother."

Kellan went off to the side, rolled his cloak into a pillow, and laid down at the base of a tree. Claude left without a word.

Eryk rested his cheek on Nicolette's head, closed his eyes, and steadied his breath. This mess needed to end.

Nicolette's ability to remain calm despite their troubles amazed him, but she couldn't keep it up. He wanted his family home behind Thornewood's walls with his soldiers to help keep them safe.

He'd let none of them out of his sight again. He squeezed Nicolette.

"Eryk," she said, sleep in her voice, "I can't breathe."

"Sorry." He loosened his grip.

"What were you thinking?" She tilted her face up to his.

Dare he kiss her?

She reached up, laced her fingers in his beard, and pulled his head down. Their lips met with gentle but insistent pressure. They held still, connected, unwilling to break apart, unable to go forward.

Eryk squeezed Nicolette and released her. He cleared his throat, sat straight, and moved away from her.

"Now's not the time," he said. "You are distraught, and I won't take advantage of your frail emotions."

"My what?" She scowled at him.

"You aren't in your right mind from the grief of your missing daughter," he said. "And the death of your father." He looked into the distance. "Your sister's betrayal." He turned to her. "You killed Francois. I killed Henri. That's a lot to deal with, and right now, you're just looking for momentary comfort."

She jumped up, pulled his cloak away, and threw it at him.

"You have a lot of nerve telling me how I'm feeling," she said.

"Hush," he said, looking up at her in astonishment. "The others will hear you."

"You just shushed me." She punched him on the shoulder. "As if I were a child."

"No, I..." He shook his head. "It's just that..." He raised his hands palms up and shrugged his shoulders.

"It's just what?" She shoved him.

He fell over onto his back, unprepared for her anger. He stared at the sky.

"Nicolette," he said, his voice quiet. "I just don't want you to want me because of convenience or gratitude or...." He covered his face with his arm. "Or anything."

"Ugh," she said. "You vex me." She stomped off.

"Where are you going?" He rolled up.

"I have to pee."

"You can't go in the woods alone," he said.

"I can. I will," she said over her shoulder. "You stay away from me for a while before I really punch you, so it hurts." She went around a wide tree. "Men," she said.

"That went well," said Kellan from his prone position.

"Must you always be a witness to my most embarrassing

moments?" He threw a rock over the fire and into the trees beyond.

"Watch it," said a man.

Kellan laughed.

"I suggest you keep quiet and still for a bit," said his brother. "Your wife will straighten you out when she's done being annoyed with your nonsense."

"What nonsense?" Eryk sat on his heels by Kellan. "I don't want to take advantage of her emotional state."

Kellan laughed again.

"Stop it," said Eryk with some heat.

"Nicolette is not some fragile greenhouse flower," said Kellan. "Consider all she's been through and how well she managed it all."

"I thought I was."

"Sounded more like you were pitying her and hinting that she wasn't strong enough to know her mind."

Eryk shook his head.

"You need to get out of your way," said Kellan, "before you ruin things with that woman. She loves you. Always has, if I remember correctly."

"How do you mean?" He held his breath.

"We all saw it from the moment you two met," said Kellan. "I think it's why Isuet hates you so. But you both do your best to keep each other at arm's length."

Kellan sat up.

"You've refused every woman who crossed your path," said Kellan. "You put on a good act, but I know you."

Kellan grasped Eryk's arm.

"I'm not the right man for her," said Eryk. "She deserves better."

Kellan punched him in the jaw and stood up, fists on hips.

"I've had enough of your bullshit about your birth," he said. "You dishonor our parents. You dishonor me. And you dishonor Nicolette." Kellan huffed. "You are one of the best men I know. Start acting like you know it too, or I'll punch you, so it really hurts." He stomped off into the woods.

He'd have to remember his behavior tonight for the next time he needed to clear a room.

He rubbed his chin with one hand and his shoulder with the other. He couldn't take any more delicate punches from the two of them.

CHAPTER FIFTY-TWO

Honey Mead

Nicolette sat in the bushes, far enough from the campsite, so she didn't have to deal with Eryk, but close enough to still see him. She jabbed a stick in the dirt over and over again. It broke. She sucked in a lungful of air, held it, and blew it out through her nose.

She heard Eryk's conversation with his brother and lost some of the energy of her anger. Eryk felt unworthy of her. She snorted. He was near perfect in her eyes. Not when he said stupid stuff to her and acted all courteous to her. She didn't want some mythical man from a ballad. She wanted that big, blundering lug. He rarely blundered.

He seemed to want her still, even knowing about Henri. There was no man better than he, as far as she was concerned.

Kellan was right that she loved Eryk from the time when he encouraged her to get on the war horse she wanted to ride.

A body crashed through the brambles behind her. She hid behind a tree, pulled her short sword, and held her breath.

A woman cried out. Cursed. More thrashing.

Nicolette used the tree trunk to pull herself up and as a shield.

Isuet fell in front of where Nicolette hid. She sat on her butt, heaving, her back to Nicolette. Isuet crawled back, coming up against Nicolette's tree.

"Stay away from me," said Isuet to the bushes.

Nicolette watched as male fingers parted the bushes. Claude ducked and emerged from the foliage, following Isuet.

"Stay away," said Isuet. "Do you have any idea who I am?"

Claude looked up and caught Nicolette's gaze. Isuet followed his look, turning her body.

"I found her stumbling around in the dark woods," said Claude. "That will save us a bit of time."

"Oh," she cried, bending forward and hiding her face in her knees.

Eryk and Kellan joined them as Nicolette stood over her sister.

"Where is my daughter?" She held her sword in a white-knuckled fist. She placed the tip under Isuet's chin and leveraged her sister's face up to look at her. "Where is she?"

Isuet whimpered.

"No," said Nicolette. "You don't get to play the victim. Tell me where Betsey is, or I will begin carving pieces off you." Nicolette pricked Isuet's cheek with the point of her blade and drew blood to underscore her point.

Isuet sobered instantly, wiped the tears from her face, and sneered.

"I found a hut and banged on the door. I gave her to some old woman for a heel of bread, a hunk of cheese, and a swallow of ale." Isuet laughed. "See how cheap your daughter's life is?"

Nicolette slapped her sister.

Isuet lost her breath and stared at Nicolette.

"Even now," said Nicolette, "when you've lost all allies and support, you remain nasty and vindictive." Nicolette grabbed Isuet's hair and pulled her to her feet. She shoved her in the direction Isuet had come.

"Show us where," said Nicolette. "We better find her, and she better be in good health, or I will kill you with my bare hands."

A hint of dawn light sifted through the leaves, and they followed Isuet with the help of Claude, who followed the trail she left as she blundered on her quest to escape.

They came upon a one-room hut near a brook that bubbled with soothing sounds. An old woman sat on a bench against a wall where a patch of morning sun warmed her small fenced-in garden.

Betsey toddled through wildflowers chasing butterflies, laughing and giggling as a puppy scampered with her.

Nicolette sheathed her sword, ran to her daughter, scooped her up, and hugged her tight. Betsey laughed and wrapped her little arms around Nicolette's neck.

Nicolette collapsed onto the ground and cuddled Betsey in her lap, the puppy jumping on them for attention.

"See," said Isuet, "no worse for wear."

"She has burns on her wrists from the rough rope you used to tie her," said Nicolette as she kissed the spots of raw skin.

"I treated them with a soothing salve," said the old woman from her perch, unperturbed by her guests.

"You bought my child for scraps," said Nicolette, turning to the woman.

"I rescued her from the crazy one," she said, nodding to Isuet. "I thought it best to separate the two." She smiled, her two front teeth missing.

"I see," said Nicolette. "I thank you for your quick thinking. Betsey looks rested and fairly well."

"She napped, ate some honey bread, and had her nappies changed," said the hag. "I still know how to care for children despite my dodge."

"You look hail and hearty," said Eryk, approaching her. "May we reward you for your care of our daughter?"

The woman laughed, shaking her whole body.

She stared at Nicolette with her one blue eye and one green. She winked.

"You, girl," she said, pointing at Nicolette. "And you," she turned to Eryk. "You both will sire a child in your line of heirs that will change the world." She smiled.

She pointed at Isuet.

"You, despite your chaos, will be the mother of kings." She cackled.

"But what of you?"

"Me? I am always and will always be," she said, blinking.

"I meant a reward," said Eryk.

"I have another child, James," she said. "Take him and raise him, along with the girl."

"Where did that child come from?" Nicolette narrowed her eyes at the woman.

"I am known to rescue unwanted children," she said. "I believe him to be of an age with your babe, and they share a father. The boy has the same hair."

"You trust us to care for another of Henri's children?" Eryk glanced at Nicolette.

"Do you fault the children for their parent's sins?"

Her mismatched eyes held Eryk's.

He shook his head.

"No," he said. "The children are blameless."

"As I thought." She entered her house and returned with a small boy with dark hair and a swipe of white in his bangs. Other than that hair, he had the look of someone else.

Eryk picked the boy up and turned to Nicolette.

"What think you?"

She could tell he was already in love with the boy. Eryk grew so big to hold all his care for the world.

She nodded.

"Yes, we will raise the boy as our own," she said.

The old woman handed Nicolette a bottle.

"Drink this at the next full moon on your wedding night," she said.

"We are already wed." Nicolette took the bottle.

"For your real wedding," she said. "My special honey mead for your honeymoon." She bent down and kissed Nicolette's forehead. "A blessing, in the old fashion."

"May we have your name?" Nicolette stood and hefted Betsey on her hip.

"I am simply Mother," said the old woman. "I will always be with you. I always am."

"Thank you," said Eryk. He reached into his tunic and removed a pouch. He handed it to Mother.

"Perhaps this will be useful for any future foundlings you rescue."

She snatched it from his fingers, and it disappeared into a pocket of her apron.

"Be off with you," she said, disappearing into her hut.

"Well," said Kellan. "Our numbers are ever increasing." He laughed.

"Let us be off," said Eryk. "I, for one, have had enough adventures."

"Adventures," said Isuet. She scoffed. "You are an idiot."

Nicolette grabbed her sister's sleeve and jerked her so they stood face to face.

"You will never speak to my husband again unless you are civil." She shook Isuet. "Do you understand?"

Isuet scowled, but she nodded.

Nicolette glanced at Eryk. He beamed at her. She felt heat rise to her cheeks.

He plucked Betsey from her arms and strode tall through the woods, a child in each arm and ignoring the low-hanging branches.

"That's one happy man," said Claude, passing Nicolette to lead the way back to their horses.

Isuet grumbled about walking back to the château, but between the lame horses, and the dead men on the backs of others, there weren't enough mounts, and no one was inclined to be kind to her.

They reached the King's palace by early afternoon, as the traitors had not ventured far.

Nicolette and Eryk took the children to their rooms and let Kellan and the other men tell the tale of the last two nights to Prince Kevan and the King.

The following day would be soon enough to see what came next.

CHAPTER FIFTY-THREE

Queen-Making

They were called to their audience with King Hugh early in the morning. Eryk's side was sore from his wound, but the physician, Dom Aimoin, that barbered Henri and doctored Tomas at the end of his life, cleaned and bandaged his wound.

Prince Kevan ushered Kellan, Nicolette, and Eryk into the King's war room. King Otto sat with King Hugh.

He raised an eyebrow at Kevan in question.

"He has a couple of interests in these proceedings," said Kevan, leaning into Eryk and Nicolette so only they could hear. Kevan gestured to a servant to show them their seats by the wall off to the side.

"Keep your hands off me," said Isuet from the hall. "I am still the daughter of a count." A soldier stumbled into the room backward, turned, and bowed.

"Begging your pardon, your highness," he said. "The Lady Isuet." He stepped out of the way as Isuet flew into the room, arms flapping.

She stilled in front of the King, curtsied, and straightened, tall and defiant.

"I did not know you married me to a traitor," she said.

The King frowned and raised his hand to stop her speaking.

Eryk watched her struggle to control her facial expressions. She clenched her teeth and mashed her lips together, forcing her words to stay in her mouth.

"Prince Kevan," said the King. "Escort the Lady Isuet to her seat to await her turn before me."

Kevan sat Isuet next to Eryk on the same bench. Kevan smiled at Eryk's scowl.

"Lady Nicolette," said Kevan. He held his hand out to her, kissed the fingers she placed in his palm. He winked at her. "The King wishes to hear from you first."

Eryk smiled at the young prince's attempt to make him jealous. He didn't have Kellan's possessive nature.

Nicolette followed Kevan to stand in front of the King. He remained by her side.

"Lady Nicolette," said the King. "Your daughter is well?"

"Yes, your Highness."

"We are glad to hear it," said the King, waving his hand to include the room's occupants. "Despite the circumstances of Elizabeth's birth, she is still the granddaughter of a queen and king."

Nicolette nodded.

"Please tell us of the events of the last couple of days," said the King.

Nicolette detailed their chase of the traitors, how she killed Francois, Eryk killed Henri, and the deaths of the other men.

"So, we must replace the Duke of Nantes, as the Ramnlf male line is at an end." King Hugh turned to Otto. "We abide by our agreement to install your nephew as the new Duke of Nantes." He tapped his finger on the table. "Scribe, make it so."

"Continue, Lady Nicolette."

Nicolette glanced at Eryk, and her eyes fell upon Isuet.

"My sister ran off into the woods with Betsey while Henri, Francois, and his brothers attacked me," said Nicolette. She clasped her hands in front of her and took a deep breath. "We had to wait to follow, as it was still night. We were fearful of what she would do to my daughter."

The King looked at Isuet and frowned.

"We did eventually find them both and another child of Henri's. A wise woman in the woods rescued the children."

Nicolette finished with the details of her story and sat back down.

"Your turn," said Kevan to Isuet. He did not address her with her title or hold out his hand to help her rise. Kevan left Isuet standing alone before the Kings.

"Lady Isuet," said the King, "you are not being faulted for your marriage to Henri." The King leaned back. "Your crime is the kidnapping and abandoning of your sister's child."

"I tried to save her," said Isuet. "Henri said the brat was his to do with as he pleased. I was merely a pawn in his dastardly deeds." She sucked in a deep breath. "Your Highness." She batted her eyelashes and smiled.

Eryk watched the Kings' reactions to her defense.

King Hugh seemed unmoved and non-believing. He drummed his fingers on the arm of his chair.

King Otto smiled, showing his teeth.

Eryk got the impression he wanted to laugh at Isuet, not because he thought her ridiculous, but because she amused him.

Isuet smiled at Otto, sensing an ally.

"Based on what we've heard here and reports from others, we understand you did not consummate your marriage to Henri," said King Hugh. "Is this correct?"

Isuet raised her chin. Her eyes slid to Nicolette and back to the king.

"I remain a virgin," she said. "Chaste and untouched."

The King's mouth quirked up.

King Otto leaned into King Hugh. They turned away from the room's occupants and spoke in whispers while Isuet stood before them.

The Kings turned back.

"A doting father indulged you," said King Hugh. "but your behavior or excuses do not amuse us. You owe the crown compensation for the chaos you caused. Lucky for you, we have the perfect solution for your orphaned state and a way to make mends to us."

The scribe placed a sheaf of paper before King Hugh. The King scanned it, and passed it to King Otto. Otto nodded and pressed his ring into wax melted on the vellum. King Hugh added his seal.

"Lady Isuet, King Otto has declared his desire to marry you," said King Hugh. "I have agreed."

Isuet gasped.

"But....," she said.

"No. You will do this. You will marry King Otto today and go with him to his home and thus help forge the peace between our peoples."

Isuet lost her balance.

Eryk jumped forward as the closest person to her and held her erect. She did not cringe from him; the shock made her senseless.

King Otto rose and took Isuet from Eryk.

"I look forward to having you as my queen," said Otto.

"But you are old," said Isuet. She shivered.

King Otto laughed.

"This will be fun," he said. He lifted Isuet's hand and kissed her fingers. She tried to pull away, but he held on to her as she shook her head.

"We consider him an excellent candidate for you, Lady Isuet," said King Hugh. "You will do as you are told."

"My queen," said Otto as he bowed to Isuet.

Isuet tilted her head and considered Otto.

"Is there a crown?" Isuet tucked a stray lock into the braids wrapped around the top of her head.

"Most definitely," said Otto.

Isuet smiled, tucked her arm through Otto's, and he led Isuet from the room.

"Let us visit the priest and then go home," said the Saxon king.

Good riddance and may they never see her again, thought Eryk.

King Hugh beckoned Eryk, Nicolette, and Kellan before him.

"I have nothing further for you," said the king. "You have my leave to return home. We are grateful for your service."

They bowed and left to pack.

CHAPTER FIFTY-FOUR

Home Alone

They took a more direct route home, lasting three days instead of the week needed to get to the capital, and avoided the border between Franconia and Saxony even though the Kings signed a peace treaty. They took roads directly south, stopping only for brief rests for the horses and personal needs, sheltering at inns and roadhouses for the night, the men sharing one room, the women and children in another.

Nicolette enjoyed this journey despite traveling with her father's body. She would never set foot in Welf again, now that Otto had the estates through his marriage to Isuet. They relaxed, told each other stories of their fathers' lives, and appreciated the spring life provided by the earth.

Maryn alternated between riding with Nicolette and Clarissa on horses and spending time with the children in their wagon.

It only took them two days to get to Hilltop Fortress. They spent one night there.

"Your time is close," said Maryn as she felt Revena's bulging baby belly.

"Oh," said Maryn as her hand rose with the kicking of a baby. She moved her hand around. A second baby bumped her hand.

"You'll need to come up with two names," she told Revena.

Revena tilted her head up to face Kellan.

"Twins," she said.

He beamed.

"My brother, the overachiever," said Eryk with a laugh.

Maryn raised Revena's feet on a stool. "The swelling in your ankles is not too bad, but best to keep them up when you aren't in bed. We want you as comfortable as possible."

They sat in Revena's solar, so she didn't need to take the stairs to the main hall to entertain her guests. Her private chamber off of her bedroom felt intimate and homey when filled.

When one of her women voiced concern about the men attending during her lying in, she made a face at the woman.

"We are family," she said. "They calm me."

The woman shrugged and glanced at Adam. Clarissa scowled.

"Will you stay with me?" Revena took Maryn's hand. "I know you've been away from home for too long...."

"I would be happy to stay," said Maryn.

"It would ease my mind," said Revena, looking down as if embarrassed, not used to asking for help.

Kellan stood behind his wife, massaging her shoulders, looking at his mother with concern.

"I have to stay for a while," said Maryn. "Nicolette and Eryk need time to settle into their new life without a mother hen interfering."

Nicolette smiled. Maryn was the least interfering person she knew. She marveled at her luck with her mother-in-law.

They reached Thornewood the next day, exhausted but elated to have their adventure at an end.

The steward gathered the household and had them waiting in the courtyard as they arrived, having received an advance rider with the news of the Count's impending arrival.

Eryk helped Nicolette from her horse, held her hand, and guided her toward the servants.

"Steward, I present my wife and the new mistress of my holdings." He grinned like a child with a purloined sweet whenever he called her his wife. His joy excited her and gave her hope for their future.

"Nicolette, Countess of Thornewood," he said, "I bid you welcome home." He swept her into his arms and carried her into the great hall.

Nicolette giggled and blushed. The thought of finally acting as a wife made her nervous.

Eryk put her down, and she organized her guests.

Clarissa was still with them. Adam seemed reluctant to leave them, or more specifically, Clarissa.

The day after arriving at Thornewood, they buried Tomas in the cemetery next to Allan, Eryk, and Kellan's father. They had a small ceremony with only Nicolette, Eryk, Betsey, James, Clarissa, Adam, and the priest in attendance. It was the end of May, and flowers bloomed around the graves to celebrate the dead's memories.

The funeral seemed to give them closure to their adventure north, the end of a generation, and the beginning of change. The world felt new and full of promise.

They had a light meal when they returned after the burial and let out a collective sigh of relief.

"I feel like we've been gone for years," said Clarissa, watching Betsey and James play with a ball on the floor between the adults.

"I look forward to a long sleep," said Adam. "I think I aged ten years, and my hair has turned gray." He rubbed his shaved head.

Clarissa laughed.

Nicolette smiled at the two of them.

"I'm not sure how to behave without royalty and enemies surrounding me," said Eryk as he rubbed his wounded side. "I look forward to just being with family." He glanced at Nicolette.

"Speaking of which," said Adam. "I invited Clarissa to visit Beustel. She has an interest in the vineyards. And we thought to give you a rest from guests. Settle into your new status as a married couple."

Nicolette looked at Clarissa. Her friend turned her face down, trying to hide her pink cheeks.

Nicolette looked at Eryk, who stared at Adam. Adam shrugged.

"Too obvious?" Adam popped a strawberry in his mouth.

"You need time alone," said Clarissa.

"You want time alone," said Nicolette under her breath.

"What's that?" Clarissa leaned forward.

"Nothing," said Nicolette. "Beustel is a beautiful estate and well worth a visit."

"Yes," said Eryk. "Adam has made vast improvements, as my dearly departed cousin wasn't much into managing his property."

"When were you thinking of going?" Nicolette addressed her friend.

"Tomorrow," said Clarissa.

"So soon," said Nicolette.

"Yes," said Clarissa. "But I will be back."

"It will be odd not having you with me every day," said Nicolette.

"Almost two years of constant companionship," said Clarissa. She reached for Nicolette's hands. "I could not have hoped for a better friend."

"You have been a better sister to me than my own by blood," said Nicolette. "Promise you won't stay away for long."

"I promise." Clarissa nodded to Adam. "He says Beustel is not far."

"Barely an hour by horseback," said Adam. "Just far enough to think before invading the newlyweds' privacy but close enough to come at a moment's notice when invited." He laughed.

"You won't return to Black Bear without seeing me first?" Nicolette frowned.

"Definitely not," said Clarissa. "There's not much there for me. While it is mine, it was never my home. We were talking about it," she peeked at Adam, "and thought it might make a good hunting lodge. It is close to the borderlands but not much in the way of a fortification, so it seems dangerous at the moment."

Nicolette breathed a sigh of relief. "I must admit, I was worried."

"Time enough for me to decide what to do with my future as long as I remain welcome here."

"You will always be welcome," said Eryk. "Consider Thornewood your home, too."

Nicolette beamed at him. Was there ever a more generous man?

The evening wore on in homey comfort, faded into a peaceful slumber, and broke into a bright new day.

CHAPTER FIFTY-FIVE

Sex on the Beach

They ate breakfast in the kitchen, reminding Nicolette of when they arrived at Thornewood less than two months ago. So much had changed and yet remained the same.

Jen spoiled them with fruit tarts topped with cream whipped to fluffy light clouds. She bounced around her domain, touching her daughters as she passed them. To say she was glad they were home again was an understatement. Jen had lost weight in her anxiety about the safe return of her children.

Fronika and Libbe had kept their mother awake most of the night with the tales of their adventures. Their stories were in demand by the rest of the household, who never even dreamed of venturing forth from the places they were born. Fronika and Libbe were now worldly wise and sophisticated.

They each had a charge to look after and new knowledge of the rest of the world to model their teachings for Betsey and James.

Fronika addressed Betsey as Elizabeth and insisted everyone else do the same.

Libbe chased the crawling children around the kitchen, scooped one in each arm, and handed Elizabeth off to Fronika. The table manners lessons hit the toddler's energy wall.

"We finished packing," said Clarissa, licking jam from her fingers.

"Perhaps you can bundle some of this wonderful food for us, Jen," said Adam. "If I eat much more right now, I will need a nap before we can leave." He smacked his lips. "I have missed your cooking so much.

Those chefs in the King's court have nothing on you."

Jen blushed and handed Adam a basket.

"Score," he said.

Nicolette and Clarissa hugged and cried.

"It's only for a few days, ladies," said Adam, waiting to hand Clarissa into her saddle. He shooed away the stable hand with the mounting block, preferring an excuse to touch Clarissa by helping her up on her horse himself.

Nicolette hoped Clarissa and Adam could be more than friends. She longed to keep her friend close.

Eryk and Adam clasped forearms.

"Send word with the all-clear when we can visit," said Adam with a wink.

Eryk looked away without one of his usual witty rebuttals.

Quiet all morning, his behavior made Nicolette nervous. She feared he was having second thoughts about them, as she did not know his thoughts about their future, as they had no time to work it out alone. She wiped her sweaty hands down her dress and waved to Clarissa and Adam as they rode out of Thornewood, accompanied by the soldiers Adam took to Verdun.

Eryk stood beside Nicolette until their friends were out of sight.

"I must meet with the steward and receive his report of the estate's status while we were away." He didn't look at her. "I will see you this evening." He left her standing on the stoop to the great hall's entrance.

She turned her face to the sun and sighed. She might have to punch him or something.

Thornewood was a well-run household. She walked around her new home, peeked into various rooms, and asked questions. She saw they did not need her and felt no energy to get involved.

She asked to have a bath prepared. While she waited for the filled tub, she played with Elizabeth and James for a few hours, insisting Libbe and Fronika take the respite for themselves. They weren't gone long.

Nicolette bathed in lavender and chamomile, hoping to soothe her nervous energy with warm water and fragrant herbs. It didn't help.

"I'm going for a walk outside," she said to her maids once they finished dressing her and braiding her hair in one long thick rope down her back.

"I'll get you an escort," said Kathe, tying the green ribbon in her hair.

"No," said Nicolette. "I need some time alone."

Grite frowned at Kathe.

"I've gone out many times on the estate alone." She plucked a shawl from the peg on the wall. "I will go out by the little pond."

Light glittered off the water's still surface like stars dancing in the sky. Nicolette loved this spot; it calmed her like no other place in the world.

She hiked her skirts up, tucked them into the belt at her waist, and waded into the pond. The water lapped at her naked thighs, sending shivers along her body.

There was a rustling in the weeds along the bank. Nicolette turned and saw Eryk sitting up, watching her, a stave of wheat between his teeth. He brushed his thick, rusty brown hair from his forehead; his gaze focused on her like a hunter stalking his prey.

She returned his stare, locking onto his eyes.

Reaching up, she pulled her braid forward, untied the ribbon, and let it float away in the breeze. She combed her fingers through her hair; the curls danced around her.

Eryk crawled closer to the water.

Nicolette raised her arms above her head, twirled, and laughed. She fell back into the water. She emerged, breaking the surface like a goddess.

Her dress clung to her body, highlighting her lush curves. She stepped onto the bank and walked towards Eryk.

He leaned back on his hands, and she saw the bulge in his pants. He wanted her.

She shivered with the thought.

She knew he would not make the first move, leaving the decision up to her.

She stood at his feet and let her eyes roam his body, smiling, happy and satisfied with what was all hers.

Still tucked into her belt, her raised skirts showed off her bare legs. She placed a foot on either side of his hips, lowered her body, and came to rest on his obvious need for her.

He groaned.

She pulled on his shirt, bringing him forward, and bared his golden chest. She placed her palms on his tight stomach, moved them up inch by inch until she wound her fingers in his beard and pulled his face towards hers.

She kissed him. Their tongues met, and they both moaned.

His hands clasped her waist, firm and gentle.

"Are you sure?" He locked onto her eyes, looking into her soul.

"Yes," she said. "I want you. Only you. Always."

He stroked her cheek and kissed her forehead, eyelids, and her jaw. His mouth claimed hers, showing how much he had always wanted her.

CHAPTER FIFTY-SIX

Honey Moon

Eryk waited at the front of the church, dressed in the deep green of the Thornewood colors. His father's blackthorn broach, with its five-petaled white flower, pinned his cloak at the shoulder. This was the first time he had worn his father's symbol.

Shade, the sword given to him by his father, sat on his hip, vibrating with excitement. He stood tall, proud to be the head of his family, no longer needing to hide himself from the world. He watched the door, waiting for his wife.

"Marry me," he said to Nicolette after they made love for the first time two weeks ago by their pond.

"We are already married," she said, laughing.

"I want to marry you here at Thornewood with our friends and family around us." He ran his fingers along her naked back, warm from the sunshine and their lovemaking. She shivered as she lay atop him, and he felt himself grow hard. He wanted her again already. He tried to control himself, but she reached between them and stroked him into worshiping her body.

When their breathing steadied, she continued their conversation.

"I will be proud and honored to marry you, Count Thornewood."

He untied the leather thong holding the dark amber stone that reminded him of Nicolette from around his neck and placed it around hers.

She clasped the stone in her fist and kissed him.

Every time he thought of Nicolette, his body quickened. So as not to embarrass himself, he looked at the people waiting with him in the chapel.

Kellan and Revena sat to his left with their twins, a girl, Beatrix, and a boy, Viator, born the day after they left Hilltop. The nannies hovered behind the happy parents, who would not give over the babies to their care.

Maryn sat next to them. His mother smiled in contentment.

His children, Elizabeth and James, played at her feet.

He laughed at the scandalized expression of their priest, who felt the occasion demanded a bit more pomp and circumstance.

The only disturbance to what Eryk considered perfection was Adam's dower expression. He stood beside a pillar, arms crossed. He had not made one joke since arriving that morning.

Clarissa returned to Thornewood last week without Adam in tow. Something had gone wrong, but she refused to tell Nicolette anything about it.

The light in the chapel's opening changed and caught Eryk's attention.

Kellan's daughters, Ema, Ava, and Gisela, proceeded down the nave, baskets of flowers in their hands. They tossed petals in the air as they approached Eryk.

They joined their parents, and the congregation's body turned as Nicolette stood outlined in the spring sunshine just outside the church, ethereal and otherworldly.

Eryk held his breath, and she stepped into the building, becoming real. Her smile dazzled him, and he had eyes only for her.

In a breath, she stood beside him and took his hand in hers.

They kneeled. The priest spoke. They repeated his words. In the blink of an eye, they rose.

"I now pronounce you husband and wife," said the priest. "You may kiss your bride."

Eryk stared at Nicolette.

"Well, Count Thorne," she said. "I am waiting."

He wrapped his arms around her, lifted her, and spun with her. His lips found hers, and he lost himself to the moment's happiness.

They sat in bed that night, propped up with pillows. The house felt quiet and peaceful, but the revels outside and in the fields continued. No one passed up a chance to celebrate the Honey Full Moon, especially when the lord of the castle married his lady-love.

Nicolette reached over to the bedside table and plucked up the bottle from the Mother of the Woods. She uncorked it.

"I know you don't drink, but it might be bad luck not to follow the old woman's instruction." Nicolette tilted the bottle to her mouth and drank. She held the bottle to Eryk's mouth. He sipped.

"That's quite tasty," he said.

"See what you've been missing?" Nicolette wiped a drop of the golden elixir from his lips and licked it from her finger.

Eryk looked at her mouth, leaned in, and kissed her. She tasted sweeter than honey.

The End